WATERWITCH

by

Helen Burton

Grosvenor House
Publishing Limited

This book is published by
Grosvenor House Publishing Ltd
28-30 High Street, Guildford, Surrey, GU1 3HY.
www.grosvenorhousepublishing.co.uk

A CIP record for this book
is available from the British Library

ISBN 978-1-906645-11-3

For CAROLE,
with love.

Prologue

The man with the camera perched himself precariously on the pinnacle of rock which jutted out from the headland like an accusing finger. From here he could look back at the village, see the houses clustered tier upon tier, climbing the flanks of the valley, look down upon the sheltered harbour with its coloured fleet of tiny craft. It seemed deserted; a toy town without its complement of wooden dolls. He peered at his watch, 10 a.m., still too early for the morning's influx of trippers, pouring down in a coloured crocodile from the car-park.

A sudden movement caught his eye. A gaggle of children was spilling out onto the head of the quay, shepherded by a young woman - perhaps their teacher - a girl in Alice blue, the neat black band about her hair adding to the Lewis Carroll image. Excited voices floated up to the watcher on the rocks. At the same time, a boat moved away from the harbour wall, reversed and turned to head towards the open sea.

He was in luck; the man with the camera, for it was an old boat, harking back to the days of the great fleets of Cornish luggers, pride of the South West as the century turned. It still carried its sails, neatly furled. There was no one on the deck but he caught the impression of a young face at the wheel, obscured now by the deckhouse. It was a glorious morning. The sun warmed the old woodwork, glinting on the pealing paintwork of the hull, green and gold.

The man on the rock thought of Flecker's verses, of the old ship which had burst into flower again from the sprouting woodwork of its timbers. '*I have seen old ships sailing, like swans, asleep,*' he murmured. But there was nothing sleepy about this old scow, pointing arrow straight for the harbour mouth, moving fast.

'Perfect, perfect!' hissed the man, camera clamped to eye. She would line herself up between those jagged rocks and sail straight into his sights. How graceful, even in her old age, how....

The sunlight was shattered by an explosion which deafened him. A blinding, searing flash filled his viewfinder; the upward rush of splintered woodwork. The rocks, taking up the dreadful sound, were throwing it back, tossing it between the cliffs and about the bowl of the harbour. And, after the last echo, there was nothing left but a few shards of driftwood and a slick of oil, still burning.

He began to run then, back toward the village. An old man, leaning over the wall, turned and said, 'There be no earthly good you runnin'. Nothin's to be done. She's gone the old Waterwitch, and the boy with her. Tide's on the ebb. It's always on the ebb when they go. 'Tes as it should be.' With Celtic fatality he turned away, face set, tugging at his pipe.

The children had gone but the girl in the blue dress remained, standing motionless on the end of the quay, tears pouring silently down her lovely face.

PART I

A Kingdom by the Sea

CHAPTER ONE

1896

'She was a child and I was a child
   'In my kingdom by the sea ......'
   'And we loved with a love that was more than a love,
I and my Annabel Lee,' chanted Tabby Cluett, stretching out amongst the short turf at the cliff's edge. 'But you see, she was never Annabel Lee, she was a Boase - Dr. Boase's daughter and more than the tilt of her nose above everyone else. Her mother was gentry and old Dr. Boase not much less. She thought she was a lady, did Annabel.'

Tabby rolled onto her stomach, there were already grass stains upon her pinafore and smudges of yellow-gold pollen. She kicked at the air with the heels of her black button boots and tore at a rusty stem of sorrel. 'And where do you hail from, Johnny Fortnight, no-one hereabouts will tell me?'

The young man shaded his eyes and grinned at her. He had taken off his shabby dark coat with its tarnished buttons, for the October sun was bright and hot and the sky the colour of the germanders which sprinkled this headland throughout the summer. He was an unremarkable young man of indeterminate age, somewhere just under thirty perhaps, with a long rangy frame, a narrow-boned face and eyes which flickered from the grey of

3

thunderheads to shore-sea green and back again as his moods changed.

'You never say,' pouted Tabby, her round child's face puckering with annoyance. 'Once a fortnight you come out of nowhere, then you're over the hills and far away with your pack and nobody sees hide or hair of you in between!' Johnny Fortnight gave her a smile. Tabby's mother fed him, a crock of hot soup and the ubiquitous pasty. It wouldn't do to antagonise the child.

'I come from Langarrock in the north,' he shaded his eyes, flat on his back now, feeling the sun's warmth on his face, 'from the river-flats and the sea holly and the ever shifting sands.'

Tabby tossed her tangled brown curls. 'Nobody comes from Langarrock, nobody at all; it's a fairy town, vanished for ever beneath the dunes.'

'You asked me,' said Johnny Fortnight, with a shrug. 'Now tell me, Tabby, pretty Tabby - about Annabel Boase.'

'Annabel Toller, the Widow Toller,' snapped Tabby.

'And is the Widow Toller walking out?'

'Why should I tell you? Why should I tell you anything?'

'Because I have a pink hair-ribbon that exactly matches your sash.' He reached out a long hand and snatched it from his pack, letting it arc up against the blue sky.

Tabby snorted. 'I'm surprised it isn't a blue one to match my eyes, like the length you sold to Hetty Varco or the green one Meloney Jelbert had of you – and what do you sell to brown-eyed maids?'

'White lace for their petticoats - to set off a trim ankle – don't digress, I have to go back to work.' Tabby sat up and smoothed out her pinafore, then began pleating its folds. 'Annabel Toller has no interest in any man round Trevander Bay, none good enough for her, I suppose, though why any should want her, she's old - over thirty - and red-headed? Are you looking for a wife, Johnny Fortnight? Mathey would hate that and Jack would see off any man whose eyes wandered in that direction.'

'Mathey, Jack? Tabby, you're infuriating!'

'Mathey is her son, we're friends. We have an understanding for the future - that is, he doesn't know about it - not yet.'

Johnny grinned. 'And how old is Mathey?'

'Thirteen, fourteen Candlemas next.'

'Oh, I see, maturing rapidly. And Jack, he's all of ten, I suppose?'

'Jack Toller is her brother-in-law and likes to think he owns her. She lets him think that way when it suits - he was her husband's brother, he'd be wed to her himself if there weren't laws against it. Instead, he's wed to the boat.'

'Ah,' said Johnny Fortnight 'the pride of the fleet. None of your smart Cornish blacks and whites but gold and green, with new-caulked timbers and russet sails and a red-haired mermaid at the prow?'

'No,' said Tabby 'a good Cornish bow-sprit, nothing la-di-dah and fancy like you see up to Plymouth.'

'I was musing, but I am right, the green with a slick of gold across the rubbing strake? Her husband had money?'

'Frank Toller? Not he, he had a pretty face and a fine body, so Mam says. Annabel set her cap at him before she left school. Old Dr. Boase was mad against it - said the Tollers were a wild crew, Old Jem nothing but a pirate and as for brother Jack, as bent as a hairpin. Frank was a good man; Mathey adored his father.'

'Lost at sea?' asked Johnny Fortnight, sitting up and beginning to sort out his pack.

'No, the typhus got him; took half the village. Before your time here else you'd remember it. Too many families went over the cliff and the young and strong went as easily as the old and weak. Annabel took it hard and the keel barely laid. That was to be her gift to him - a love gift. When Dr. Boase died, 'Fosfelle' came to Annabel as the only child - her mother had gone before - oh, ten years before. Annabel loved Fosfelle, who wouldn't - but she sold out to the Deverels and that was to pay for the Waterwitch and new gear.'

Johnny Fortnight knew 'Fosfelle'; he called on the Deverels every visit. Gabriel, the perpetual bachelor, had given in to fate and was soon to marry Hetty Varco. Hetty was a frivolous chit of a girl, there'd be rich pickings for a packman when she had money chinking in her purse. He shaded his eyes and looked back at the village. Trevander clung perilously to the curve of the bay, houses set back into the cliff, straining, one above the other, roof and gable and upper window, to peer out across the water or down at the anchored fleet which was its livelihood. Fosfelle, old and grey and mellow, clung high above the modest cottages of the crewmen and fish-workers; honeysuckle-clad, rose-fettered, shaded by tamarisks, a tortuous path wandering down to the roadway through the fuchsias, the veronicas, the patches of crimson corn lilies, the tenacious pink of valerian, the iridescent blue spires of larkspur. It had been a wilderness when Jane Penrose had married Edward Boase and clawed colour and harmony out of arid patches of whin and stubborn tracts of yellow furze. And Annabel had grown up in the enchanted garden and learnt to love every tree and pathway and startling patch of colour. She had relinquished it all to build a boat for her lover - green and gold with a russet sail - mused Johnny Fortnight. As true a craft to be laid down this side of Plymouth these last twenty years. Set down your pack and shake the dust out of your shoes, Johnny, there's a life beyond the sandy byways of the north in the green country of the south. It's time to go courting, my lad! He put a hand to his pack again and pulled out a fistful of ribbons, deep as the violets nestling below the hedgerows; violet to match her eyes......

Diggory Martyn was publican at the Moonraker; large and rosy and rubicund, with a flamboyant taste in waistcoats and an enviable collection of clay pipes at his disposal, lined up in racks behind the bar. He had, it seemed, stepped straight from the frames of those eighteenth century paintings still to be found hanging on cottage walls, foxed and faded, mottled with age and damp; the cheery publican, feet firmly planted before a blazing log fire, tankard in hand, regaling a motley collection of his patrons, eyes bright and nose aglow. Diggory, on the surface, exuded the same geniality, but he was not a man to cross, even so.

When Johnny Fortnight asked for Mrs. Toller, Martyn inclined his head towards the stout, panelled door to the parlour and said:

'Share out.' This conveyed little to the packman, the intruder from Up-Country. He nodded to the publican and strode across the floor. His hand was on the latch before Diggory's deep voice boomed out. 'That's no place for you, son!' The packman could have halted and turned in his tracks but perhaps he was deaf or ignorant. He opened the door and stood resolutely between the jambs.

The panelled parlour was softly lit by a trio of oil lamps and the log fire of a hundred paintings, well stacked against the fire back. The corners were dark and uncertain but the group about the stout table in the centre of the room were well illuminated and flattered by the lamplight. All eyes turned toward the stranger, all conversation ceased.

There was a boy, fourteen, maybe younger, with a fresh complexion and tousled fair hair, sprawled untidily in his chair, obviously the son, Tabby's intended, young Mathey Toller, and the big man, tough, compact with thick hair, dark as lamp black, and, at thirty two, a face already seamed and folded by the power of wind, sea and sun - this was Esco Cluett, Tabby's father and already known to the packman. But the young man he did not know - fair hair and louche grey eyes and a mocking smile to his mouth. If this was a party, a celebration, and by the white linen cloth spread out on the table and the tempting array of pies and patties and good Cornish beer, then Jack Toller was making no effort, still clad in the navy Guernsey and high sea boots of his calling. But to these three Johnny Fortnight paid little heed. His eyes had fastened themselves upon Annabel Toller. She was tall for a woman, narrow of waist and shapely - he had watched her before now, ahead of him in the street, long black skirt hiding even a glimpse of an ankle, hips swaying easily, shoulders back and that neat red head of hers perched on top of a long slender neck as precisely as a

ball in a fountain. He liked the way those rebellious
tendrils slipped out of their pins and sprang about her
nape with a will of their own. Today she wore a crisp
white blouse, pin-tucked and pleated and rising high up
her throat, virginal and puritanical and sending prickles
up his spine. She was not a beautiful woman, she had too
much fire in her for such a passive adjective but she was
probably finer for the years she carried than when Frank
Toller had wed his carrot-topped, ringletted, school mate
and taken her down to the house along The Strand with
the green front door and the stout shutters and the rioting pots of geraniums which spilt their vermillion petals
along the cobbled walkway. She lived there still, even
after Fosfelle became empty and she came into the inheritance. Some said she dared not go back, that once the
walls had enclosed her they would not let her go again
and she needed all her resolve to put it up for sale. But
those who knew her better said she stayed along The
Strand because she liked it there, down on the sea's edge
with her handsome husband, her small son and a ram
cat, ginger like herself, half wild and just as untameable.

The packman bowed, not too low and smiled his
easy smile.

'Johnny Fortnight!' she said, angry at this intrusion
into their private world.

'John Maddaver,' he said 'and always at your service.'

'This is a private function. You intrude, Maddaver,'
said Jack Toller looking Johnny Fortnight up and down
and approving what he saw and disliking his own
approval because any man with any presence about him,
any man who could raise himself above the care-worn
and the hang-dog in these difficult days was a threat to
his own security.

'I apologise,' said Maddaver 'but I thought to speak with Mrs. Toller. The occasion seemed apt, the yearly share-out, I gather?'

'Speak out then,' said Toller, rising and moving to the fireplace, kicking at a protruding log, sending the sparks flying. He was four inches short of Maddaver. It didn't normally matter. Today it irked him.

'I came to speak to Mrs. Toller,' said Maddaver firmly.

'We're kin, you can speak out.'

'No,' said Maddaver easily enough and

'No!' said Annabel forcefully. 'I'll hear him, Jack, in private as he asks. We've finished here. Go home with Mathew, I'll see you later.'

Jack swore, only half under his breath, turned and grabbed for his coat and blundered out. 'I'll be at the boat. Mathey, Esco?' The boy and the big man who was Tabby's father, followed slowly as if they were half ashamed to be always at his beck and call but knowing that they would always do as he bid; habits too hard to break.

When the door closed behind Esco, Maddaver, unbidden, took a chair opposite Annabel. She noted his presumption and frowned. The brows beneath the red curls clustering her temple were darker, finely drawn.

'Be brief, Mr. Maddaver.' She saw him look down at his hands, placed before him on the table, and knew he was nervous and would not look at her as he began to speak. It should have given her a sense of power over him but she disregarded it. The hands were long and pale and tapered; those of a stained-glass saint, not the rough, chapped, hardened fingers of the men who cleared nets down on the quay.

'The Waterwitch - you can't possibly manage with two men and a boy, you need four men grown.'

'Times are hard, a bad summer,' said Annabel 'and that would mean six shares.'

'Six?' hesitated Maddaver 'I said four.'

'Six shares, Johnny Fortnight, you know nothing. One for the boat and one for the gear, one for each of the crew.'

'Only a half share for the boy,' said Maddaver genially.

'The boy is my son, he takes a full share. We manage. Take on another hand and that would cut Jack's share, and Esco's. If you're offering yourself for hire the answer is 'no'. A year and you wouldn't have the half of Mathey's knowledge.'

'He is a likely boy,' agreed Maddaver 'but you're giving him a hard life, Mrs. Toller, and a fraught one. A boat undermanned like that, a force eighter, a freak sea…. You could lose him.'

Annabel laughed; she was quite pretty when she laughed. 'I would lose you faster, Johnny Fortnight. I'll think about it. I'll speak to Jack and Esco. An apprentice on a half share? Perhaps we might give it a try.'

Maddaver smiled. 'No, Mrs. Toller, a full share, a man's share. You built the Waterwitch. You own her. Make it your decision. Brother Jack will do me no favours; that I'll warrant. A full share.'

'But you're not my son,' said Annabel.

Maddaver rose, he was facing her, leaning over, palms flat on the table between them.

'No, Annabel, but I intend to become your husband.'

Her lips parted in the 'O' of recognised effrontery as his lips came down upon hers in the lightest, most tantalising of kisses and he was away across the room before she had time to think of slapping his face. He turned at the door and swept her a low bow before retreating and closing it behind him. She heard him laughing as he crossed the tap room floor.

'Jack would obliterate him for that!' she thought. But she did not tell him, only that Johnny Fortnight thought to become a fisherman and they laughed about it together.

'I can handle this myself,' she thought. 'I don't need Jack to fight all my battles. But that wasn't the reason, it had more to do with the thought of the long white fingers battered and bruised in a fist fight and a bloody gash where the hard firm lips had been. In the house along The Strand Jack was drinking tea, dark as creosote, from the thick china pot. He lifted his cup and grinned at her maliciously. 'The old toast,' he said 'to Fish and Tin, and death to the pretensions of up-country pedlarmen. Drink up, Annabel!'

Maddaver didn't try again for some time but he saw her often, standing at the pump with the other women, leaning over the harbour wall, calling down to Mathew, skirt kilted up like a fish-wife; climbing the steps to Church for Hetty Varco's wedding, gowned in lavender grey, the lightest of muslins, hardly more than lip service to the mourning which lay more lightly upon her these days and sent hope leaping in the packman's breast.

There were many who noticed that Johnny Fortnight's visits were becoming far more frequent and would soon necessitate a change of nickname.

'If it isn't Johnny Twice-a-week,' giggled Tabby Cluett as he stood at her mother's door, doffing his strange battered hat and drawing in the mixed aromas of oxtail soup and fish pie.

On his way up hill to Mrs. Cluett's he had to pass along The Strand, pass Annabel's house, Chy-an-Lor - House of the Moon in the Cornish tongue - with its climbing geranium, its green panelled front door with the sturdy brass knocker - a Saracen's head, grinning fiercely at any who dared to take him by the beard. Chy an Lor was the grandest house in The Strand. It was once the home of Captain Abel Turk, one of the old Cape Horners and skipper of the Mexica which took him to the bottom of the Skaggerac one wild November night. He it was who had adopted the Saracen's head as a visible pun upon his own name and planted the turk's cap lilies in the tiny plot of garden at the back where they still flourished under Annabel's hand. Maddaver could see himself as master of Chy an Lor, as skipper of the Waterwitch but most of all as master of Annabel herself, with the wild red hair running through his fingers and the imagined white of her body close under his own.

He would stand at the end of The Strand where the path wound away up to The Burrows and the winding coast path and leant against the comforting stone wall which seemed as if it alone could hold back the cliff; grey and lichened, festooned with curtains of ivy, and the upright candles of pennywort, where in summer the bees droned lazily and the joyful pink of sturdy valerian sprang out, striving toward the sun.

Johnny Maddaver had strayed north, over the Tamar, to the verdant pasture lands of Devon, to gentler green hills and the scented blossom clouds of the apple orchards, to the busy brightness of Barnstaple, to the grace of Exeter But the Duchy had hauled him back again to its rocky sea board, to its grey hidden ports, to the smell of sea and wet, of salt and pilchard oil, of green turpentine and the Borneo Cutch they used for curing the nets, of tar and bladder-wrack and the evil stench of the mud sucking round the keels when the tide is out, and the smell of the spring born on the south-westerlies. Cornwall had claimed him long ago.

Chapter Two

It had been a bad summer, would they ever admit otherwise? The pilchard shoals had kept away from their usual hunting ground eastward toward the Wolf Rock and switching to Dogging in October and November had brought little reward. But yesterday, Job Varco on the 'Hopewell' had returned with his fish holds brimming with living silver; the pilchards were back up channel! Usually a little cagey, he had reported the shoals out between Polperro and the Eddystone and plenty for all.

The Waterwitch was thirty eight foot of English oak, caulked and painted, decked with pitch-pine and supporting two fine masts. Her foremast carried a large dipping lug sail, her mizzen a smaller standing lug, warm russet against the blue skies of summer. When they shot her drift nets it was necessary to lower her foremast though the mizzen remained set to enable her to ride comfortably in a seaway.

There were narrow walkways to connect the partial decks fore and aft and between the decks lay her fish and net holds and her six foot wheelhouse. Below lay the cabin with its bunks and lockers and the friendly bulk of the coke stove in the corner. Waterwitch had been built at Polruan at the mouth of the Fowey River. 'No finer shipyards in all the Duchy!' declared Esco Cluett. He had been there at her launching and seen her slip gently into the river, bright with bunting. Afterwards, they all stood on the quay and drank the last of the champagne from Dr. Boase's cellar.

Jack, Esco and the boy were down at the boat after lunch on Friday, hauling aboard twenty nets and coal for the stove. As darkness fell they sailed out on a light south-westerly, looking about for gannets those tell-tale harbingers of the pilchard shoals. It was Mathey's sharp young nostrils that first caught the whiff of fish oil on the water and they shot their flotter net, first of the twenty, in the bight of the Rame within sight of the dark shore line; the Eddystone light winking away on their other side, comforting, friendly somehow.

'Handsome night,' said Esco, though his position at the head rope gave him little chance for star gazing. Jack, working at the leech, grinned back at him; two shot and eighteen to go, it would be a long night. They marked the flotter net with a hurricane lamp and watched it bob away from them. Every now and then Esco allowed himself to turn and curse the boy at the wheel but Mathey wasn't a bad lad, a dreamer when all was said and done, but who isn't at thirteen?

Later, they had time to go below and sit about the stove with a mug of tea and a pasty. At first there was little said. They knew, all three, how to hold a lengthy and meaningful conversation in monosyllables, enriched with a twitch of the head, a sniff or a snarl - economy of effort whilst they refuelled their aching bodies for the long haul ahead.

Esco, not averse to riling Jack purely in the cause of healthy argument, lit his pipe and settled comfortably onto his bunk.

'That Maddaver be fair set on your mother, Mathey. How do 'ee fancy a new father to clip 'ee about the ear?'

'I don't and she wouldn't!' said Mathey darkly 'Marry him, I mean. She couldn't think to marry again!'

'Be realistic, lad, your mother's a handsome woman. Women always want more babies. They didn't break the mould when you appeared.'

'She wouldn't do that to me! Jack wouldn't let it happen.' He turned to his young uncle, stretched out on a bench, hands behind his head. He was a good-looking rogue, too much of his piratical old father there, Esco thought. A real bad 'un some folk said. Esco was used to him, you couldn't fear a man you had striped enough times when he was a boy.

Jack only smiled his slow, louche smile. 'There'll be no wedding bells for Annabel,' he said 'never fret. Now get your oilskins on, we'd best start hauling!'

It was a good night's work. They hauled and cleared and the fish hold began to fill and Esco, wiping sweat and salt from his forehead, might have been Simon Peter on the Sea of Galilee and all other fishermen in between. The pleasure was there over a good catch, even though there was a morning's work ahead of them, counting the fish into baskets.

Annabel was on the quayside when they arrived back in harbour as she always was. There was no need to ask if it had been a good trip. The brimming holds, the looks on their tired, strained faces were enough. Jack tossed up his bow rope and she hitched it competently to the top of the wooden skids, the notched baulks of timber fixed to the harbour wall in lieu of ladders. She was aboard as soon as they were secured, helping to count the catch out into the wicker maunds, giving a hand to Mathey beginning on the laborious task of checking the nets for damage before they could be stored away again ready for the next trip. The boy was tired out; his movements mechanical, the long-lashed lids drooping, flickering over sore eyes that would no longer focus. Once he slipped, manhandling a full maund. Esco caught him and set him firmly on his feet again.

'Bed,' said Jack 'I guess there'll be a brick in yours, eh Annabel? A pity there's nothing in mine,' he laughed, prodding Mathey in the right direction. 'There was plenty out there last night and the weather set to stay fair.' He ran a hand through salt-encrusted hair.

Annabel, the wind whipping her own red locks out of their pins said. 'You can be out by sundown then?'

'The gear's in good trim; no real problem.' Jack took her by the shoulders and shook her lightly.

'Girl, since when did Sunday forget to follow Saturday? It is Saturday - unless the whole fleet has downed tools and taken a day off for an early Christmas!' He motioned towards the line of luggers already berthed, gear stowed neatly, sails furled, hatches fastened down. But Annabel's violet eyes held a challenge. He said, 'Esco, shall we chance it again tonight? I'll have you back in time for chapel or take eternal damnation on myself.'

'Sabbath breaking?' said Cluett. 'Is this your idea, ma'am?'

'It's been a hard summer,' said Annabel 'perhaps our luck has changed.'

Jack said, 'I'll see you down here again about six o'clock. Right?'

'Damn you, boy! Mrs. Cluett will carve me up with that tongue of hers. Six o'clock it is.' He went striding off along the quay, hardly heavier of step than when he had appeared the previous evening clutching the brown paper parcel containing the night's provisions.

Annabel said, 'Come home with us, no point in trekking up the cliff.'

'Annabel, the village matrons will crucify you for this, you know that. That red-headed wild-de-go, putting her own child to sea before he's scarce weaned, kilting up her skirts and gabbing with the men along the quay about the price of fish and her own good man only gone these past four years.'

'And that brother-in-law of hers' continued Annabel, 'worse than his wild rake-hell of a father...' They had turned off the quay and out along The Strand. Jack continued: 'And her sainted mother and good old Dr. Boase turning beneath the turf for sure at her ungodly ways. Burn her, burn the Waterwitch!' He pushed open the door to Chy an Lor and pulled her behind him into the dark warmth of the hall, not more than a broom closet in size. Then he kissed her full upon the mouth, pulling her towards him, feeling for her breasts beneath her coat.

Annabel said, 'Brothers-in-law don't kiss like husbands – so I've always understood.'

'No more they do,' said Jack and kissed her again.

They went out on the flood in the winter darkness and left Annabel on the quay. There were mutterings but after all it was still Saturday and they had lobster pots to the west, there were many reasons for a short trip down the coast. No cause for real comment or suspicion. Only they didn't sail to the south west, they were off east again, back towards Rame Head and the pilchard shoals, and Saturday slipped into Sunday and they did not come home.

If God was mocked by their presumption he did not withdraw his bounty. The nets they hauled over the starboard side were blue-white with a flickering phosphorescence, here and there weighted dangerously with a spat of pilchards whose bulk was likely to take the net to the bottom and cost them the loss of the whole net. But the worst did not happen and the weather kept fair and the stars were white asters, bright enough to outline the coast and the curve of Whitesand Bay.

It took them seven hours to haul and clear the nets and the sun was climbing, if invisibly, In lowering cloud, when they made for home.

'This is the life, isn't it, Jack?' said Mathey.

His uncle didn't smile. He only said: 'When we moor, you get straight on home and you stop for nothing and you talk to no one, you understand me?'

'It's a free country. What's stopping them following us?' said Mathey. 'The Varcos'll grump about us. Who's scared by the Varcos? I can take it, Jack.'

'You'll do as you're bid or you'll know about it,' said Jack, at the wheel, taking the Waterwitch clean into the mouth of the harbour. Mathey put two fingers up to his uncle's back and Esco clouted him.

'Jack, you might have held back until they were all in chapel!'

Annabel was waiting upon the quay, already surrounded by a vociferous crowd of women, clad in their Sunday best. The clouds which had banked up as the Waterwitch headed for home now released their snowy burden, thick white flakes that whirled about the group on the quay like the glass snowball which sat upon the mantelpiece in Annabel's parlour.

'It's against all the laws of Church and nature!' said Jenna Varco. God help us, Annabel, but your Frank was a good man, a good neighbour, he'd never have set foot aboard on a Sunday, a Christian husband if ever there was one.'

Jack Toller, sprinting onto the quay said, 'death confers sainthood upon the strangest people. Did I have such a man for a brother, Jenna?'

'And your poor mother,' said Jenna, ignoring him, 'twice to Church every Sunday, God rest her!'

'And her father turning in his grave!' shouted Jack above the snow wind.

"Es, surely,' said Jenna.

Annabel had left the group to their doom-laden prophecies. 'For God's sake be silent, Jack, they're fuelled high enough as it is. Wait till the menfolk get here, they've no love for you at the best of times.'

'And who sent me out, walking on the water? It was a good night's work, Annabel, I've sent Mathey home.'

'I'll give you a hand.'

Later, there was a deputation round to Chy an Lor. Three good men and true, feet planted firmly on the Turkish carpet in the parlour, hands behind their backs, looking uncomfortable in their Sunday suits.

Annabel faced the Sabbath Keepers, demure in a crisp white blouse. Pearl buttons and pin-tucks were her armour. She was Frank Toller's widow again, a young matron and mother.

'It can't happen again,' said Job Varco, clearing his throat.

'The Sabbath is the Sabbath.' This from Esco's brother-in-law, Tom Lethaby.

'You'll give us your assurance and no more will be said.' Joseph Honeychurch was Minister at the Chapel. He didn't hold with the Tollers and the Deverels who trekked off to the church on the hill of a Sunday.

'Gentlemen, no promises. I make decisions as and when it's necessary. The Waterwitch is my property, she sails when I direct it, as she'll lie up when I think fit, and you can line up all the village elders here on the rug , you'll get no more from me. I've noted that we've irked some of you ......'

'Irked,' snorted Varco, 'a mild word, girl. Set the village by the ears; cat among the pigeons.'

'Fox in the hen coup?' snapped Annabel. 'Trevander won't be the worse for a shake-up, sleepy Sunday or no. Please leave!'

'I don't think you understand how high feelings are running,' said Honeychurch.

'Oh, I think I do. You know where the door is, Mr. Honeychurch.'

'Listen, my girl...'

'I'm not YOUR girl!'

'It's no use,' said Varco, 'her father would have spanked her.'

'Out!' shrieked Annabel, and sent the snowscene spinning toward him. All three ducked and it hit the door post to shatter on the floor. They shuffled out speedily and Mathey, who had been hiding on the stairs, ran in to find her kneeling on the floor, dusting off the little man with the umbrella; his crinolined partner was headless.

'Oh, mother, you didn't!'

'I'm afraid so, they descended upon us like the leaders of the Sanhedrin, what did they expect? Mind the glass splinters. Your father bought me this.'

'You won't' said Mathey, eyes dark-circled, 'marry John Maddaver?'

'The packman? The Lord of Langarrock?' laughed Annabel. But she only said, 'fetch me the brush and crumb tray. It was a good catch, Mathey. God isn't against us.'

'Then we'll go again?'

'Does it worry you?'

'Not when I'm with Jack, nothing scares Jack. He's the sort of fellow you could follow to the end of the earth and back and never a qualm.'

'Be yourself, Mathey. Never be Jack's shadow. You were born into the world an original; don't seek to die any man's copy. Lecture over! Go to bed, darling.'

She sat for a long time in the darkness, the firelight gleaming on brass and silver, the middle class legacy of Fosfelle which set Chy an Lor above all others along The Strand and set Annabel aside as a lady rather than a fishwife. The sounds within were magnified, the tic-toc of the long case clock, the creak of furniture settling itself for the night, once even the patter of mice behind the wainscoting. Beyond the walls, far out into the night she could hear the murmur of the sea and the sound of the snow wind. Annabel felt like the little headless lady of the snowscene, standing there whilst the world whirled about her. Her life with Frank seemed so far away, divorced from the day's happenings. Frank Toller was lying under a green mound beneath the same moss covered headstone which marked his mother's resting place. Janniper Boswell had been of gypsy stock and her wildness had suited old Jem Toller. Jack was so much more their son than Frank had been; handsome, genial, dependable Frank who had set the world on an immovable axis. But Frank was in the churchyard and Johnny Maddaver away in the north in the lost lands of the Atlantic sea-board, but Jack Toller, the gypsy's brat was here in Trevander, head down in the tumbledown cottage up the hill towards The Burrows and Jack had a touch to send fire through her body and a love and loyalty for the two she loved; Mathey her son and the Waterwitch. And if she lost one she would as likely lose all three, out off Black Head in the eye of a storm as Emily Trevose, two doors away, had lost a husband and two sons when the Rosebud had foundered three winters before; her youngest was barely sixteen, full of fun and eager for life. Annabel rose and lifted an oil lamp and the shadows jumped and swayed. Somewhere a shutter clattered against an outside wall. Her shadow followed her up the narrow wooden staircase to her room. She stood at the window looking out over the last lights of the village, caught up in the snow storm.

CHAPTER THREE

That first time, to fish on the Sabbath had been reckless, a second such trip was outright folly and ensured another visit from the village hierarchy, and the women in knots on the street corners had shaken their heads over young Jack Toller and murmured that the devil looks after his own and Jack had grinned behind their backs and sauntered on, his sea boots slapping the cobbles. On the third trip the Waterwitch came home early for her holds were brim full. Annabel had not expected them. When she reached the quay, still pulling her shawl about her head, the Waterwitch was already moored and there was a sizeable crowd gathering. Light-footed she ran towards them and they gave way a little, stood back and hissed at her like angry geese. Selena Cluett said, 'Tes my man you've got on board there, Annabel Toller. My Esco's a good man, a god-fearing man.'

'Your Esco,' snapped Annabel 'has a mind in his head and a tongue behind his teeth. Out of my way, Selena Cluett!'

'There's sauce for 'ee, Selena,' said Jenna Varco. 'I'd box the minx's ears!' She clutched at Annabel's shawl and with a toss of her head the girl freed herself of its encumbrance and thrust the unfortunate Jenna aside, a hand on the flat of her ample chest. Mrs. Varco, skirt billowing about her, sank like a galleon after a sudden, disastrous shift in cargo and she landed with a thud on her less well-upholstered rear. Annabel made her escape down the stout wooden ladder affixed to the quay.

'What was all that about?' Jack hardly looked up, still clearing nets.

'That harridan,' spat Annabel 'Jenna Varco, holier than thou and a face on her like the Medusa. Talk about the crock calling the kettle smutty if ever I heard of it!'

'Christ, what was that!' said Jack as something thudded beside him on the deck, followed by another missile.

'The devil take 'em, they'm stoning we!' said Esco, pushing his cap up from his eyes. What're 'ee about?' he yelled. 'Garn! Let a man go about his lawful business!'

'Tisn't lawful on a Sunday!' yelled someone. 'Tisn't God's law. There were witches up on the moor not so long since. They've come down to Trevander now, it seems!'

'Dear God,' said Jack 'a skinful of preaching and fish pie and they'll be seeing piskies before the afternoon's out!'

'Mother, look out!' yelled Mathey, his uncertain voice ending in an undignified squeak. He was bending to collect the missiles, mostly cobble stones and hurling them back with uncanny accuracy into the crowd when Jack grabbed him by the scruff of the neck.

'Below and stay there!'

'Jack, I'll miss the fun!'

'You'll do as you're told unless you want a rope's end round your rear. That'll be no fun at all. Make your mind up.' Mathey threw him a look of hatred and disappeared down the cabin hatch. Esco was bawling up at his wife about as oblivious to the raining cobble stones as the Rock of Gibraltar in a hail storm. Jack had been caught in the face, a jagged cut on his right cheek bone; it bled profusely. He looked terrible. Annabel was at his side, her wild eyes blazing fury.

'Jack, you're hurt, you really are hurt!'

'Annabel,' said he 'did I ever tell you you were beautiful?'

'You'm mad,' said Esco. 'Us all are. They'll never let us land the catch; it'll rot in the maunds. By God, Selena, I'll have something to say to 'ee, standing there screeching like a whitneck! Let us up now!' But his words were met with a barrage of projectiles, clattering on the deck boards, splattering in the open fish hold. They never heard the one that caught Annabel on the temple and sent her to the deck; slow and graceful and unreal, like a scene from a magic lantern running out of steam. She lay like a discarded doll, in a froth of petticoats too richly edged in lace for a fisherman's widow.

'More like a city chorus girl,' said Jenna Varco jealously, 'a fisherman's widow or a fisherman's whore!' Her gimlet eyes met Jack's grey gaze.

'She's hurt!' sobbed Mathey, bursting up from below decks. 'Can't you see she's hurt?'

In Cinderella, it was a Fairy Godmother; in Aladdin, it was a Genie. In Trevander on the Sunday before Christmas it was Johnny Fortnight, elbowing his way along the quay, shouting them down, threatening, swearing, the constable, panting along after him, and it was Johnny Fortnight with the long legs, clearing the ladder two rungs at a time until he was beside Annabel, one long hand feeling for the pulse in the fine white neck.

'She'll live,' jeered Jack.

'I'll take her home-along,' said Maddaver, 'get the boy and clear us a path. Esco, bide with the Waterwitch, I'll be back and give you a hand.'

'We're even nearer to Christmas than I thought,' said Jack.

'You're damn fools all of you,' said Maddaver angrily, Annabel, coming round in his arms, decidedly groggy and with blood in her hair. Between them they got her up onto the quay and Maddaver swept her up into his arms and strode away towards Chy an Lor. Jack had a strong arm about Mathey's shoulders.

It was Maddaver who carried Annabel upstairs to her bed and fetched water and bathed the cut and set Mathey to keep an eye on her whilst he and Jack returned to the Waterwitch. He worked with a will, counting pilchards into maunds, though his back was breaking and his fingers were raw. Jack, taciturn and silent most of the time eventually shot him a sidelong glance and a wry smile. 'It's one way of getting your feet under the table, I suppose, working towards being indispensable. But a berth on the Waterwitch doesn't guarantee you'll ever lie between lavender scented sheets and wake up in the weeds of her hair.'

'I could,' said Maddaver, 'I should, decorate the other side of your face.'

'But you won't,' said Jack 'because you want a fair fight and wouldn't see me disadvantaged. Whereas I, they'll all be pleased to tell you, never fight fair. Get off the magic carpet, Maddaver, before it gets tugged from under your feet!'

Sitting by the fire, faces near as white as their bandaged heads and as acquiescent as you were ever likely to find them, Jack and Annabel let Maddaver's easy bantering voice wash about them. It had a soporific quality combined with the mulled wine, poured generously from a jug on the hearth. By the end of the evening it would

have seemed ridiculous and more, churlish, to have
turned down his offer of a hand with the boat and before
the midnight chimes from Ann Boase's grandmother
clock had died away they were almost in agreement that
in the name of peace and harmony in the community
they should curtail their Sunday excursions. And so,
effortlessly, insidiously, Johnny Fortnight laid aside his
pack, gave up his bare, faceless room on the north coast
and settled in with the Cluetts where it was possible to
feed well, and get your laundry done and where there
was a fire in the bedroom between October and May and
bright chintz hangings and lavender scented sheets and a
vase of deep purple lupins on the dresser. Years later, the
peppery scent of lupins could always conjure up that
room, that haven against the storms to which he would
so willingly retreat after a day's fishing; a warm crackling silence after Jack Toller's scathing sarcasm and
Esco's lashing tongue and Mathey's scorn. Sometimes
even thoughts of Annabel's white body could not
compensate for the pain of his hands and the bone-
weariness, and only an inherent stubbornness kept him
hanging on grimly. But he was learning.

Every week, looking back, it seemed the chalice of a
brimming, infinite knowledge of sea-lore bound him
closer to the Waterwitch in all her moods, as changeful as
a woman, as wilful as Annabel who kept him further than
arm's length, allowing no liberties. But he was prepared
to wait, to sit back and watch village life pass by in colourful vignettes, lives that hardly seemed to touch his own
self-containment. Had he stopped to consider he would
have known that he was waiting for Jack to make a move,
handsome, passionate Jack who belonged to this envi-
ronment, complemented it and was trapped by it, all at

one and the same time. No painted subject ever belonged so to his creator's canvas, effortlessly melting into the scene yet standing forward from its mundanity not Napoleon on the Bellerophon or the Mona Lisa amongst her rocks. To see him striding along The Strand or climbing the steep cobbles to The Burrows, haggling in Market Street or leaning over the quay wall, fair hair tousled, faded blue Guernsey clinging to his lithe young body, sea boots and rolling gait proclaiming his trade, was to place Long John Silver on board the Hispaniola or Ham Peggoty in the flat sea-scape of East Anglia. But Jack was young and healthy and anything but a philanderer. He had loved Annabel since he was twelve years old and though there had been experimental trystings in Pellymounter's net loft there had never been a serious commitment. Running errands once for Peter Trinnick the baker, bounding up the steps from The Strand through the little wrought iron gate which lead into the gardens of Fosfelle, he had found her lying on the daisy spotted grass, gazing deep into the lily pool, her white skirts spread, her red hair clouded about her. It had been enough.

'He'll give in,' said Jack cheerfully. They were clearing the deck for the return home, 'He'll go back to the byways again and be glad of it.'

But Esco shook his head. 'Will 'ee wager on it? No, the lad's got more about 'un. One thing to your advantage though, 'un'll never have the stamina to afford Mrs. Toller any pleasure. Not like your brother who put the sea behind 'un with the closing of the bedroom door.'

'Oh, all for the conventions was our Frank!' laughed Jack who had caught the typhus and survived. 'She wouldn't get as far as the bedroom if I had my way, Esco, the rug before the parlour fire would do us very well....'

'Mrs. Toller pays me,' said Esco. 'That's dirty talk so you'll refrain. I'm still bigger than you, lad. A man can have his dreams but you'll keep your tongue from such profanities, d'you hear me? There be whorehouses in Plymouth if 'ee have the need.'

Jack laughed. 'I don't reckon to Plymouth. Annabel *is* a whore, she just doesn't know it!' He leapt the net hold coamings, agile as a goat, when Esco lunged for him. But the feint was half-hearted. It must have occurred to Esco too.

In May, they decided to go spiltering for mackerel, which meant a change of gear for the Waterwitch. Away with the baskets of lines and hooks used for longlining and out with the finer lines used for spiltering.

They kept their nets and lines in the loft above the Nankivell's sail yard, and it was a hike down along The Strand and round the corner into Fore Street but it gave them the room they needed for mending nets and storing floats.

Mathey and Maddaver were at the boat, painting the coamings a smart sea green. Annabel, lured by the warmest of Mays into white muslin, leant over the wall above their berth, swinging down a couple of pasties, swathed in cheese cloth, from the end of a boat hook, waved a hand and set off along The Strand to Nankivell's with a third dinner for Jack.

Even above the smells of fish and tar and mud which permanently pervaded the village, it was possible to sniff summer in the air and the cobbles were spattered with the creamy snow of may blossoms, blown down from the stilted hawthorns atop the cliffs; sweet and cloying on the wind. Someone was singing deep inside the bakery, way below the level of the street. Diggory Martyn at the

Moonraker doffed his hat and called, 'summer's come, ma'am!'

'It has indeed, Mr. Martyn.' She gathered her skirts and ran lightly up the outside staircase above Nankivell's, calling for Jack.

In the net-loft it was velvet blackness after the sunlight of Fore Street. She hesitated in the doorway, a perfect silhouette against the light, like a child's shadow picture. Jack was sitting on the window-sill, one knee drawn up, one arm linked about it. He was smoking; she could see the white spiral curling against the blue of the sky.

'Dinner,' said Annabel. 'I'm pleased to see you working so hard.'

'I hate sarcasm in a woman,' grinned Jack. 'Come here!' She picked her way carefully through an obstacle course of coiled ropes and discarded danns, and tumbled hurricane lamps. There was a fine view from the glassless window, a roofscape of greys and duns, patched with yellow lichens and tufts of coarse and tenacious grasses, of glinting windows under shadowed eaves, of blue glimpses of Trevander bay, all criss-crossed with a lattice of gulls' wings. Below them, the Nankivells' squat apple tree was a pink and white parasol of blossom, alive with the lazy hum of honey bees.

'It's beautiful,' said Annabel 'like a soft cushion of cloud.' She leant out; drawing in deep breaths of its sweetness, watching the Katie sweeping into the bay, back from checking her lobster pots.

Jack could only catch the scent of Annabel's perfume, light and floral. The touch of her sleeve on his bare brown arm caused him to flinch involuntarily. He laughed at himself and said. 'You have blossoms in your hair, here, let me.' He drew her back from the window, plucking at the tiny creamy petals, blowing them out over the sill from the ends of his fingers. And, when there were no more of the miscreants to flick away he began upon her hair pins, laying them in neat rows upon the sill.

'Jack, I'll have it all to do again before I go up the street!' She admonished him, laughing, pushing him away with a slender hand. Not as smooth and white as her mother's - Jane Boase had never cleared a net or counted pilchards - but it was still a neat, woman's hand, a lady's hand. Beneath it she felt the roughness of his Guernsey, male and uncompromising. He caught her against him, one hand locked in the red hair, his kiss upon her throat.

'I've loved you for too long, Annabel, I can't go on wanting, not like this.' He knew every inch of the net-loft and steered them backwards towards the tarpaulins which covered the mesh of their pilchard nets. The whiteness of her dress, her face pale above it, made of her a ghost in the gloom; floating, incandescent.

'Jack, no. I can't!'

'Yes, you can, you want it as much as I. Frank died almost five years ago. I said I'd take care of everything.'

'And this is the care you have for me?' Annabel held him off. He was not so much taller than she, but he was lithe and young and strong.

'I can't,' said Jack 'let you go out of the family, can I?' And, as she made to move aside he tripped her neatly onto her back in as dirty a move as he had ever used up on The Burrows, wrestling with the boys from nearby Penherrit. The nets and tarpaulins were buoyant enough, she came to no hurt and he was down beside her, kissing her again. Her hands were pinned beneath him; one of his own was free enough to tug her skirt upward.

'Greater love,' he gasped on a laugh 'hath no woman than that she raises her petticoats for her brother!'

'That is blasphemy,' snapped Annabel through her teeth. 'Well, if you're going to, why don't you? If I scream we'll have the Nankivells up here two at a time. Hurry it up, little brother; I've a mound of washing waiting for the copper. Don't take all afternoon!' Her derisory words hit him like a shock of cold water. He let her be and sat up.

'I'm sorry, I never meant to - that is, I thought you wanted it too. I love you, Annabel; I've never loved another woman. I can't go on any longer wondering how it would be. I'll leave. I'll leave Trevander, find a ship, get as far away as I can ....'

'Fool, you'll never leave Trevander,' said she softly. 'And what would we do without you, Mathey and I?'

He lay on his back. 'So I'm to stay and go through this torture at your nearness every day of my life? No, I'll ship out from Plymouth, end of the week.' But he knew she would never let him go. She was leaning over him, her hair whispering above his face. She was kissing away the beads of sweat clustered upon his forehead.

'Jack, there's a madness in my blood. It's May and five years is a lifetime. Let me know I'm still alive!'

The rafters were strong, seasoned ships' timbers, but the loft was barely floored over. The Nankivells below were used to the sounds of industry above, especially on winter days when the crew of the Waterwitch were all gathered, working away mending torn mesh, splicing rope, checking their floats .... There were a hundred and one sounds and the Nankivells took no heed. But it was May and Jack Toller was alone until Miss Airs and Graces arrived in her bridal white. Jimmits Nankivell had noted her taking to the stairs as light-footed as a schoolgirl and she hadn't come down an hour since. And there had been laughter and whisperings that carried all too well, and other sounds, all too familiar if you were a family man like Jimmits with six mouths to feed. But he might have kept things to himself had not Gwen arrived, laden with shopping, disgruntled from traipsing around the market, and Gwen had never forgiven Annabel for the Sabbath Wars. She herself was a Saturday night woman and the fewer of those the better. Wednesday dinner time seemed to make such behaviour more outrageous.

'Christ himself forgave the woman taken in adultery,' pointed out Jimmits in mild tones, hoping his wife was not going to make a scene.

'Tesn't adultery, since neither be married. 'Tes more like incest, he being her good-brother. The Church speaks out against fornication, then so should we. That little hussy who puts herself above the rest of the village, bedding down with that young ruffian like a tinker's whore!'

Jimmits sighed. Tinker's Whore was the strongest Gwen would go to - both being abhorrences set upon this earth to try honest folk. She stayed only long enough to watch Annabel Toller's departure down the outside stairs; gown crumpled and dusty, hair tumbling from its hastily re-arranged pins, before she was off on a progress across the village to burst in upon a Temperance Society meeting in the Methodist Hall, where she found it her duty to inform her sisters, both collectively (and later singly in more graphic detail), that Annabel Toller had taken her drawers down for brother Jack - such junketings and a Wednesday too!

The winged errant, rumour, fled from house to house like wildfire. Unlike the Angel of the Lord it passed over no door but knocked and found entrance with the highest and the lowest. Esco found Mathey crying in the cabin of the Waterwitch, sat down on his bunk and drew the boy to him. It was all foolish, wicked talk of course. He mustn't heed any of it. But Mathey was a sensible child and a worldly wise one – he sniffed, blew his nose and said that if it was going to happen he'd rather it was Jack than any other man, when all was said and done, but couldn't they have waited until they got home behind locked doors?

Esco privately agreed with him. There was talk of Annabel having to do penance at St. Petroc's on Sunday. That would be a blow to the Methodists but they would of course put their spies amongst the Anglicans.

'You can't go, ma'am!' said Esco. He was at her door early on Sunday. She wore a hat with cherry red ribbons and another white gown. The lobby smelt of bluebells, there was a huge jug spilling over with them on the hallstand.

'That's absurd,' said Annabel 'a bunch of old wives tittle tattling. If I stay at home it will add more fuel to their fires. I'm grateful for the warning, Esco but I'll not be intimidated by Gwen Nankivell and her harridans.'

'Then do 'ee have a care for the boy, ma'am, have him stay behind.'

Annabel was wavering at last. 'Yes, you're right. He can stay at home today. I'll think of some pretext. Don't fret, Esco, you'd best be going to chapel before Selena starts chaffing. I'll see you tomorrow, down at the boat.'

She closed the door and leant against it. In the mirror her face was white above the white gown. She pinched some colour into her cheeks and went to speak to Mathey. There was a scene as she had known there would be. He refused to stay behind and she ended by locking him in his room before she set off along The Strand to climb the hill to St. Petroc's, high on its sea cliff, where the tumbledown memorials of Trevander's dead perched perilously above the jagged rocks at the entrance to the bay.

Mathey was adept at climbing out of his bedroom window. Moving gingerly along with his toes gripping the string-course he was able to climb into his mother's bedroom where he let himself out of the front door and ran along The Strand and up to The Burrows and the Toller's tumbledown cottage. Jack was still in bed. His father, old Jem Toller, wouldn't even let his grandson over the front door step. He had no love for children and this grandchild of his was just another brat like the ones who pushed their way through the tangle of his holly-hocks and threw clods of earth at his windows and called him names.

Mathey went on hammering at the door until Jack's fair head eventually appeared at the window, unshaven, hair tousled. He looked terrible.

'Christ, what harm can come to her up there? Your wits are addled, Mathey. Go home!'

'No, I'm not leaving till you come down here!'

'If I do it'll only be to box your ears.' Jack slammed down the sash window and Mathey turned away, tears of rage stinging his eyes. He stood irresolutely in the middle of the road.

'Mathey, playing truant from church?' Johnny Fort-night, like Jack Toller, had little use for church or Chapel - High Days and Holidays maybe but on a sunny May morning there were other pleasures beckoning. Mathey shook his head. 'I'm not to go today. She locked me in only I climbed through the window; I always do. But something awful is going to happen to her. Esco came to warn her but she wouldn't listen. I don't know what to do.'

'Suppose you tell me what all this is about.'

'But you must know what they're saying!'

Maddaver shrugged: 'Maybe. I don't pay much heed.'

'I think it's true,' said Mathey in a low voice. 'I'm sure it must be. And now they say she'll have to do penance at Church, to atone for her sins. She should have let me go with her. Jack won't help. I guess he had a skinful last night!'

Maddaver grinned wryly: 'I expect you're right. Now go home and wash your face and don't fret. I'll go up to the church and see that all is well.' He set off up the hill with his easy, loping stride.

Somehow, Mathey felt comforted. He turned for home.

To be shunned by the women of Trevander was nothing new to Annabel Toller. To be leered at, to be given a second raking glance by the men was a disconcerting experience. Vanished forever was the louting respect traditionally awarded to Annabel Boase, the doctor's daughter. Even after the Sabbath War and that period of ostracism she had still been acknowledged as a cut above the country women in their rusty black skirts, the fisherwomen with their chapped hands and soiled aprons. She had been raised to that high plain inhabited by the Deverels, Lords of the Manor since 1429, and by little Miss Tweedie, the up-country schoolmistress from the smart side of Exeter. Now she was cast down from her pedestal, the stones flying; the woman taken in adultery or, if not exactly taken, overheard enjoying the experience which was the greater sin. And indeed, she showed no regrets today. She mocked them all in her virginal white, her maiden sprigged muslin, with too much on view of her freckled neck and shoulders and too much colour in her cheeks.

The experience had only brought the awakening of a hunger for life, a desire to step out of Frank Toller's shadow, to feel his grasp finally letting go, the wraith of his presence at her shoulder slipping back into the grave upon St. Petroc's Hill.

The wind blew in from the sea as she turned to step into the shadow of the lych-gate, and it lifted the hat from the red hair, tugging resentfully at its pins. It fell in loops and coils about her shoulders, adding to the abandonment in her heart. It was the most exhilarating moment in her life and moving towards the porch, between the mounds of the old graves, sprinkled with knots of spring flowers, she realised that as she had cast away the shadow of the beloved husband, she had also loosed the fetters which bound her to his young brother. His way was not to be her way and though there were no regrets for that sunlit afternoon and the darkness of the old sail loft and she would never forget the fire of his touch, she was free of him at last.

She entered the ancient darkness of St. Petroc's, passing between the pews where heraldic glass sent bright splashes of colour onto the grey flagstones, their chiselled skulls and chilling prophecies all but worn smooth by the shuffling of centuries of communicants - 'As you are now, so once was I!' Gravely, she was flanked by the Churchwardens, Mark Denbow and Ralph Combellack, escorting her to a seat at the entrance to the chancel, a penitent's seat - a scold's seat, she mused to herself. There was no help but to sit where she was bidden and await whatever came. There could be no undignified squabbling over a seat in her usual pew, no headlong flight out into the sunlight.

The familiar words o the liturgy floated over and around her and she could not feel herself a part of the day's events. The Reverend Mr. Trefusis was a vigorous man in his early forties. He did not mince words or shy away from a delicate topic like the grey old parsons of grey old hamlets set in the hollows of mist-haunted Cornish coombes. There would be no skirting round duty in the name of delicacy.

His sermon was all fire and brimstone, his subject - always one to hold his congregation in thrall - fornication; thrills for the virtuous and the savouring of guilt for the sinners - Revelation, Chapter Two, Verse 20.....

'*Thou sufferest that woman, Jezebel, which calleth herself a prophetess, to teach and to seduce my servants, to commit fornication, and to eat things sacrificed unto idols.*

'*And I gave her space to repent of her fornication; and she repented not ...*' His voice boomed out and lingered among the beams of the roof. '*Behold, I will cast her into a bed and them that commit adultery with her ....*' He was moving wildly about the pulpit now, one finger stabbing through the air, toward the woman beside the chancel steps.

Gwen Nankivell sniffed, 'she has no need of a bed, our loft was soft enough for her frolics, and where is he to be denounced, that arch-fiend of a brother-in-law?'

There were one or two men in the congregation who privately thought it the lightest of punishments to be flung into a bed with Annabel. Trefusis had set aside Revelation and was descending the worn stone steps from his airy seat. He stretched out a hand toward the young woman.

'Come, my daughter, rise and kneel with me and confess your faults and do penance. Follow not in the steps of Jezebel and be condemned to the everlasting bonfires for your harlotry!'

There was not a sound in the shimmering air of the nave. Two hundred souls held their breath communally. These were wonderful words. Who would have thought their parson had it in him! Annabel rose because there was nothing else to do, and at that moment the trump of doom rang out!

Johnny Fortnight had been standing in the shadow of the south doorway, now he let it slam behind him, breaking the parson's spell. Two hundred heads swivelled round on two hundred necks and watched him stride down the aisle, a strange figure in his ill-fitting Sunday suit. The rainbows from the climbing sun shattered upon him from the east window, leaving him in tatters of colour; ruby, emerald, sapphire and amethyst. Jane Nankivell was twelve years old and favoured Browning. She said into the silence. '*His queer long coat, from heel to head, was half of yellow and half of red...*' And, indeed, he looked a Pied Piper of a fellow, loping forward like an animated scarecrow. He gave Trefusis a nod and took Annabel's arm.

'No more of this, sir. I come to you today with a request that you should read the banns of marriage for Mrs. Toller and myself and I find wild accusations against her virtue. If I am pleased to consider her as the mother of my future sons, what faults should other men find in her? If you should be pleased to read our banns next Sunday, sir, there will be opportunity enough for gossip to point a finger or else forever hold the peace. Come, Annabel!' He tucked her arm into his, shortened his stride to her own and walked her down the nave. From the shadow of the south porch came a slow hand clap. Then Jack Toller moved swiftly out of sight.

'I shall not marry you!' hissed Annabel. 'I will not do it!' But she knew she had no choice.

'Oh, bravo!' said Jack from the dark shelter of a wind-riven yew tree. 'I underestimated you, Maddaver, fool that I was. I suppose I bow out now and wish you as much joy of your thousand and one nights as I had of her in an afternoon. But only remember that I had her first!' He turned on his heel in a violent movement and left the churchyard by the back way.

'So it was true?' said Maddaver quietly.

'Did you doubt it? Thank you for that, and for the loan of your name. You seem little likely to gain from your gallantry. I am not to be coerced into any man's bed!'

John Maddaver smiled into the may-scented air. 'Oh, I am well-satisfied,' he said.

CHAPTER FOUR

In spite of obvious disappointment amongst the church-goers of St. Petroc's, there was general relief in Trevander that an unsavoury episode was to have such a prosaic ending. Maddaver was generally well-liked, apart from the unfortunate fact of his being an outsider to the village. He would keep Annabel Toller in right ways, set her to child-bearing and let her take up a domestic role.

The wedding was an exceptionally quiet affair. Annabel wore lavender grey - very fitting for a second marriage. Jack Toller spent the evening in the Moon-raker, as drunk as anyone had ever seen him, and Mathey had been packed off to his Great Aunt Polly in St. Keverne for two or three days. If he had been grateful to his new step-father for rescuing his mother from appro-bation and shame he never showed it and in the weeks before the wedding, the boldness of his insolence fuelled with Jack's approval was growing daily.

Maddaver was now installed at Chy an Lor with feet firmly under the table. His place in his wife's bed was a more perilous acquisition. There was to be no question as to his taking to another room. He had to live in the same house as Mathey and to have been banished to the third bedroom - they only had three - would have been too great a source of rejoicing for the boy. So they occu-pied separate sides of Frank Toller's great bed, exchanged perfunctory kisses in public and privately had little converse. Maddaver was content to bide his time as he had all along, knowing that it infuriated and piqued Annabel that he could climb into bed beside her, snuff out his candle and turn his back upon her. She could never know how much this ritual cost him. The one crumb of comfort in this doll's house existence was that Annabel's pride would never reveal to Jack Toller that her marriage was an empty sham. Esco knew and sadly shook his head to himself. 'There's no bloom on the maid,' he muttered 'no bloom at all.'

The richest pilchard grounds in the West Country stretched between Lands End and the Scillies and for several weeks they set sail for the Wolf Rock, landing their catches at Newlyn, berthing the Waterwitch there for the weekend and travelling back to Trevander by train. Into September, with catches depleting they stayed nearer to home, sailing out beyond Polperro toward the Eddystone where there was an unseasonable glut.

They had been plagued by south westerly gales but that evening, the wind eased for a few hours and they decided to risk a trip. They went down to the Waterwitch at seven in that grey autumn dusk which renders all landscape into monochrome and softens and blurs the edges of the shoreline as the first of the Michaelmas mists found Trevander Bay.

They set out together, Maddaver, Mathey, Esco Cluett and Jack Toller, toward the red rocks of the Eddystone reef and the dubious comfort of the light. They shot their nets successfully and set the mizzen to keep the Waterwitch head to wind before breaking thankfully for tea and a bacon and egg supper. Usually, Esco found that time, sitting about the stove in the comfortable fug, one of contentment far approaching happiness, but today the atmosphere could be cut with a knife. Mathey's increasing animosity towards his step-father, encouraged by Toller, was reaching new heights and making life uncomfortable for them all. Esco, as the outsider could view all their problems with some detachment: Maddaver's wish to become a decent step-father to the awkward, insolent young boy whose life he had just turned upside down; Jack's chagrin at finally losing Annabel to the stranger from the north with whom he was forced to work and obliged to call Skipper, and Mathey's fear of being ousted from his mother's affection and ruled by the man who had all but tricked his way into their home.

Esco had boys of his own, if Ben and Santo were yet younger than Mathey Toller, and he could read the signs. The boy was merely testing the water, seeing how far he would be allowed to go, letting Maddaver pay out the rope and waiting for him to haul it tight. When Mathey was sent up on deck to take his share of the watch, Esco lit his pipe and said quietly, 'you'll be needing to make a stand, Skip, show 'un who's master. I know you've pussyfooted around 'un lately, courting popularity perhaps - being more than fair-minded, but 'tesn't working. A pinch of healthy hatred as long as it's seasoning for a deal of respect won't hurt you. But the respect you must have. Clear the air with 'un and set boundaries!'

Maddaver acknowledged that he was right. They donned their oilskins and went up on deck, hauling the boat astern by the spring rope until they reached their first net. Esco heaved the roller onto the starboard side and they proceeded to haul in a healthy catch; Esco on the leech, the main body of the net, Maddaver on the headrope; Jack clearing the mesh of the living silver hoard and Mathey stowing floats and coiling rope. They were so busy, working automatically, that they hardly had time to mark that the wind was veering north westerly. The water was blue-white now with phosphorescence and the net too heavy; a sudden splat of pilchards was dragging it to the sea bed. The fish were dying before they could get them aboard and their dead weight forced the net down - the dream catch turning, as they so often did, into nightmare. They were hit by a sudden squall which turned the bows to the shore so that Waterwitch cut across her own nets. Jack fled for the wheel, motioning Mathey to take over clearing but the boy was smarting from an earlier reprimand and was taking his time in all he did. Maddaver was noting and totting up scores for later.

As Jack brought her back, Esco's foot slipped on the streaming waterway so that he slid helplessly for'ard and the over weighted leech which should have had two men to hold it ran from him, back over the side with Maddaver at the headrope powerless to stop it. He yelled to Mathey to grab the leech, grab it anywhere to halt its reversal whilst Esco, nursing a numbed and useless forearm, struggled to his feet in the driving, blinding rain.

'Mathey, for God's sake give him a hand!' yelled Maddaver above the wind. The boy shrugged and muttered, 'What did you say to me earlier? If you want something doing round here it appears you'd best be doing it yourself. Well, why don't you!' and he turned his back on the nets. Esco, swearing, was lunging for the lost net but it was too late. Even with Jack's help now it was beyond retrieval and with it went several stone of pilchard; the back-breaking work of many hours gone to waste!

They had to cast it adrift and abandon it. Mathey retreated to the stern as they ran for home, away from the sharp edge of Esco's tongue. Pilchards were money and you don't toss your silver overboard!

The seas were high now; they were coming home on the flood. Mathey, too far gone now in rebellion to make amends, ignored Maddaver's orders to help clear the nets and when he finally deigned to move, he was concentrating too much on languor of movement and upon maintaining a bored expression that he forgot to duck the mizzen boom which clouted him on the shoulder and sent him neatly overboard.

Jack had heard him yell and was issuing orders in a moment. The sea was with them and running fast. He stopped only to divest himself of his oilskins and sea-boots and was over the side. Esco and Maddaver turned the Waterwitch into the tide and Esco grabbed a Tilley lamp. Jack's fears that the boy might be unconscious were unfounded and though he wasn't the strong swimmer his uncle was, he was making towards the boat. Esco threw them a line and together they hauled the boy aboard, followed by Jack.

It was Jack who held him choking and retching until he had rid himself of a large part of the English Channel and Jack who was gentle with him as he sobbed and gasped in his arms but it was Maddaver who eventually dragged him still spluttering into the smoky warmth of the cabin, dumped him unceremoniously upon his bunk, tossed a blanket over him and, jerking his head up by his streaming hair, said levelly, 'When we get home we have business together, you and I. Think about it!'

~

John Maddaver propelled his step-son in through the front door, to be met by a startled Annabel.

'Mathey, whatever happened to you?'

'He took a ducking. Went overboard. He's fine,' said her husband, still gripping the wet, bedraggled Mathey by the collar. Don't fret.'

She said, 'I'll get dry towels and a hot brick. I'll bring them up.' She turned toward the kitchen. Maddaver shook his head. 'Later, leave it for now.' He was pushing the boy toward the stairs. She thought he looked grim and tired. He forced the boy before him up the wooden staircase, flung open the door of his room and sent him sprawling across the bed.

'Get out of those wet things. Now!' He took his own jacket off in a more leisurely fashion, turned and stuck the peg in the latch of the door, then bent down to remove the tarred rope's end tucked into the leg of his sea-boots before rolling up his sleeves with meaningful deliberation.

'You can't!' said Mathey. 'You don't have the right. You wouldn't dare!' It was the last thing Maddaver allowed him to say.

When he had done what had to be done and all without a sound from the boy, Maddaver tossed down the length of rope, picked up the boy's nightshirt and thrust it at him. 'Put this on and sit up. We have to talk.'

'I don't see why!' The boy's voice was muffled as he pulled the shirt slowly over his head. Maddaver jerked it down further so that the fair head was level with his own.

'Because I say so!' It was the retort of every exasperated parent. The young face, far from chastened held a belligerence which boded ill. He stood before Maddaver, hands stubbornly at his sides when he must have itched to rub his hurts.

'I suppose,' he said 'that this is where you sorrowfully tell me that was all for my own good and I'll learn by it and it pained you to do it!'

Maddaver couldn't help a grin. 'Really?' he said. 'I didn't know; I suppose I'm new to this fathering. As a matter of fact, I enjoyed it. I've been longing to lay hands on you for weeks, and you'll change the tone in your voice unless you want a second helping!' He felt he was beginning to sound like his own father; echoes of years ago. 'Now, we'll have an end to this nonsense of yours. Dear God, Mathey, I never sought your implacable hatred, though you're welcome to it if that's the way things have to be, but not when it puts your own life at risk or the lives of the crew! If I have to I'll haul you up here every trip for a repeat performance until it's fixed in your thick skull that there are right and wrong ways of ordering your life. Do you understand me?'

'Oh, yes,' said Mathey with a toss of his head, 'I understand. There's no joy to be had with my mother so you'll take it out on me!'

'What are you talking about?' Maddaver was towering over the boy. Mathey said, 'I'm not half-witted. I know you never bed together. I've lived in this house all my life. I was eight years old when my father died but I can remember the creaking of the marriage bed well enough. Oh, I was too little to know what it meant but now I interpret the silence much better.'

'Ye gods!' said Maddaver, thrown completely; at a loss for a suitable retort.

The boy, confident he had struck home and with a vengeance continued. 'Oh, we laugh about it often, Jack and I, especially at night when we're up on deck, taking the watch.' Maddaver had taken an involuntary step towards him then, danger in the grey-green eyes and Mathey realised that he had gone too far. In panic he snatched the rope's end from his bed and lashed out, bringing the tail slicing down Maddaver's cheek, leaving an immediate scarlet wheal which brightened into pinpoints of blood as he watched fascinated and horrified. Maddaver twisted the rope from his grasp and flung it to the farthest corner of the room. He had the boy's arms in a firm grip, steering him backwards towards the only chair in the room, uncompromising, unyielding oak. He sat him down hard. The boy yelled then and swore at him.

'I'm very sorry,' said Maddaver cheerfully. 'Call it self-indulgence but you deserved that.' He knelt in front of the boy and took his cold wrists, forcing him to look him in the eye. 'Mathew Toller, I never thought, when I fell in love with your mother, that you would loathe me so, I never saw the need for it. I suppose I was exceptionally naive. I watched you on the boat, night after night, doing more than a man's work, with your back breaking, your eyes stinging, your hands chapped and no complaints. I've seen the support you've given to your mother, your loyalty to Jack. I've liked and admired you for all that. All I ask is that you give things a chance between us.'

'I can't, oh I can't!' Mathey was sniffing now, with nothing to wipe his eyes on as Maddaver still had his hands imprisoned. 'I can't back down now, all 'yes

Skipper, no Skipper, three bags full, Skipper'. I can't lose face with Jack and Esco, how can I!' he wept. Maddaver found his own handkerchief, a crumpled over large affair, and wiped the boy's nose for him as if he were three years old.

'That's the most idiotic thing I've ever heard you say. The worst they could suspect you of is growing up a little. Stop wriggling, I'll let you go in a minute, and stop crying, you never cried before and it must have hurt a lot. Just think things over. Now get into bed, your hands are like ice.' He picked up his coat and retrieved the rope's end, tossing it across to the boy. 'Have this as a keepsake. Second thoughts, put it in your bottom drawer; I'll know where to find it when next it's needed!' he added with a laugh and strode toward the door.

Mathey said unsteadily, 'John - I lied to you. I never told Jack, I never told anyone. I couldn't do that to mother.'

'I know that - I didn't believe you for a minute and I told you to get into bed!' He took the peg out of the latch and turned to go.

'Johnny?'

'Well?'

'Johnny, I am sorry.' They were both aware of the magnanimity of this gesture and of its cost to the boy. Esco would have stridden back into the room and given him a bear hug. Jack would have paused to grin and ruffle his hair. Johnny Fortnight said without turning. 'Well - we'll see, shall we?' And let the door close behind him.

He took a deep breath and went downstairs to the parlour to seek Annabel. She cried out when she saw his face.

'John, whatever has happened!'

'A tarred rope's end, my dear. Your offspring thought I needed chastening!'

'Mathey did that?'

'Oh, it serves me right for trying to play the heavy father. It was fair exchange; I gave him a dozen or more across his backside!'

She only winced and said. 'I'll get the wych hazel.'

Maddaver followed her to the kitchen door. 'I should leave him be, he won't thank you to be fussed over.'

She laughed. 'Oh, Mathey wouldn't mind but this is for you. Sit down and let me see to your face.' He sank onto the sofa, compliant whilst she stood over him, dabbing at the stripe. It was the first concern she had ever shown for him.

'I really should have warned you about Mathey. I know he needs a firm hand but I felt it would be an imposition on you.' He flinched from the sting of the wych hazel and pulled a face.

'And I was frightened to lay a hand on him for fear you'd turn on me for it!'

She laid down the bottle.

'No, it's time he had a father again,' she took his face between her hands and gently leant to set her lips the length of the lash 'and it's surely time I had a husband.' Her mouth found his own.

'Will you come upstairs?'

'No!' he said the light of panic in his eyes, 'That is, it's warm down here, before the fire. Let me see you in fire glow.' He watched as she unbuttoned her blouse and leant out to caress her shoulders - she was powdered with golden freckles.

'Annabel, dear girl, you've held out against me for far too long.'

But she laughed and said. 'You could have had me weeks ago; I was hungry enough for it. Oh, I'd have clawed and scratched a little but I wouldn't have done that to your face!'

'Dear God,' said Maddaver in amazement 'and I lay burning beside you in that hideous bed and all for nought?'

'I'm afraid so and I'm glad of that if it was so but what is wrong with the bed?'

'It creaks.'

'You wouldn't know!'

'Mathey told me.'

'What!' She sat up in her chemise, her hair about her shoulders.

'Man to man, of course,' said Maddaver solemnly and kissed her again.

'God, I hope you left him smarting. He will when I next get hold of him!'

'Why not just change the bed? Get something more modern.' He had stripped her chemise from her shoulders, exposing the full, creamy breasts, as freckled as the rest of her. 'Annabel, we've wasted so much time.'

'And are like to waste more,' she said dryly. 'Would it be indelicate if I were to point out that a lady's drawers fasten at the back?'

He pulled her down and at last made love to her in the wreck of her own lace-edged frippery, with an unleashing of the power and the passion he had kept in check for so long. And afterwards they lay in each other's arms with only the crackle of the fire and the soft sighing of the wind, coming in from the sea.

The old bed went for firewood and a new one was installed and Esco was pleased to note that the bloom was back again on Mrs. Maddaver and Mathey, whilst he was not moved to obey a request from John first time of asking, settled for second and an uneasy, wary truce. And Maddaver learnt to say 'upstairs!' in the chilling tones of the most feared patriarch though it never came to anything more. The promise in his eyes that one day it might was always enough. Only Jack Toller who had lost Annabel and now felt the boy slipping away from him was restless and uneasy.

CHAPTER FIVE

Annabel gave birth to John Maddaver's son one unseasonably wild night at the end of May. They christened him Drew to honour Maddaver's father.

Drew Maddaver little resembled either of his parents but at least he had none of the Toller fairness to set tongues wagging. Annabel privately felt he favoured the Boases - true Cornish stock - and Johnny felt there was more than a look of his mother in the tiny dark scrap.

Drew's birth was the turning point for Jack Toller. He had come to the end of the road where his hopes for Annabel were concerned. If he had ever thought that she would regret her liaison with Maddaver he realised that this child's birth had set the seal on their union. He needed to get away, as far away as possible, to start again somewhere where he need never see her, to cut her out of his mind and out of his heart. But he needed money; he would not traverse the world to arrive a penniless mendicant.

That summer, Maddaver's mother died and he went home to spend a week with his sister, to arrange the funeral and help sort her affairs; Annabel and the baby went with him. Jack once again took charge of the Waterwitch and with Mickey and Esco set sail for the Scillies to arrive at Newlyn with a miserable catch and finally back at Trevander with more than netting and marker buoys in his holds.

The Scillies were the playgrounds of the French Coopers, fishing boats which fished only as a blind for other activities, smugglers who left the French mainland with holds full of contraband; the old cargoes of brandy, tobacco and perfume. The Cornish bought at cheap rates and sold back at home; there was enough mark up on the mainland to make it worth everyone's while. Every now and then, the customs officers staked out shop or warehouse and attempted to follow up the route from ship to shore. Sometimes they succeeded; often they failed to do other than confiscate the goods from the unfortunate shop-keeper.

This would not be Jack Toller's first sortie into the world of the Free Traders. His father had been known for a smuggler years ago when there were still brandy kegs to row ashore on moonless nights and donkeys with muffled hoofs to traverse the sandy cliff top paths from the coves to the east. Jem Toller had even had a spell in Bodmin Gaol but it had not proved a deterrent.

Maddaver had put a stop to such expeditions but Maddaver was on the north coast and Mathey and Esco were nothing loath to go back to the old ways. They would rendezvous with La Jouette in Crow Sound and haggle exuberantly with Mathey's scattering of schoolboy French. Satisfied with the deal they shot four nets off the Wolf Rock, just for form's sake, and sailed into Newlyn shaking their heads, grim faced. There were some who wondered at their bad luck when the Barnaby had berthed with holds brim full; there were some who did not wonder at all!

They set sail immediately for home, congratulating themselves, and Mathey sang at the wheel and Jack got out his mouth organ and played 'Spanish Ladies' and

'The Mermaid' and Esco, who had been a navy man in his younger days, did the hornpipe and a jig in the confined space of the foredeck.

They overshot the entrance to Trevander Harbour and sailed quietly along the coast toward Spanish Cove, a deserted beach hidden between the rocky outcrops which jutted from the cliff foot. Jack flashed a pre-arranged signal with the Tilley lamp and received an answering signal from the shore. He took them further in, close among the rocks, using the sweep oars, sent another signal and then they heard the sound of oars in rowlocks and a small dinghy came out to meet them. It was an elderly man with a thick thatch of grey hair sticking out round his head, scarecrow like - he rowed well for his age.

Mathey, leaning over the side said, 'Granfer!' in amazement and Jem Toller, gap toothed, grinned up at him.

'Who else would a Toller be puttin' his trust in, eh young un?' And they loaded their contraband onto the small boat and watched Jem return to the shore. When he signalled that all was well, they put out to sea again and turned for home.

Jack said, 'he'll stow the cargo in Kitto's Cavern, the boat too for tonight. I'll go round tomorrow and collect.'

'The old devil!' grinned Esco. 'Your Dad should be putting 'un's feet up at his time o'life, Jack.'

'Not him. Says he'll be staring at his toes long enough from his coffin. I've promised him a drink at the Moon-raker. I bet he'll make it before we do!'

They collected the cargo next morning in a potato sack; Esco had allotments along the cliffs like many of his neighbours. It all went up to the Nankivells' loft.

After that, distribution was easy as Jack had his contacts and had already primed them. He was not foolish enough to flood the little shops of Trevander; he went further afield, to Penherrit over the hill or to Nanvallock to the west. Less than twenty four hours later they set out again. Mathey had slipped a bottle of perfume marked 'de Paris' in Annabel's dressing table drawer. He did not tell Jack or Esco who would have disapproved. Annabel had turned a blind eye to their adventures in the past but could now be concluded to be 'siding with the enemy'.

La Jouette was there again, just off the Eastern Isles, blue sails above a green and glittering sea, an eye painted upon her bows so that she might see the better in the night and the fog, her French crew chattering away like exited monkeys. Mathey wanted to go aboard and they let him this time. He came back with a string of onions round his neck and they made onion soup whilst they waited for the obligatory four nets to fill.

Jack was happy, standing at the wheel, the stiff breeze filling their mains'l, a loan gull at the masthead and the rocky coast of South West Cornwall hazy off the port bow. If only life could always hold this element of anticipation, this thread of danger!

They arrived off Spanish Cove and Jack gave their pre-arranged signal to an answering light from the shore.

Esco said, 'that's not the one he gave last time, Jack!'

'Nor is it.' Jack was frowning. 'If that old scarecrow is drunk again I'll throttle him!'

'There it is again,' said Mathey. 'Look it's wavering; he is drunk!'

Esco shook his head. 'No, there's someone else there. We can't risk it, Jack. Let's get out of here!' But Jack was already at the wheel, ready to turn the Waterwitch for home.

'Mathey, get to the halyard, we're going about!'

And then it happened. From the shelter of the jutting rocks east of the cove shot a fast revenue cutter. They had no chance of running before her with Mathey fighting to change the halyard and forestay to the far side of the deck as they changed direction. They were far too slow to take avoiding action. The cutter was overhauling them, the skipper with a megaphone ordering them to heave to. It did not take the boarding party long to discover their haul for Esco had moved it all from their hiding place in the fish hold, ready to pass it down to Jem Toller as soon as he was alongside.

They took Jack on board the cutter, manhandling him over the side but they did not touch Esco or the boy. They seemed willing to accept that the two were under Jack's orders and had little choice but to obey his dictates. Jack Toller was a familiar enough face to them, and known for an insolent young devil. They had already caught his father on the shore. Up to no good though he swore he was only out for a night's fishing.

They let Esco and Mathey take the Waterwitch back to Trevander. Jack was to accompany them in the cutter - under arrest. Esco and Mathey berthed at the quay and went first to the Moonraker to alert the skippers of the fleet. If there were any with goods to secure they had best look to it before the crew of the cutter came ashore. When she docked they brought Jack up along Fore Street, handcuffed between two coastguards, one eye closed up, a bruise on his chin.

Diggory Martyn stood on his step, surrounded by the men of Trevander, the same who had cursed Jack Toller in the days of the Sabbath Wars but, after all, he was one of their own and they were men of the Duchy and Free Traders almost to a man. Even Gwen Nankivell was heard to say, 'What need to rough up the lad weren't two of them enough for him!'

'Chin up, Jack!' shouted Esco. 'Annabel will have you out of hold!' Jack grinned at them and forced his captors to a halt, but they dragged him along again. And it seemed that the whole of Fore Street was out on the cobbles or leaning from upper windows, jeering the customs men. Someone even emptied a chamber pot and narrowly missed Toller. But it was the most triumphant progress he had ever made, with the children cheering him on and the women waving handkerchiefs.

He was taken to the lock-up next to the Police House and there installed for the night, to be handed over in the morning and taken to Bodmin Gaol. Constable Hicks was an accommodating man. He fetched extra blankets for the small bare cell and his wife arrived with hot water to wash in, salve for the bruised jaw and a bowl of rabbit stew, steaming hot and packed with herbs and vegetables. After Jack had eaten his fill Constable Hicks fetched a stool and a pack of cards and they sat down together to while at least half the night away.

'The Maddavers,' said the Constable 'will get you a good lawyer. You'll get off.'

'Yes,' said Jack, 'I'll get off, this time. I wonder what they've done with the Old Man.'

The Constable smiled, 'sent him home to bed, or so I hear. He gave a good impersonation of being totally gaga.'

'He is that,' said Jack. 'He doesn't need to act, he tends to overdo it. Still, it usually works with his creditors. That's three pounds I owe you. Christ, that's the price of a new net. I think I'll turn in before there's further damage done. You couldn't rise to a night-cap, could you?'

'Mary,' said the Constable 'makes a nice cup of cocoa. You should remember, Jack, you spent enough time in here as a boy!'

'Cocoa,' said Jack faintly, 'would be wonderful!'

Annabel and John arrived home to find a worried Mathey, a shame-faced Esco and Jack in Bodmin Gaol. Maddaver said very little, he set about finding a good lawyer. Annabel sold her mother's clock.

Jacob Roose travelled up from Penzance on the Flying Dutchman as far as Liskeard and thence by coach to Trevander. He was a bespectacled, aesthetic young man with a perpetual cough and what the Cornish called a dark brown voice. Jem Toller, summoned to a family conference, eyed him suspiciously.

'What good will 'un be, limp as a dish clout and looks as if a puff of wind will blow un over!' But Roose was a competent lawyer:

Had the Waterwitch been searched immediately on boarding? Yes, it had.

Was the Skipper, Mr. Jack Toller, given the opportunity to dock at the Customs House in Fowey or any other port to declare the disputed goods? No, he wasn't, he was apprehended and handcuffed and removed forthwith.

Was there direct evidence that the aforementioned Mr. Toller had had no intention of doing so? No, only the case of the strange old man, father of the said Jack Toller, who was reeling drunkenly about on the shore waving a dark lantern.

Was it Mr. Jack Toller's honest intent to declare the aforementioned goods? 'Of course it was!' declared Esco and Mathey indignantly in unison. They were on the way to Fowey when the revenue cutter had spotted them. Well, perhaps they were headed in the wrong direction. It had been a misty night, hadn't it? Well, patchy perhaps. They'd overshot the river mouth perhaps, well, a few sea miles, what was that? They had just realised their mistake and were about to turn. And weren't the goods up on deck? Was there any evidence that they were being hidden away from the eyes of the excise men? No, of course not!

At the end of the evening Roose declared triumphantly that there wasn't a case to answer. No court would convict on such evidence. Leaving Drew in the care of Selena Cluett, they all travelled to Bodmin for the hearing. Roose was right, the magistrate dismissed the case with speed; he had a long morning ahead of him. 'Lack of criminal intent,' he said his eyes boring into Jack's bland grey ones. Mr. Toller should stick to his trade and avoid the lure of the Coopers in future but he was free to go. And so Jack was bought for the price of a grandmother clock and the return of a favour of years ago when Jacob Roose had been down on his uppers and John Maddaver had made him a timely loan. He was, said Roose, entitled to collect his interest.

Jack wanted to shake his hand and offer profuse thanks but the young lawyer only shrugged, declined the outstretched hand and said. 'Thanks for what? Perverting the course of British Justice? You sir, are plainly as guilty as hell!' With a nod to Annabel and a wink at Maddaver he shambled out of their lives.

'You might,' said Maddaver 'have lost us the Waterwitch.'

'I might,' said Jack 'have made us a fortune!'

'Us? Oh come now! You'd have kept quiet, all three of you.'

'Not with Granfer being in on it,' said Mathey 'what chance the story wouldn't have been all over the Duchy?'

'Would you like to make an issue of it?' Jack smiled lazily and raised his fists.

'Not particularly, you'd best me, you know that. I know that. If it happens again you're out, Jack, finished with the Waterwitch, no second chance!'

The summer turned toward autumn without further incident. The Coopers were not mentioned again although it was known that there had been a number of profitable trips out to the Scillies by the Barnaby. October ushered in gales and there were many days when the fleet were stranded in harbour or had to run before the storm to make safe haven. Caught out one wild night off the Runnel Stone, a streaming, tilting deck beneath them, Maddaver was thrown back against the main mast and fell, breaking his left arm. It was, luckily, a clean break but it was to lay him up for a time. With the worsening weather it made little difference and Annabel was pleased to have him at home. As soon as the weather cleared he was anxious to be back at the boat.

Blue skies, scudding cloud and the gold of the cliff tops where the bracken had turned and the furze blossom still lingered, made a beautiful backdrop to the Waterwitch, her russet sails set, as Jack, Esco and Mathey left harbour without him, bound for the Scillies. Jack took them quite close to the Manacles, those deadly outcroppings of submerged rock between the Dodman and the Lizard. On such a perfect day it was impossible to believe that death had lain in wait for countless souls on this stretch of coast. It was then he told them that they would be making for Crow Sound again in search of the Coopers.

Esco exploded, saying he was having none of it. John Maddaver paid him and John Maddaver had forbidden them to have further truck with the Coopers. They wrangled about it heatedly until eventually Esco washed his hands of the whole enterprise and called on Mathey as witness that he was to be absolved of all participation.

'And you, Mathey Toller?' asked Jack, emphasising their kinship. 'Are you for a safe road with Esco or are we together as we always used - all for one, remember?' Put that way there was no reneging. Mathey spat on his palm and clapped Jack's hand; the partnership was sealed.

The pick-up was uneventful; a good supply of jaccy and as much brandy as they had the money to barter with and the space to stow it. The voyage home was smooth and fast with the westerlies behind them. They would not be calling upon Jem this time; he had proved too much of a liability. Instead, they were to land to the west, taking the goods ashore by dinghy, stowing them in one of the many caves hidden in the cliffside; haunts of the smugglers of old. Then they were to go aboard again for the journey home. Jack said to Esco, 'any trouble, don't wait for us, cut and run for home. We can't afford to lose the Waterwitch.'

Esco said dryly, 'and Mathey, he is expendable? You would put the boy at risk?'

'What risk? It's negligible. Cheer up, Esco, if anyone gets their backside kicked for this it will be me.' Jack had known he should have waited for dark of the moon but with Maddaver so conveniently laid up and the weather set fair it was too good an opportunity to miss.

The rocky inlet he had chosen was bathed in moonlight, the waters lapping gently at the rocks. Mathey climbed into the dinghy and waited for him to hand down their contraband. Esco's last sight of Jack was sitting athwart the gunwale, fair hair blowing in the light breeze, handsome in his dark guernsey, trousers tucked into his sea-boots, tops turned down - and that was when Esco stopped - at the gleam of metal protruding from the leg of his right boot.

'Jack, you fool, you bloody fool!'

Toller only shrugged. 'I've told you, ordered you, at the first sign of trouble, cut and run!'

'And the boy?'

'I'll look after Mathey, you see to the boat. I'm ordering you as skipper...'

'Then it'll be the last order, lad! You'll skipper no more boats for Annabel Maddaver!'

Jack only smiled, a long, slow smile. 'Shake hands then, for old times, at least wish us luck!'

'No, damn you!' Esco growled, going to the wheel, taking out his pipe and turning his back on them as the boat moved away toward the creek. He wished, afterwards, that he had felt able to say something, anything, to hold out the hand of friendship for the last time. He never saw Jack Toller again.

Chapter Six

They unloaded the goods in the shallows where they were just another mound of shadows amongst the rocks: tobacco, well wrapped and waterproofed against the weather, and brandy in the keg. Then they started the climb up the tumbled cliff face to the hidden mouth of the cave - not until they were inside in the welcome darkness below the grassy overhang of the cliff top did they dare to light a lamp. The narrow opening gave onto a narrower tunnel where they had to bend double for a hundred yards before it opened out into a cavern high enough for them to stand upright comfortably. The rocky walls were conveniently stepped, providing natural shelving, the floor of soft sand and shale.

Mathey said, 'when did you last come here, last use this as a hideaway?'

Jack shrugged, 'not for many a year. Why?'

'Look at the floor - footprints, signs of something being dragged into the shadows. Someone used this very recently.'

Jack was down on hands and knees with the lantern. 'That's sharp of you. Well, there's nothing here now. Come on, let's haul the stuff up. Put the lamp on one of the shelves, we'd best not keep Esco chewing his nails any longer than necessary.' They left their lantern glowing on a rocky outcrop and set off again down the cliff to be about hauling the goods up to the cave mouth. They could see the outline of the Waterwitch, riding to her anchor, rocking gently, showing no light. They had to make two journeys and it was hard work. They were yards from the cave mouth on the second haul when a figure emerged from the bracken and gorse just above them to challenge Jack with a shout of 'Hold hard!'

Jack turned quickly, 'run, back to the boat, I'll hold him off!'

Mathey was a few yards below him. Jacked lunged then at the intruder, aware that he could not be on his own, he must be at least expecting back up. In that second he cursed himself for a fool, for using the cave again when it had so obviously been another's hiding place. There were none could know the Waterwitch would anchor where she did that night but this man could be one of a party sent to stake out another's expedition. Jack leapt at the man, grappling with him there in the dark. He was a big man, thick set, powerfully built but he could give Jack fifteen years or more and hadn't his speed and agility. Mathey stood still and agonised over the order, half of him wanting to flee down to the boat, push off toward the Waterwitch and make for Trevander, the other part of him knew he could not leave Jack.

'Run, you fool!' Jack hissed over his shoulder and the distraction cost him his footing but he took the big man down with him. As they hit the scree which littered the cliff path, something slithered down towards Mathey with a metallic clatter. Like a sign from heaven or a bolt from hell, Jack's handgun landed at his nephew's feet. Mathey knew he carried it; they had been fooling about one hot afternoon on a walk toward Penherrit, lying at the edge of a cornfield potting rabbits. Now he seized it, and with a steady hand took measured aim and fired.

The two men were flung apart, Jack to end sprawled across the rocks, coughing in the sand they had stirred up, the other man to lie spread-eagled across the path, silent and still. Mathey dropped the gun as though it had burned his fingers. Jack scrambled across to his assailant's side. The bullet had entered his back; it had passed straight through his heart. He turned to Mathey, 'he's dead,' he said simply, soberly. The boy was trembling.

'I never meant, I never meant it. I thought he would kill you. I had to do something!'

Jack put an arm round him briefly. 'I know, and thank you for that. He can't be on his own, we have to think fast.'

'Can't we bury him?' said Mathey, deathly pale.

'No, of course not, this isn't one of the Penny Dreadfuls. They'll find him and they'll know which boats were out tonight and there'll be questions.'

'But it was an accident. We'll say it was an accident! We'll say I didn't mean to kill him!'

'It won't make any difference. Listen, Mathey, I'm going to make a run for it. I'd meant to clear out anyway as soon as I'd raised the cash on this little lot. I've tied myself to your mother's apron strings for years enough and now she has John and Drew and I know she'll look after you and Granfer so I've no reason to stay. Now, let's get down to the boat. Can you swim out to the Waterwitch? Good lad. Then make for home. If Maddaver and Annabel want to know where I am you dropped me off in the dingy and left me to it. You would have none of tonight's work. You never saw this man, you never heard the shot. Can you stick to that story?'

'Yes, but you - if they catch you....'

'They won't catch me. If I can I'll ship to the Americas. I won't be coming back.'

Mathey wouldn't be sidetracked, he repeated, 'if they catch you, if they catch you, you'll hang!'

'They'd hang me anyway. Now, out to the boat, keep to the story for everyone's sake and keep it inside you for the rest of your life. You understand?'

'Yes, but ....'

'No buts, Mathey. Guilty secrets aren't easy; an albatross about the neck, but it's for the best. I'm relying on you. Now go!'

Mathey was crying, he flung his arms about his uncle's neck until Jack prised them free, gave him a shove toward the brink of the water, watched him strike out toward the Waterwitch and finally climb aboard her. The dingy he stove in but there was little chance it would not be found and recognised. Then he made his way up the cliff and set out toward Nanvallock and the south west. He looked back once to see that they had set the mains'l. Esco and Mathey were making for home, for John and Annabel and Drew, for Chy an Lor along The Strand. He could not watch them out of sight; he had lingered for far too long with the boy. He turned away, almost amused to find that his eyes were blinded with tears......

In the days that followed he was often to wonder about the outcome of that night and its effect upon them all in Trevander. It felt like a stone in his heart, not knowing, suddenly catching him unawares when life seemed fair, eating him away almost.

That night he travelled without a rest, keeping to the cliff top paths and field ways, avoiding the main highways. He had little money on him for they had paid over

almost all they had between them to the coopers. He had
the thought of making for St. Keverne and his Aunt Polly
- she must have a little nest egg somewhere. She was
always lavish enough with Mathey on his infrequent
stays there and it would only be a loan, it would be
returned and with interest, even from the far side of the
world. He would await the cover of darkness and slip
into the village.....

It was a blustery night, the wind east-south-east and
blowing a moderate gale; the seas were high. He had left
the main road which meandered down from Falmouth,
where it crossed the Helford River and had skirted the
coast; Mawgan to Manaccan, to Flushing, Porthallow,
Trenance. He spent his last shilling at the Inn in Porthoustock. He would wait awhile until the streets of St.
Keverne were deserted before slipping into the shelter of
Aunt Polly's sturdy, lime-washed porch. He was still in
the tap-room when the call came for the lifeboat to be
launched and the bar emptied in seconds. It seemed wis-
est to follow them down to the slip, stranger or no, to
keep with the crowd. No man should point a finger and
note him standing aloof. And no Cornishman would be
found a laggard when the cry went up for all hands. Off
the point lay the Manacles, that reef of rocks a mile
long, stretching down to Lowland Point north of Cov-
erack, and a full mile out to seaward. Jack Toller was familiar enough with those jaws of death jutting from the
green waters on a sunny afternoon. At night, in high
water springs, they were invisible; the graves of num-
berless ships and countless unfortunates, the brave and
the foolish alike. The mournful tolling of the bell buoy
warned of danger on a quiet night but with the gale de-
veloping....

'She's a steamer, a big one at that!' A man from Rose-nathan had been tending his sheep above Manacles Point; he had seen her with her lights ablaze; he had know then that she was in mortal danger; that it was too late to save her. He watched her strike Maen Vasses, the Outer Manacles. Her lights went out and he began to run.....

They filled the lifeboat with willing volunteers. Jack hung back at the head of the beach but when the Second Coxswain arrived, breathless, asking for volunteers to take another boat out from the beach he came forward. There were four of them. Jack pushed off with a long oar then he stood in the stern, steering as they made for the reef. Mr. Cliff, the coxswain, soaked his necktie in paraffin and made a torch so that they could be seen from the wreck. They found her because they knew the waters and they knew where she had struck. She was a four-masted giant, the Mohegan of Hull, one thousand, two hundred and eighty tons. She had left Tilbury with a crew of ninety seven and sixty passengers, carrying a mixed cargo of beer and spirits, toys and tin, lead and antimony, church ornaments and artificial flowers. She was bound for New York. Listing at forty five degrees and down by the head she had gone before the coxswain and Toller could reach her; only her masts and her funnel were visible, but there were men and women clinging to the rigging, climbing the masts.

Cliff cupped his hands. 'Hold on where you are. She's on the bottom and can't move. Help will be coming very quickly.' He knew that by now they would have launched the lifeboats from Falmouth and Cadgwith and Polpeor but none knew the Manacles like the men of Porthoustock and the ship would be difficult enough to find in the darkness with so little left visible.

They managed to pull a number of men from the sea and one woman, still clinging to a door. Then, fearful of being swamped, they made for the shore; difficult enough to row round the Shark Fin Passage as the sea was making fast with a strong tide running. They reached land at ten o'clock, at the same time as the lifeboat. The Charlotte was towing one of the Mohegan's own boats, with twenty four shivering, shocked souls aboard and water half way to the gunwales.

The Charlotte put out again, this time with the indomitable Cliff aboard. He had the idea of swimming out to the wreck with a line. Jack Toller soaked through and bone-weary spurned the offer of soup and a blanket at the Inn and wandered out along the rocky shoreline. It was still possible to hear the cries of those stranded in the rigging. He wanted to shut his ears to it but there was a fascination in the sound which appalled him. There were bodies along the tide line, washed into gullies in the rocks. He had a storm lantern, snatched from the slip and he laid it down and bent to the gruesome task of hauling corpses above the high tide mark. There were a number of women, hampered in the waves by their long skirts, men in city suits, a baby, no older than Drew, dressed in long white robes....... It would be a long while before any walked again on this terrible shore, so strong was the belief that the shipwrecked dead walked again, hailing their own names!

At last he took his lantern and turned to leave; there was nothing living now in that boiling sea and the dead would wait until the silver grey of a Cornish dawn. Then the light caught the edge of the tide and for a moment he halted. Another body, rolling over and over in the current? But no, this was a living man, still fighting strongly and dragging another with him. Toller stood down his lantern and was into the sea.

'Hold on there, I'm with you!' He fought to keep his balance in the strong undertow and grabbed for one of the swimmers, his hands beneath the arm pits. It was a woman. He could see her hair, long and black, swirling upon the creamy foam of the combers. He also knew that she was dead. He hauled her up onto the rocks and laid her down, going back for the man. He was exhausted, unable to help himself further. He lay on his side too weak even to retch. He was a big man with a neat beard and short dark hair, he wore good clothes but he was no longer young and the effort had weakened him. He moved an arm feebly, his hand fluttered. 'Consuela,' he muttered 'my daughter.' He had an American accent, a pleasant southern drawl. Gently, Toller placed the hand with its heavy gold signet upon the cold fingers of the dead girl and he seemed content. It only took a few seconds for him to die.

Jack Toller, sitting back on his heels, tired and wet and strained, hungry and homeless, remained there for a long time before he shrugged his shoulders and bent to remove the ring and pocket watch with its heavy gold Albert. The man was carrying a purse in his inside pocket, crammed with American dollars, and a gold cigarette case inscribed John Alfred Talbot O'Brien.

'Well, old man, you won't be needing these again and I am in desperate straits,' muttered Jack. 'I would as soon you had lived to take your riches back to America but a higher authority decreed otherwise.' He turned to collect his lantern again. The light fell upon the face of the dead girl, lying tumbled in a pearl embroidered evening gown of bridal white, the weeds of her black hair about her like a veil. Even in death she was the most beautiful creature he had ever set eyes upon. He smoothed away the dark hair from the porcelain face and touched her earrings, still depending from the bloodless white of her lobes; jet black and studded with tiny pearls and what looked like diamonds.

'Consuela,' he let the name roll from his tongue 'just a keepsake. No malice in it, just a remembrance.' He unhooked them from her lobes, fumbling with the catches which had held them firm through the threshing waves that had killed her. 'Sleep soundly, Consuela O'Brien.' Then, on a sudden whim, he took his new briar pipe, which Annabel had had carved with his name for Christmas last, and placed it in the pocket vacated by John Alfred Talbot O'Brien's cigarette case. They would not find a Jack Toller on the passenger list but would they check before they buried him at St. Keverne with the men and women of the Mohegan? He thought not. Jack Toller, a murderer on the run, laid in a mass grave with this American princess. He rather liked the idea. He tucked his ill-gotten gains away and went back to the inn. The publican's wife only saw a weary young man with the horror of the night still in his eyes. She gave him a bowl of soup and a bed for the night. Next morning he was gone. The masts of the Mohegan remained and whilst her dead slept at St. Keverne, the houses in the villages round about acquired elegant furniture and crested plates and cattle in the fields drank from her lifeboats. Men would hunt the bed of the sea for the treasure of her cargo long after the men of Porthoustock, who had put to sea on that fateful night, had gone to their own quiet graves.

PART II

Strange Meeting

CHAPTER SEVEN

1915

The bright world was not good enough for Drew Maddaver; he inhabited a dark place of his own. He had been a changeling child with none of Annabel's fire in his colouring and little of Maddaver's fine-boned chiselling and Byzantine narrowness of face. He was a true Cornish darkling, a throwback to the old stock, with a thatch of dark brown hair, blue eyes and a surly tongue when he chose. The antithesis of his easygoing father, the sea was his element; it had never been more to Johnny Fortnight than a way to earn a living, to secure a boat, a wife And, after the assassination at Sarajevo, when Europe had gone to war and Mathey Toller and George Deverel, who had been the nearest to friend Drew had ever found or ever wanted to find, had marched away with the Naval Reserve, he had gone back to sea, out into the bay on the Waterwitch, with Esco Cluett at his side and a boy named Colan Denbow who was fourteen years old and needed constant watch set over him. And Denbow leeched away some of Maddaver's boyhood, leaving him feeling old at seventeen.

'He'll learn,' muttered Esco. 'Us all have to learn. You did, your brother Mathey did.'

But out there, after Herring in Bigbury Bay or off round the Eddystone, there was no war. Even at the weekend when Annabel and Tabby, who had married Mathew Toller as soon as she turned sixteen, sat in the back parlour of the Moonraker and wound bandages and knitted comforts for the troops, even then it did not seem as if the war could ever touch Trevander. Even on cold winter evenings, in the face of a force-eighter, patrolling the cliff tops, policing the coves, waiting for nameless treachery from some unguessed source, Drew still found it unimaginable.

Sometimes the girls accompanied him, muffled in long scarves and waterproofs, identically hatted in bright woollen berets. His sister, sixteen year old Lowena wore green to set off her red hair. Not for this elfin sprite her mother's honest carrot, ripe for teasing, but a rich dark crimson, with untameable ripples of its own, cascading to her slender waist in Pre-Raphaelite splendour. At her side in cherry red, pom-pom bouncing walked Emelynne, her bosom companion, George's scapegrace sister, all mud brown braids and bright dark eyes and wind-whipped, rosy-cheeked cheerfulness.

'Oh, I would go!' said Lowena for the thousandth time, standing on tiptoe at the lookout point above Drumgarrow Rock, so that the wind filled her coat like the belly of a sail and she seemed poised to take off above the crashing waves which tore at the cliff foot. 'I couldn't stay here with Europe ablaze - not if I were a man and fast approaching eighteen!'

'How convenient that you're not!' said her brother dryly.

'He'll go,' said Emelynne, 'all in his own good time.'

'He won't,' said Drew. 'It's not my fight.'

'Any man's death -,' said Lowena, jumping down from her pinnacle of rock. 'The bell tolls for thee, Drew

Maddaver! If you were eighteen you'd be getting white feathers and every girl in the village would be pointing you out for scorn!'

Maddaver grinned, showing an even set of white teeth. 'How do you know that there is a war out there? Are the stars cast adrift and jumbled up? Is the tide stayed? Is anything changed at all? Every night the storms keep us in harbour it's 'Who'll patrol tonight? Oh, Drew will, Drew's nothing better to do, keep him out of mischief.' I've plenty to do. I've nets to mend and sails to bark and once it was all important in this town, a man's work, and now no-one counts it for anything! War fever is all that matters. Who will turn to and feed this bloody country if every man who can set a hand to sail or oar takes off adventuring?'

'Oh, dear,' said Lowena, 'its feathers are ruffled. It's on the defensive.'

'I fear so,' sighed Emelynne. 'Never mind,' she put an arm through one of Drew's. 'When we get back we'll all set to and help with the nets. I'm half as fast as you and twice as fast as the Denbow boy.'

'Lowena won't,' said Drew 'she'll not soil those lily white lady's hands of hers!'

Lowena put out an exceptionally pretty pink tongue. 'Not so white, brother dear, as your lily white heart!'

'That,' said Emelynne, troubled, 'was more than unkind.' Drew had stalked on ahead. Lowena shrugged. 'He doesn't really have a heart, you know. He has a little piece of ice instead, like the boy in the Snow Queen.'

'I expect he has a tortured soul,' said Emelynne 'sort of all Keats and Shelley; I expect he suffers.'

'Oh, yes!' said Lowena, blue eyes flashing. 'He suffers from a mother who dotes upon him and a father too indolent and fond ever to lay a finger upon him and ….'

'And a sister who's green-eyed with jealousy?' smiled Emelynne. 'I had a letter from George today. All I can say is I'm glad that Drew is here at home with us while George - oh George never complains but I know it's hell on the ships and I wish it was all over and he was safe home again, leaning over the wall up at Fosfelle, his pipe in his hand, talking nonsense. Oh, Lowena, we can't lose Drew too. He's the most arrogant, the most stubborn, the most impossible boy this side of the Tamar but imagine going down to the quay and seeing the Waterwitch sailing out without him at the wheel and knowing that he's out there somewhere, beyond the horizon, hurt and broken under the noise of those terrible guns. Drew!' The words were torn away from her as she gathered up her skirts and tore along the cliff top path after him, slipping on the wet rocks, snatching her coat from the clutch of wet, lichened blackthorn and stubborn flitches of gorse. 'Drew!'

He heard her at last and stopped, hands in his pockets, face set. Emelynne, who was a deal shorter than he, jumped up and kissed him on one cheek.

'What was that for?'

'It was from Lowena, to say she's sorry. We've decided we don't want you to go away.'

'Don't I get two kisses, one in your own right?'

'That wouldn't be proper. Besides, I promised George - no fast ways. We have to keep faith with the men at the front.'

'He might be gone a long time,' said Drew, stirring to her nearness, the feel of her wind blown hair against his face, the warmth of a small, gloved hand upon his wrist.

'You were one of those who said the war would be over by last Christmas,' she retorted.

'I was wrong and you might die an old maid. He wouldn't want that.'

'Maybe I'll put it to him next time I write.'

'Do you write often?'

'Oh yes, but the replies take an age. Besides, Lowena has promised to wait for him.'

Drew scoffed. 'Only because he's the only man in the village with enough money to warrant her attention. Its not George brings the sparkle to her eyes, it's the thought of Fosfelle being returned to its rightful owners!'

'I think she's fond of George, I really do. And you, Drew Maddaver, if your sister is a fortune hunter what does that make you?'

'Oh, I wasn't proposing marriage, Emelynne, heaven forbid!'

'What then?'

'Just notches.'

'Notches?'

'Marked up on the bowsprit of the Waterwitch - you could have the honour of being the first!'

'You beast! You cad!' gasped Emelynne, cheeks as scarlet as the bobbled beret. She began flailing at his chest with her fists.

Lowena, sauntering, had caught them up.

'I thought you were worried about Drew's health and safety, apparently I was mistaken. Shall we call in on Tabby? The children will be in bed, she'll be glad of some company.' And leaving Drew to continue his lonely cliff-top patrol they turned away from the path and opened the green gate into Tabby's tiny garden.

Penolva, Jem Toller's haunted, derelict cottage, had become a place of sunlight and hope after Granfer died and Mathey and Tabby moved in to rear their two little girls. Now it was a whitewashed, scrubbed, chintzed idyll and even here, in the darkness, the torn scrap of a moon illuminated the flower beds along the path and silvered the tamarisks. There was even a pisky on the brass door-knocker. Mathey had laughed out loud when Tabby bore it home from a shopping spree. 'It looks just like Granfer - I suppose he's never really left!'

Tabby came to the door with a lamp in her hand, a faint beam of light spilling out into the storm. She was pregnant again, quietly confident that it would be a boy this time. Her condition showed only in the height of her waist and the glow of her skin. She smiled and bade them welcome, lifting a hand toward Drew, lingering at the gate. He turned up his collar and set off again into the darkness.

In the weeks before the war started, it was said that John Maddaver had spent little under £400 to equip the Waterwitch with an engine. 'And for what?' muttered the Nankivells and the Varcos - so that his mad-cap young son could tear round the bay wasting precious fuel on unnecessary speed trials, coaxing and cosseting this snorting devil's machinery into further feats, setting the gulls wheeling and crying and the echoes rebounding from the cliffs. Almost reluctantly others followed suit and, if engines were still not commonplace, they had become acceptable and much coveted by the impecunious.

Even with an engine, pilchard drifting was hard work for two men and a boy but the summer came early in 1916 and Drew and Esco had the Waterwitch ready for the Wolf Rock with sails barked, hull scrubbed and painted, mast oiled. They hauled aboard twenty nets, topped up their fuel tank and hefted coal on board.

Annabel and Johnny came down to the quay to see them off, standing arm in arm as the Waterwitch warped out. Clearing the harbour mouth, Drew hoisted the russet mizzen sail and they headed south west.

'Handsome day, 'tis,' remarked Esco. Drew only flashed back his white smile and called to Denbow to ease the mizzen sheet. Nearing the Wolf Rock they set to look out for gannets and the oily waters of the pilchard shoals. They gave the rock a wide berth, respecting its circling tide races. Denbow was put to the engine where he could do least damage as they set to lower the nets.

'Knock her out, Colan!' Maddaver waited until the boy had put her into neutral before standing to the head rope. With Esco on the leech they shot their nets, marking the dann buoy at the end of the flotter with a hurricane lamp. Twenty nets take a deal of time to shoot but at last they secured the spring rope, switched off the fuel and left the mizzen to keep the Waterwitch head to wind. It was dark now, the Wolf light a strong, comforting presence in a sea almost devoid of other craft. To the North East they could see the Longships Light. They sent the boy below to get some sleep and stayed on deck with a brew of tea and a complete star map of the northern hemisphere above them.

Esco thought that Drew looked as contented as his restless spirit ever let him be. Stretched out along one of the waterways, hands behind his head, he let Cluett talk of the old days, of the early voyages with Frank Toller and brother Jack, of his father's first hilarious attempts to take to the life and, when he had finished and got to his feet because it was eleven o'clock and time to start hauling, Drew only said quietly 'It isn't my war - this is my country, out here.'

They pulled on their sea boots, donned oilskins and called Colan Denbow up from his bunk. He came out into the starlight, knuckling his eyes and yawning. They lit the fishing lights, shipped the roller onto the starboard side, switched on the engine and began hauling. The last net was the hardest, with a splat of pilchards weighing it down dangerously. Hauling and clearing had taken them over five hours and the sun was coming up over the rim of the horizon when they had time to look about them. They turned for home with a favourable wind, proceeding under sail and making six knots.

Leaving Esco on board as lookout Drew and Colan went below to start breakfast and soon had bacon sizzling on the stove.

'This,' said Colan 'is the time I like best of all!'

'Philistine!' laughed Drew and 'Christ, what was that?' He was up on deck, Colan at his heels, even as Esco was bellowing down at them.

'Bloody great shell!' said Esco. 'Fired over us. Bloody sub - if she catches up with us we be done for. Remember the Mary Ann, out of St. Ives and eighteen mile from land? Seven men forced to take to the jolly boat whilst the bloody Hun shot them up - lucky to make it home.'

'At least they had a sporting chance,' gulped Colan, 'we don't have a boat!'

'I had noticed,' said Maddaver, running the engine at full speed. 'Hell, get down Colan!' as another shell took the mizzen with it, mast and sail. The next shot fell mercifully short and they were making ten knots and heading west for the shelter of the Scillies. Later, under the aegis of Smith Sound, with St. Agnes to Port, they rigged up a jury mast with one of the sweep oars and the fore-stays'l.

'We've lost them,' said Esco. 'We were too small a fish. Thank God for the engine!'

Colan had been sick. Whether from fear or sheer excitement, no-one bothered to enquire.

'Bloody, bastard Hun!' spat Drew, lashing the oar to the stump of the mizzen. 'What right, what bloody right – what harm could we have done to a bloody great sub. Couldn't they have found anything smaller? They would have sent us to the bottom, Esco...' Face flushed, fists balled, he was shaking with rage.

'I'll brew up the tea,' said Cluett mildly. 'I shouldn't let it worry you, boy. Tisn't, after all, your war.'

Drew ran a hand along the rail beside him. The indignity! His beloved Waterwitch entering Trevander with a botched jury mast, the catch stowed anyhow and Colan Denbow being sick every five minutes.

'You'm flogging the engine to death,' said Esco equably. 'Don't take it out on the boat.'

'I'm not. Anyway, taking what out on her?'

'Being wrong,' said Esco. Us all make mistakes, even Maddavers. Perhaps they have to fall harder.'

'I want to be on the other end of a gun,' said Drew grimly.

'Don't 'ee be dramatic. I'm glad I'm not going to have to cope with your white feathers. I was planning an eiderdown for Tabby's girls. You can be an arrogant little toad, skipper. I'll look after the boat as if she was my own. I'll get old man Jelbert along to help us.'

'You've got it all planned,' said Drew. 'How long?'

'Oh, ages. I knew the worm would turn eventually. I took bets out. There's a book on it in the Moonraker.

But, Christ, boy, I don't want to lose you, whatever's been said, so you'll take care and have a thought for what you'll be leaving behind: nights like last night, mornings like this one.' He put an arm round the boy's shoulder and squeezed it briefly. They sailed into Trevander bay, honourably blooded, and it seemed as if the entire village was assembled to greet them; they had been sighted before they opened up the point by a sharp eye with a telescope.

Willing hands helped with the catch. Colan Denbow's mother bore him away home but Esco and Drew sat on the quay head, surrounded by a captive audience ready for a yarn and they told of their adventure, then again for late comers, then someone else wanted a third run until a man came pushing his way through the crowd, kit bag over one shoulder, tall and blond and broad shouldered. Able Seaman Mathey Toller gave his young brother a brief fraternal hug, gave Esco a bear's handshake and propelled them both down to the Moonraker. By the last and greatest telling the enemy submarine had loomed large and shadowy over their port bow and there had been more shells fired than rockets on Guy Fawkes Night. The version which had reached the 'Godolphin' at the far end of the village by nightfall had the Captain on the conning tower issuing a salvo of guttural commands and threatening to plough the gallant little Waterwitch into a watery grave. Drew left Trevander a hero, with hugs at the station from his mother and sister and Tabby and a kiss from Emelynne behind the luggage office.

The Waterwitch put to sea without him.

CHAPTER EIGHT

Maddaver found himself drifting in and out of consciousness, the noise of the guns still pounding in his ears. Wild
nightmares brought the terror of the sinking back to him
again and again. The grey bulk of the Nereus rearing
above him, the towering green sea and the face of the man
beside him in the water, urging him to hold on; his
brother's face. Mathey and he had been proud to belong
to the same ship's company. The Nereus had been a K-
Class destroyer and sister to the Nimrod; a fine ship.
Now he could only pray to God Mathey was safe.

He was aware that his head was swathed in bandages
and that there was a weight across his feet. But the
weight displaced itself and proved to be a rather manic
young man in faded, shrunken, striped pyjamas who was
chirping away to his crutch-bound companion in a chair
across the ward in accents unfamiliar south of the Tamar
or way north of it either.

'*Well,* he says, twirling his moustache, *what wuz you
in civvy street, my lad - strong lad like you, fine figure of
a man,* well, those wasn't his exact words; he didn't have
my command of the English lingo – like. He bloody
didn't. So I fixes him fair and square with these two eyes
and butter wouldn't melt. *Rocking horses,* sez I, I paints
the eyes on rocking horses. Skilled labour that is,
specialised. Need a steady hand and a sharp eye - who

wants a cross-eyed nag. Can't have his peepers ending up down by his nuts. The bugger took it all in, solemn-faced, he did. Said his little fraulein, his liebling, had a fine horse, plush saddle and all the trimmings. *'Bring it in,'* says I, *'any time you want a re-spray,'* I tell you, I was creased, doubled up. It started me off with the squirts again. God, he's come round at last. This one must be in for real. What's your name, mate?'

'Maddaver - Drew.'

The boy looked very young. His fair hair stuck out about his head. 'Maddaver Drew? It don't sound like much of a Limey name to me.

Maddaver's head ached abominably. 'Drew Maddaver,' he said 'and it's Cornish. Where in God's name do you come from?'

'Australia. Lately from Cairns but I bum around a lot. Leastways, I did before this little lot. O'Brien's the name, Alfred T. O'Brien - I say T cause I don't like what it stands for - me mates call me Alfie, so Alfie'll do for you. So you really are a head case? Spud over there's in with earache; difficult to prove he aint got it, and me, it's the Petty Mal. Every time they look like turning me out of 'ere I have one of me fits, writhin' and groanin' and frothin' at the mouth.'

'I'm sorry,' said Drew alarmed. 'That must be rotten for you.'

'Oh, no, I learnt how to fall years ago in Coober Pedy. Got matey with a clown. Talk about Tumblin' Kelly! It's easy when you know how. I can go down to order like a skittle. It's the toothpaste that's the art. Got to get up a good froth but it's only a little tube and there's lots would like to get their hands on it. I'd share anything with a mate, God's honest truth, but the Hun - well, he knows the British aint a nation of epileptics, so I keeps it to myself. I can tell you 'cause you won't need it, being legit.'

'Yes, I'm legit,' said Drew faintly. 'How long have I been here?'

'A week nearly, in and out, mostly out of it. Where was you brought in from?'

'HMS Nereus – well, I'm not really supposed to say - went down off the .....Well, anyway it was very sudden. I got in the way of one of the guns - knocked straight out and into the sea. They say a man dragged me aboard a Carley and lashed me down with his belt then I was out. I need to know what happened to him!'

'We all need to know things, pal. They don't volunteer much in here but it's better than the labour camps. I should become a hamkneesiack if I were you, a pitiful jibbering wreck. I can teach you a good jibber. Your own mother wouldn't know you was a fraud.'

Drew managed to smile. At least, his facial muscles seemed to be operating; he kept twitching his mouth and eyebrows experimentally. 'How did you get here?'

'Before the camp, you mean? Oh, via Mucky Farm and Pozieres. Pozieres Ridge is more densely sewn with Aussie sacrifice than any place on earth. Well, that's what they're saying – Australia's finest hour they're calling it; I've known better but if it gets me a medal and a seat on the tram it'll be worth it when I'm back in Oz. Served under Lieut. Col. Leane. They called us the Joan of Arc Battalion – d'you get it? Made of all Leane's – Maid of Orleans.... only an Aussie would think up a name like that.' He paused for a moment. 'Lost a lot of mates though, good mates. You too, I expect?'

In the suffocating darkness of the night hours, Drew lay on his bed with a head that throbbed still to the rhythm of the Nereus' engines and the recoil of her guns, his nostrils filled with the stench of cordite and the sweat of fear. Beside him, on the nearest pallet, the hoarse whispers of the irrepressible Australian droned through his nightmares and found root in some unoccupied corner of his fevered mind.

'Of course, we'd need clothes - nothing flash, nothing out of the ordinary and it ought to be warm, this is a bloody wet country - and I suppose you can't get far without papers - papers will be difficult. We'll need outside help. Women are the answer! With my youth and your beauty, mate, we'll conquer those little Walloons - make their toes curl inside their clogs. Me, I have a way with women. Didn't I ever tell you - well, I expect I did - that leggy blonde in Bendigo - wedded to her tennis racquet ...'

'Alf, will you bloody shut up - I want some sleep - I need some sleep - the whole ward needs some sleep. Can't you keep your mouth shut for just a couple of hours?'

'Enough said, cobber - why didn't you mention it before? But you will won't you? You do want to get out?'

'Of course I do, more than anything on earth!'

'Then it's settled, we'll shake on it. Now, before common sense gets the better of you.' There was the sound of fruitful spitting and a hand groped for Drew's in the darkness. 'There you are, mate, signed and sealed. I should get some sleep if I were you - get your strength up.'

In the end, it was Kenneth Graham who gave them the idea. Before the last century was out, Graham had come to Fowey Town and captured the enchantment of the river in 'Wind in the Willows' and Maddaver had been sent a copy for his ninth birthday by Great Aunt Boase who lived at the better end of Truro. It had arrived wrapped securely in brown paper, tied with garden twine and sealed with scarlet wax. Within its covers dwelt the doings of Mole and Ratty and the scurrilous Toad. Drew used to wade out to Enys Du the Black Island across the little causeway lined with silver pebbles and lie there on its flat top in the summer sun, soaking up adventures.

It was Toad who gave him the idea. Toad who had escaped from incarceration dressed as the prison washerwoman. O'Brien thought it was a brilliant idea; Gilbertian, Shakespearian even in its lack of subtlety, its simplicity - a simplicity that just might work.......

There was a gaggle of women who were allowed into the camp with butter and eggs for the guards; black clad peasant women, stolid with resignation - for the most part stout and ungainly - but two were young and one was pretty and Alfie persuade them both to strip off their outer layers and allow themselves to be tied and gagged so that the wrath of the prison guards would be avoided.

So in the end they walked free, arms linked, young faces close together under the peasant scarves, and it had been hard to foot it trippingly along the road without breaking into an unladylike gallop - and all the while, hands clammy, spines perpetually a-shiver, waiting for the shot and the fire in the back and the last of the light. Wanting desperately to turn and knowing they must not. And at last, the road curved and they were out of sight of the gates and they could breathe and release each other and O'Brien had to be sick in the ditch, sweat pouring down his face. They buried their skirts in the same ditch and left the road for the fields. The voluble

Alfie said not a word for a full hour, until they collapsed in a small spinney and dared to take out their precious hoard of black bread and a square of cheese.

'When do we move on?'

'As soon as it's dark. There'll be moon enough to light us on. We have to make for the coast and get hold of a ship, anything we can. But we'll hole up during the day – too dangerous to keep going once the sun's up,' said Drew.

Morning found them burrowing deep into the hayloft of a ramshackle barn. Not for this farmer the beautiful lines of the traditional Dutch barn, four square against the rains of Flanders. It looked as if the next winter would toss this one down into the midden which surrounded it. But if the wind was cold the straw, at least, was dry and clean. Surprisingly, they both slept well, exhausted by the day's adventures and they woke at last to the sound of voices - children's voices.

'I know there's someone there, those are not father's footprints, nor Dirk's and who else comes here?' It was a girl's voice, clear and certain.

'Come and gone, I expect - gypsies again.' This time it was a boy speaking. Drew edged closer to the edge of the loft until he could see them - a girl of ten, the boy perhaps a year younger.

'Did they fly out?' said the girl. 'Idiot! These prints all lead in the same direction. They're still up there!'

'Then we'd best tell father,' said the boy backing away slightly, hating to show that he was nervous.

Alfie whispered. 'We'd better show ourselves. Say something or they'll have the whole neighbourhood down on us!'

Drew said, 'Let them go and we'll make a run for it!'

'No, let me try to talk to the girl - I know a little of the lingo and she may be a half-pint size but she's still female, I don't usually have any trouble!'

Drew had to smile at that though his hand moved in a gesture which would have cost him a clip round the ear from Annabel. Alfie rose from the depths of the yellow straw like a satiated Rumplestiltskin.

'Don't go, little Mevrow, we won't harm you. See, we have no guns.' He stood up, arms waving like the leader of a minstrel show who has forgotten to black his face, though it wasn't far off, being streaked with mud and every imaginable filth.

'You are Engleesh?' said the little girl, opening enormous speedwell eyes.

'Yes, English. Rule Britannia and Keep the Home Fires Burning - Your Country Needs You!'

'I speak Engleesh, I speak at school. My Engleesh is better than yours.'

'Well, yes, so it is, but don't go. Tell me your name. I want to tell them back in England how pretty the Flemish girls are.'

'Are all the Engleesh liars? What is his name?' She pointed to Drew, a straw-stuck scarecrow but obviously more to her taste.

'Drew,' he said.

She nodded, not finding that strange. 'My name is Marietje.'

'That's a beautiful name,' said Alfie.

'I talk to him!' flashed Marietje. 'You are from the fighting?'

'Yes.'

'And you are hungry? Of course you are, they all are. I will get my father.'

'No!' Alfie was halfway down the ladder. She looked at him scornfully:

'We have helped many but you mustn't stay here, Mynheer.'

'We'll leave. Just give us ten minutes start.' Drew was down the ladder too.

'You don't understand. My father will take you to a safe place. You will be happy there. The girls will look after you. Bill and Harry were happy. Now they have gone.'

'Well,' shrugged Alfie, 'what's good enough for Bill and Harry's good enough for me, I'm sure. Lead the way!'

'No, you stay here, you will be seen. Engleesh are fools!' She was away across the yard, dragging her brother behind her.

'Do we go or stay?' asked Drew.

'We toss for it,' said Alfie. But they didn't have a coin between them. Eventually, stiff and hungry they retreated to the loft to burrow back into the warm straw.

He was a comfortable man, Dries Steenwyck; solid and fair and tough - and he carried a shotgun. He left them in no doubt that it was loaded and they knew that he would use it if he was less than satisfied with their story. He, in his turn, saw two very young men, tired and hungry, with their natural bravado hanging in shreds about them. He had brought with him a pail of milk and drew a packet of sandwiches wrapped in grease-proof paper from the inside pocket of his overcoat; sausage followed. He watched as they ate ravenously, satisfied.

'Here you must stay until dark, my friends, then Joop will take you into town; the girls will hide you for a few days then we will see.' Drew mumbled their thanks through a mouthful of sausage.

'What a family!' he said afterwards as they settled down again in the loft. 'Do you suppose the mother is in it too?'

'In what?' O'Brien was removing his socks. Drew edged away from him.

'The escape line. It takes courage. The Huns could shoot the whole family.'

O'Brien shrugged, 'I expect they'll be pretty, Marietje's sisters.'

'You treat them with respect, you hear me?' said Drew severely. 'You don't look a gift horse in the mouth.'

O'Brien grinned wickedly. 'A Flanders Mare, you mean. Like that Ann of Whatshername. She wasn't no beauty or old King 'Enery wouldn't've topped her.'

'He didn't. Don't you have schools in Australia?'

Eventually, they subsided, watching a grey, damp afternoon sink into a grey dusk.

'I'm going south,' said O'Brien, 'when we get to England - South West, that is, to your country. We'll travel together, I expect, take the train down through the flat country of the Summer Lands, King Arfur's land. Oh, I've read plenty of books. And then, on through Devon where all those old sea dogs came from. And I'll be able to see Plymouth Hoe and the statue of Drake, and look out to the Island. Then we'll travel on, over The Bridge - Isambard's bridge with the boats pottering underneath us. Then we'll travel inland for a while, finally dropping down to the coast. We'll hitch a lift with the milk cart after and arrive before they're astir...... There's a bridge,' said he 'over the stream - only it's never to be called a stream, it's always The River, out of respect for the winter when it's in spate. And the bridge as just a single span, the low parapet topped with Delabole slate, and it's icy and clammy to the touch in the winter and in the summer it's like a sizzling hob and all the cats stretch out there in the sun. But when we arrive its going to be spring - spring moving into summer when the grey-silver dawn is flooded with rose from the emerging sun and the sleepy houses warm into three dimension; a higgledy piggledy hotchpotch of worn grey stone and dazzling whitewash, swimming out from the liquid gold pool of the tiny harbour and ....'

'You know it too - you know Trevander!' marvelled Drew at last.

'Through another man's eyes,' said Alfie shrugging, and for once he wasn't smiling.

'I've never been to England, have I? But did you think it was coincidence I watched over your sick bed, tender as a blooming mother? No, mate, you babbled in your sleep - familiar names, familiar places and I knew where you hailed from and I thought to myself 'Here's a star worth hitching your wagon to'. You see, my father came from Trevander. Born on the east side, above the old sea wall where the pennywort grows and the cliff sheers straight away to the foam. The house'll still be there, it has to be there, doesn't it?' He added ingenuously.

'I never,' said Drew carefully 'recall any O'Briens. To us that would be a foreign name.'

'And what's in a name?' said Alfie. 'I guess he changed it when things got too hot to handle perhaps - or just for fun. I remember once, him sitting with my mother on his knee, teasing her, pulling at her yellow hair. 'I chose a good name for us,' he said 'a rich man's name. He never missed it, he just didn't need it any more' and then he wouldn't explain what he meant by it and she twitted him about it all evening and refused him a kiss. But I guess they made it up later by the creaking of the bed boards. They suited each other fine, him and Amy, but he still left us when the wanderlust was on him. Went north after a fortune and we never saw him again. Maybe he'll come back one day with his grey hairs upon him and a limp in his step and she'll be happy again.' He shrugged his shoulders and buried himself deeper.

Eventually, Dries and the boy, Joop, appeared and made them change into the shapeless dun-coloured garments of peasants the world over, the most successful camouflage they could find. Later, Dries disappeared and returned with a small cart pulled by a disinterested dun-coloured pony, blending comfortably into the rain-washed, rutted landscape.

'He'd hardly make the chariot race in Ben Hur,' sniffed O'Brien. They apparently did have picture palaces in the Bush. Joop was helping his father load up the cart with turnips.

'Now, one of you on the box with Joop, the other on the back. You've no papers so if you're stopped you'll need to make a run for it. Joop will say you stopped him and asked for a lift into town - he will play the innocent and we shall all pray.'

'Oh, we've been doing that a lot in the past forty eight hours,' grinned Drew. They clasped hands with the big Fleming and took their allotted places. Joop flicked at the horse with his whip and they moved at snail's pace out of the farmyard and down towards the high road.

The pony had one pace only and pace wasn't the word for it.

'We get there by next week?' asked O'Brien tartly. Joop opened enormous blue eyes, so like Marietje's.

'Nein, Nein, Mynheer, tonight. We get there tonight and you will have beds with sheets, and food.'

'Well, if you say so, old man, suits me fine. Give me the whip; I'll see if I can ginger Prancer here up a bit.'

Joop looked indignant. 'Nein, he is old, that one - now be silent, mynheer, we are reaching the first houses. They must not hear you, there are many who have no love for the British, they would hand you over for a good meal in their bellies. You should remember that!'

'Point taken,' hissed Drew. 'Put a sock in it, Alfie!'

They slid through the suburbs in the lampless darkness, the cart wheels rattling mournfully, like the progress of a plague cart. There were few people about, scurrying along to beat the curfew, huddled into shawls or overcoats.

'We go the back ways,' murmured Joop. 'We cannot arrive at the front door with these.' He waved a hand over the turnips. 'We go to the tradesmen's entrance. Not far now'.

They turned into an alley, the cobbles rousing the rattle of the wheels into thunder. They were losing turnips at a fast rate before Joop drew rein and they were at their destination; a tall, four-storied villa with fine Dutch gables, peeling stucco and a bell-pull which would have warmed the heart of Count Dracula. Joop did not pull it, he rapped smartly on the door with his whip. It opened a crack and a white hand beckoned them inside. Drew hesitated and the hand grabbed his wrist. Behind him, Joop had given O'Brien a push and he stumbled after. The door closed, they heard the rattle of the cart wheels. It appeared that the old pony had found a second wind.

Inside the dark hallway someone lit an oil lamp and the light flared up, sending shadows up the well of a deep staircase. From the shelter of a stout banister rail six faces stared down at them, six female faces whose ages, at a rough estimate, ranged from eighteen to a year or two short of fifty: two red heads, three blondes and an ebony black. Drew thought that if these were Dries' relatives they were a motley crew but O'Brien was there before him, taking in the generous use of hair dye and face paint, the bright satins and tawdry lace, the low décolletages and the choking miasma of cheap perfume which seemed to ooze from the faded wallpaper; his grin stretched from ear to ear.

'Drew, me old mate, we've fallen feet first this time. This, my son, is a Flemish bawdy house! What a way to win a war!' He winked at the youngest and blondest. 'Alright, I'll lay down my arms and come quietly, but not too quietly!' But a plump arm shot out and grabbed him by the collar and he squirmed round to face a stout virago with a redder head than any of her younger compatriots.

'You are fortunate to have found sanctuary, my very young mynheer. You will keep your hands and anything else with wanderlust strictly to yourself. What you want you will have to pay for, same as any other man. Any transgressions and you will be handed over to the Bosch. It is necessary that we do this from time to time; it convinces our conquerors of our loyalty. In other words,' she hissed into his face, 'don't push your luck, sonny!'

Later, lying on a straw pallet in the attic, Alfie began to sort through the motley assortment of possessions he kept secured in a small chamois bag round his neck.

'There must be something I could trade in. One night of bliss is all I ask, that's not too much, surely?' He turned the bag inside out. It was like a schoolboy's pocket - all string and ball bearings. Drew pounced on a tiny compass.

'Not this. God knows what happens next but if we're on our own again, we'll need it.'

O'Brien shrugged. 'What good would it be to a whore? You don't need a compass for the horizontal.'

'Earrings!' said Drew. 'You're crazy. Why in hell's name did you go to war with a pair of earrings next to your heart?'

O'Brien flushed. 'They're mum's. She never really had the gowns to wear them with or the coiffures, so she said. She thought I might pawn them, I don't know, raise a few shillings, but I shan't. They're the real thing; they're for my intended when I meet her. They're classy.' He took them from Drew's palm and dangled one from the tip of each little finger. Consuela's diamonds caught fire from the stub of candle. 'I've hung onto them all the way from Oz, all through the hell of Pozieres.' He put them back into the bag and drew the neck together again. 'I'm just slipping below, just to the dunny. I may be away some-time, as old Captain Oates put it.'

'And if the old hag keeps her word and hands us over, they could shoot us this time.'

'Oh, I reckon the barks worse than the bite there. Somewhere behind that mound of flesh there was a twinkle. Besides, it's Sunday. I reckon even whores can please themselves on a rest day.

'Rest!' scoffed Drew. 'You'd exhaust a spinning top. Get some sleep!' But O'Brien was nudging him in the ribs and he turned to see the door quietly opening inwards.

It was the youngest, the blondest and the prettiest. She put a finger to her lips. 'Shhh, Engleesh - mynheer Drew, there is a fire in my room. It's cold up here. You will come with me?' She held out a hand. She was about Emelynne Deverel's age but with her Flemish blondness, about as far removed from berry bright Emelynne as one could wish to meet.

'Blondie, he's not interested. He's a virgin, he's keeping himself for - what are you keeping yourself for, Drew? I know, the priesthood. He's going to be a Holy Father. You know, a padre - St. Augustine and all that. *Give me chastity and continency ....*'

'But oh,' said Drew '*do not give them yet!*'

'Take no notice of him, Lottie.' The odds on life had shortened when the Nereus went down. Emelynne and Trevander were light years away. He slipped out of the room after her. O'Brien hurled his pillow at the door. It burst and the feathers filled the room like a glass snow-ball. He lay back on his pallet then and started to laugh, picking goose quills from his hair. Madam stood over him in a cream peignoir; best Brussels lace cut away to reveal generous portions of soft, white flesh. Her hair, if a raunchy crimson, appeared to be her own - it was echoed in more intimate regions.

'That is your little friend taken care of; Lottie owes me a favour. How about a night cap?'

The return to England was an anti-climax - de-briefing by once dapper officers who had lost all interest in the war, followed by weeks in a transit camp on rations which would have shamed the prison camp; a rough sea-crossing; another camp and doses of influenza, the scourge which was marching its way across Europe and claiming lives faster and in greater numbers than the Hun. But, through it all, they stuck together, bound by a 'Boys' Own' pact in which they would catch the train down to the South West and take sleepy Trevander by storm together.

CHAPTER NINE

Lady Jacqueline Lambe was an aristocrat to the finger-tips - more than that, to the plump toes of her sensible shoes. There was blue blood on both sides but whilst it was flaunted on one side, on the other it was alluded to only in whispers - an injudicious liaison in the last century - and the Lambes had been making them ever since. Even Jacqueline's elder sister, the Lady Jennifer, had married for love and married a pauper. He was a man of the cloth, a quiet country parson with a nose for the ancient and crumbly and a passion for the Bronze Age. This coupling had not fulfilled Jacqueline's notions for the romantic so she had joined the VADs. She put her straight blonde hair under a series of preposterous caps and stepped forth with dreams of angelic ministrations to handsome young officers in grey field tents, 'Somewhere in France'. It took less than a week for the scales to fall from her eyes and the starry dream to vanish for ever. But she had persevered doggedly, bolstered no doubt by her illustrious antecedents; Lady Hetty who had withstood a Cromwellian siege in 1644 and helped hurl down missiles from her own battlements, and Lady Bess who had occupied the Tower at the same time as the doubtfully virgin queen and had survived to re-emerge in not exactly smelling of roses, at least putting a brave face on her rheumatism.

Jacqueline was proving a very capable young woman and an excellent nurse. She never made Passchendaele alas, being confined to one of the London teaching hospitals and being passed back and forth between Geriatric and Gynaecological wards. The bells were already ringing out across London for the Armistice when Matron summoned her to the presence and, far from declaring 'for you the war is over', assigned her to the St. Alphege Convalescent Home, a clearing station for the flotsam and jetsam of the field hospitals and the prison camps. Thus, finally, fate threw her into the paths of Drew Maddaver and Alfie T. O'Brien.

In the beginning, setting out from Surrey, there had been dreams of a gracious, red-brick mansion, ivy-covered, set in terraced parkland where wounded officers would begin their rehabilitation ferried about the grounds in wheelchairs by respectable young ladies of their own class. And it was always spring with the magnolias in bloom and the scent of lilacs. Lady Jacqueline arrived at St. Alphege's with the dream as far away as ever, for this was a home for 'other ranks' and it was far too cold a winter's day to take to the lawns and the meagre fruit trees were leafless and there was no lilac - only the all-pervading odours of cabbage and Lysol. But the disappointment had to be pushed into the background. Lady Jacquie was a game girl - plenty of spunk her cousins always said, always one to take part in their escapades - not a milk-sop like Lady Jennifer, far too worried about her peaches and cream complexion and the state of her hair.

And now it was Christmas and they were all far from home. But there was a tree in the ward and Lady Jacquie had scaled a steep pair of steps with an apronful of icicles and stars and a rope of tinsel and not a few remembrances of Christmases past.

Alfie O'Brien lay back on his bed in the fading light of the greyest of afternoons, hands linked behind his head, and watched the pirouetting of the trimmest pair of ankles he had seen in a long time and, when she had stumbled in the descent, putting out a hand to grab for her errant cap, and he had cried out in alarm, she had turned and smiled at him and the lamplight had caught the silver-blonde of her hair.

They lit the candles when darkness fell and, led by Matron, the nurses processed down the ward between the forest of iron bedsteads. Wrapped in their scarlet cloaks and carrying lanterns they sang 'Hark the Herald Angels' and she was there, the angel at the end on the right flank, with the golden hair still managing to escape from the cap. 'O Little Town' followed and then 'It came upon the Midnight clear'.

'It gets you, doesn't it;' sighed O'Brien, 'really get to you down here.' He was searching for his stomach. Drew was absorbed by Matron's chins, throbbing in time to the music. He was thinking of the church upon the hill and imagining them all, the Maddavers and the Tollers, trooping to Midnight Mass: Annabel and his father, Lowena and Emelynne, Tabby and the little girls - and remembering the way the wind tossed the sound of the bells about the village as if they were hiding round each corner as you changed direction, taking flight from the hills and coming in from the sea.

After the carols they relaxed a little and had an impromptu concert. Sister Purvis - they were on Purvis Ward - recited 'The Wreck of the Hesperus' and the red-headed nurse with the cold hands who rejoiced in the name of Jemima, led them in a few choruses of 'Keep the Home Fires Burning' and 'Goodbye Dolly Grey'. Then there was a fair amount of female twittering and giggles and blushing whilst they rooted around for further performers and someone pushed Lady Jacquie to the fore. She stood there between two little brunettes with swaying lanterns, as alike as andirons. Hands primly clasped before her, eyes raised heavenwards, she topped the two by a head - more than common tall - and sang 'After the Ball is Over'. She had a tolerable voice, Drew supposed idly, a little too clipped, a little too breathy but well-enough. O'Brien thought it was heaven. His blue gaze fastened upon her.

'Many a heart is aching
If you could read them all.
Many a heart will be breaking
After the ball.'

It was only then that she lowered her eyes and caught his wrapt gaze and blushed visibly and, wonder of wonders, returned his smile.

'Did you see that!' he breathed to Drew.

'Forget it. That, my lad, is class, real class; blue blood, silver spoons and all. She's out of your stars.'

But in their last week, when they were allowed out into the town and even tired old London seemed paved with gold, he invited her to the theatre and she agreed to accompany him, provided that Drew asked Jemima along too. So they caught an omnibus out west and got seats in the gallery for Chu Chin Chow. And, whilst Drew gazed about him at the mass of humanity, all eager to escape from post war doom and gloom, and Jemima's nimble fingers scuttled their way through the box of chocolates he had provided, Alfie fumbled for Lady

Jacquie's hand, found it and held it throughout the performance. Afterwards, they walked back to St. Alphege's and Jacqueline's dream of tea under the magnolias with a handsome, dark, officer in neatly pressed uniform, dissolved and reformed into a brash young Australian in crumpled khaki with chaotic blond hair and an infectious smile, and the scent of lilacs was the sooty dampness of a London pea-souper, the clack of her heels, the sudden squalling of a cat the only replacement for bird-song that night. They parted on the corner for were Sister Purvis to have espied one of her gels arm in arm with a patient would have meant instant dismissal.

Their discharge papers came at last and though Drew made plans for their journey south, invitations came for four or five of them to join a party at the Lambes' ancestral pile. And, because the summons came from Lady Lambe, with her husband's blessing and because the hospital and the armed forces had discarded them, there was no bar to the visit.

Surely, thought Drew, when she sees him on her own home territory; ill-fitting suit, his rough ways, that colonial outspokenness, and she compares him with her own kind, she will wish to end this madness of theirs and send him packing back to his own class. For a while, no doubt, the endless wagging tail would sink between his legs until two stations past Paddington and he'd become maddeningly chipper again.

But Lady Lambe, her noblesse oblige polished to perfection, determined to do her bit to entertain these conquering heroes and give them a weekend to remember, had obviously lectured all, from Lady Jacquie's Etonian brothers, Rupert and Freddie and the grave young cousin who had left a leg at Mons to butlers and boot boys and the motley collection of retainers too old or too young for the fight who had remained to polish the silver and cultivate vegetables. The visitors were to be treated with respect, there was to be no tittering and whispering when their hands hovered over the battery of cutlery flanking the Sevres dinner plates, no smirk, no snide comments.

Comberton Court, rising from its smooth green lawns, with pillar and pediment, balcony and balustrade, was lit up like a fairytale palace for their last evening, in readiness for the grandest ball since the summer of 1914. Lady Lambe wore ice blue silk, stitched with bugle beads. She swept down the grand staircase into the old banqueting hall on her husband's arm, beaming goodwill upon the upturned faces below. Alfie had his hair plastered down with macassar oil and looked more like a barrow boy. Drew looked better but still very much out of place. Lady Jennifer, the one who had married the vicar and become poor as a church mouse, was small and plain and mouselike herself in oyster satin but her smile was genuine and Drew liked her at once. Lady Jacquie was late and flushed - it might have been supposed that her rushed arrival had brought the roses to her cheeks. She teetered at the top of the staircase and descended alone, her hair a brushed golden halo, piled into a chignon, clipped back with a spray of tiny diamond blossoms which shivered on their fragile stems. She wore white silk, stitched with glass beads, light as gossamer and the white satin shoes which peeped out from below her hem were walking upon air as she spied Alfie and held his admiring gaze and came down to them all. Only Drew and O'Brien noticed the love light glowing in her brown eyes. To the young Australian she had everything he found most irresistible. She had breeding and beauty and the challenge of her virginity and she was incontrovertibly in love with him. She spent most of the evening in his arms for he was not afraid to dance and soon picked up the steps. And if Drew noticed and was sad for her, Lady Lambe heaved a sigh of relief that tomorrow he would be gone to pastures new.

When the formal part of the evening was over, the young people began a game of hide and seek, running along the gallery above the main staircase, calling down to one another, spilling out onto the formal, lantern-lit terrace and dispersing amongst the dark pathways leading to the Chinese pagoda and the Ninth Baronet's over-stuccoed Italian grotto. But others, failing to be seduced by the cold wintry air, clattered up the servants' stairs to the attics and along, at roof-level, to the twisting staircase leading down to the old nursery wing. Alfie found Jacquie in a tiny, firelit room, with Victorian flowered wallpaper, old chintz curtains and a battered sofa, half hidden by the lace shawl carelessly thrown over its back. There was a cat licking a front paw, too bored to stop and look at him. Jacquie was sitting on the rag rug before the fire, face rosy, hair warmed to russet, and the flames found an echo in every one of the tiny glass beads sewn to her bodice.

Alfie O'Brien cast a quick look about him, at the open work box on the little table, spilling its jewel-coloured embroidery silks, at the old books stacked, higgledy-piggledy against the wall: Edith Nesbit and Mrs. Ewing, at the tea tray discarded, still bearing a lone sandwich, a slice of angel cake and a china bowl, half full of tea slops

'I suppose,' said Alfie 'that the old witch has gone off to stop the Sleeping Beauty from pricking her fingers. Whose room is this?'

'It's Nanny's room. There's always a fire lit in the grate so that if she wants to get away from the servants' hall there's a cosy niche for her up here. She won't be back tonight. She was nodding over supper. Someone will lead her off to bed eventually and clean up in here tomorrow.

'And, didn't you know,' she added softly 'it's too late for the Princess, she can't be saved'.

'Not even with a kiss?' grinned Alfie. 'At least let me try.' He moved quickly and quietly to the door and put the pin in the latch, then he turned down the lamp and moved softly towards her. Kneeling down beside her he took her into his arms.

Later, on the day bed, he slept for a while, fair head in the froth of her ball gown, whilst she stared, unseeing, into the firelight, listening to the wind in the chimney and the rattle of last year's dry leaves against the window pane - her mind in turmoil.

'I meant what I said,' he murmured, only half awake 'I do mean to marry you but I have to get things together first. There'll be my dad's place, I've got to look it over and see about a job. You won't live in a palace any more but we'll be together. You do believe me?'

'I think so. I want to. You know I'm in love with you.'

He grinned. 'Don't I just. Your sort don't give much away, my lady. I guessed that was for real. Look at you, as dishevelled as a schoolgirl, bank holiday on Manley Beach. You tidy yourself up, my girl. I can't face your mother tonight.'

'I can't face her ever,' said a voice inside him. Elopement was a better idea; it would appeal to her romantic nature. 'I'll come back for you soonest, I promise. Look here's earnest of what I say.' He had a hand inside his shirt, looping a leather thong over his head. He still carried the little draw-string bag which had accompanied him across occupied Europe. He took out the earrings, Consuela's legacy. Jacquie, smoothing her skirts, trying to re-assemble her blonde coiffure turned to him, wide-eyed, recognizing their value.

'They were mum's,' he said in explanation. 'Tell you what, take one for a keepsake. I'll hang onto the other for now, so you know I'll come back for you. Then you can wear them for me. Keep it safe now.' He pinned her arms to her sides and kissed her again and felt her hunger for him. 'Got to go now, give it time before you come down. I'll be away early tomorrow with Drew, its best that way - no goodbyes, I can't bear goodbyes.'

'No,' she whispered. 'Your father's house, does it have a name?'

'Oh yes,' he said 'Penolva - pretty name, aint it? It'll be a pretty place. I've got to go.' He blew her a kiss from the doorway. When he had gone she looked at herself in the mirror over the fireplace, face flushed, eyes over-bright, lips moist. How could she go down amongst them all again? How could they look at her and not know what had gone on in this room. Nanny would call her a fallen woman. Oh, how could one fall so low assailing such lofty heights? She took one last look around her and softly closed the door.

❧

They had dreamed of travelling south in the spring but in the end were glad enough to be away. Pacing up and down the platform at Paddington, trying to stamp some life into the feet, glad of the soot-laden air for the warmth it seemed to bring as each engine chugged away.

They settled in their seats; Alfie still with the triumph of his conquest upon him, chirpy and outrageous; Drew, self-contained with a burgeoning excitement within him. In the end, they slept for most of the journey and climbed out at Liskeard, that little grey town on the edge of the moors where the wind whipped away all trace of the London smog and left them fresh-faced and hungry. Drew saw one or two faces he recognised and hands were shaken and greetings exchanged.

CHAPTER TEN

They came home on the tail-board of a cart as Alfie had always said they would. But it wasn't the milk-cart heralding a silver dawn but the carter from Penherrit braving a force-eighter for an urgent delivery to the Godolphin. There was no shelter to be had and the south wind, straight off the sea and roaring through the coombes took them full on the back of the neck, driving the rain under their collars, plastering hair to the head, numbing fingers. Coming down from the moors it had been a bare moonscape of wind-blasted tors followed by a rolling landscape, red-brown winter fields and withered thorn hedges desperately clinging on to the last scarlet berries of a prodigal autumn. Here and there hidden grey villages, where hardly a dog barked, slid round the bends misty with wood-smoke. Only at the last mile did Drew twist his stiffened body round so that he could face forward and see the road beyond the driver's shoulder and over the ears of the patiently plodding nag. Alfie followed suit, his feet were frozen solid in his boots:

'Are we almost there? Funny, I thought it would feel like a homecoming and there's nothing here of the mind pictures after all.'

'Oh, its home,' said Drew. 'This is the home-wind; not south and sighing but letting us feel its presence along every street and alleyway; the feared wind which funnels into the harbour and drives the tide up the main street. Last night they will have drawn the boats up high and fastened their shutters against the rattle of shingle on the panes and boarded up their doors.'

'Loved and feared,' said O'Brien.

'Oh, never loved before today,' smiled Drew.

'There should,' said O'Brien, 'be brass bands and children with flags and pretty girls in white dresses strewing our way with flowers.'

'I'll settle for hot soup and a fire of pine logs.'

'And one of Mrs .Cluett's pasties?' grinned O'Brien, delighted as always when one of his father's folk memories, tumbling from his own lips, caught Drew unawares.

But by now they were enfolded by the damp, smoky darkness of the coombes, where every dwelling strained to let at least one of its windows lean out towards the sea, as if they jostled to peer over each other's shoulders. Beside the road the river, in spate, gathering red soil and clattering stones from the moors, chattered on, winding beside the road. Drew had never sailed an Armada of paper boats like the children of land-locked cities, he had grown up with the real thing, glimpsed them from his own windows, sat nose pressed to the glass on winter evenings and seen the fleet go out, the rubies of the port lights jostling through the narrow harbour mouth.

And then they had ceased ascending and the road, if winding, was flatter now. The last corner brought them to the harbour, with the boats drawn up into the street to escape the marauding wind. It was hard to see where harbour ended and quay began. But here was the bridge and in the distance the lime kiln and the pilchard palaces where the women worked, and the bark house where they tanned the sails and cordage and.....

'We'll get down here,' said Drew 'and walk the last half mile. If walk we still can.' He lowered himself stiffly from the tail of the cart, pulled up outside the stores. He turned and gave an arm to his friend and so Jack Toller's son came to tread for the first time on Trevander soil. And if the heavens were displeased they showed their ill-favour equally to Drew. But Drew had abandoned him at the bridge and was running along the quay, threading between the salvaged vessels drawn high and the flotsam of any fishing village: lobster pot and wicker maund, trailing nets and cork floats - until he found what he was looking for, moored against the main quay, hatches battened down, sails furled, badly wanting a fresh lick of paint but the same loved contours. He was down a ladder and onto her deck, feeling the boards beneath his feet, running a hand along the sheer of her sides.

'I'm home, old girl,' he said aloud.

'So you be, lad. What kept you so long - the lights of London?' and Esco was out of the deck-house, slipping a wicked knife into a nearby rack so that he could grip him by the shoulders.

'Praise God you were spared. Go to your mother, boy. She needs to know that one of her sons has truly come home.'

'Mathey?' said Drew. 'Mathey never....'

'No, he's gone no hope for news now they say, and Tabby with the three little ones. He never saw his son. That's hard.'

'He saved my life,' said Drew. 'I'll look out for the boy. What did she call him?'

'Tristan,' said Esco, 'after my father. I was pleased at that. She's a brave lass, is Tabby, I think she always knew she would lose him. Go to your mother, Drew.' But the lightness was out of Maddaver's step now and O'Brien had the sense not to ask him what was wrong just then. They walked along The Strand between cottages and fish factories, feet ringing on the cobbles. Cats vanished before them. There was a parrot, on his perch by an open window, his splendid plumage, scarlet and blue, livened the monochrome of the afternoon. He cackled at them and shifted on his perch. 'Pieces of eight!' grinned Alfie.

Two girls, baskets over their arms, heads together conspiratorially, were coming towards them through the rain; shawls thrown over their dark dresses; they might have been sisters.

'Drew, Oh Drew,' cried Emelynne, feet light on the cobbles, and she clung about his neck. Her brown hair smelt the same, rinsed through in rosemary every Wednesday - was it still Wednesday? She looked older somehow, the softness had gone from her face, the child-ish plumpness had fined down. She was lovelier than ever she had been in his dreams.

Alfie stood back a little way, amused. The other girl did the same. She was slim with a pretty, pert nose, a translucent skin and ripples of dark red hair. He remem-bered his father saying 'She had the reddest hair and a chin and a nose set higher than the rest and I wanted to possess her more than anything else in this life!' Alfie looked from the red head to Drew and back again. So this was his sister, the haughty Lowena, this was Annabel's daughter. He winked at her. She tossed her head, eyes cold. And from that moment Lady Jacquie ceased to exist.

Alfie moved in with the Maddavers and became an immediate hero. For him the natural reserve of the Cornish melted away. His rough colonial ways had a novelty value and charm of their own. Besides, he was Drew's companion in fortune or misfortune; he had seen one of their sons safe home. He was welcome everywhere, plied with drinks and invitations to tea.

He went with Drew to visit Mathew Toller's widow at Penolva. Jack would never have acquainted this clean, neatly swept cottage with his father's hovel on its cliff perch, draughty and cheerless - the cottage where Frank and Jack had grown up. But to Alfie it had always looked like this; gleaming glass windows, copper and brass you could see your face in, a bright fire in the hearth. But Alfie said nothing for a while, for reasons unknown to himself he kept his council and forbore to tell Tabby they were kissing cousins and that even Drew and Lowena were a kind of step-cousin. Instead, he basked in their welcome and their kindnesses, pretending not to notice when Drew drifted back to Fosfelle and the old easy friendship with George and Emelynne Deverel.

George had been badly wounded and when they at last got him home he had needed a deal of nursing. From a distance, standing waving from the Vantage, George was the same young man, debonair, gallant, lazily smiling, bronzy hair ruffled by the wind, pipe at the corner of his mouth. As you drew closer the changes became apparent; the taut lines about the mouth and eyes, movements strained and a little jerky. He limped now, trying to turn a walking stick into an affectation.

And Lowena, Lowena the red haired valkyrie who had urged him, urged all their menfolk to take up arms against the foe, had long ago tired of the war, of her own dull existence with them all away, of the sight of proud women, stoically tearless, dressed in black, carrying on their daily tasks with the telegrams proclaiming their loss tucked into the pockets of their dreary skirts. She had grown weary, trying not to flinch as yet another old schoolfriend limped home, blind or maimed, sightless, limbless or shattered in mind. And Lowena the heedless and frivolous had been too proud to reject George Deverel. He had given her an opening, a way out, told her in all frankness that there would never be children, the doctors had been kind, kind but blunt – his injuries were too severe. He understood that women wanted children; he had wanted them too, thought wistfully of it when he was away. He was saddened that there were none to follow him should he fall, none to help him grasp at a kind of immortality. But he could not expect her to give up a woman's need of motherhood. She must consider herself freed of their engagement. And though somehow she supposed that she pitied him, she knew that when she told him that she still wanted the wedding to go ahead and soon please, it was only the thought of that finger of scorn which would be pointed at her if she abandoned him - she who had been first to talk of white feathers, to goad the peacemakers into enlisting.

In the lemon sunshine of a mild march Sunday it was warm enough to sit out in the shelter of Jane Boase's tiny gazebo, set into a corner of the garden wall. Emelynne, in the dress she had worn for church, let Drew undo the brown knot of her hair, too preoccupied to chide him for his importunities.

'She shouldn't marry, she shouldn't!' Her brows were furrowed, the brown eyes distressed.

'He's your brother, for heaven's sake!' said Drew. 'He's loved her since he could walk and talk. I'm happy for them, Emmy, it'll be the four of us together again - for always if you like, as we meant it to be.'

Emelynne was staring out across the harbour, watching the sun touch the early gold of the gorse, watching the fleeting cloud shadows drifting across the cliff top.

'He was dreadfully wounded,' said Emelynne guardedly.

'But he's fine now. That limp - well, a girl wouldn't throw a chap aside for that - not even the Lowenas of this world!'

'It's more than that,' said Emelynne, 'they can't - he won't be able to have children. They were engaged on his last leave, you know. When he came home for good he offered to release her. It broke his heart to do it but he could not deny her the hope of children. It was the right thing to do, wasn't it?'

'Yes, it was right.' Drew's eyes were grave. 'She still wears the ring.'

'Yes, she wouldn't allow it. She'd set her heart on George when she was three years old. But she shouldn't go through with it now.'

Drew said, 'she set her mind on Fosfelle, isn't that what you mean?'

'Oh no, it was what we always said but I can't really believe that that's all he means to her. She's fond of him...'

'Being fond isn't enough,' said Drew 'not for a lifetime together. I've more than fondness for you, Emmy.'

She pushed him away. 'Lowena will never be really close to anyone, but George will give her security.'

'It will keep her pretty feet out of the mud of the foreshore and her head in the clouds above the stench of pilchard oil,' said Drew grimly. 'Oh, I'm glad for old George, he'll be happy on any terms and I imagine she sees it all as a kind of martyrdom. Perhaps she never wanted children. Alfie says he's never seen a girl like her, he's quite besotted. But then, Alfie never met a girl who didn't come to his bidding. It's chalk and cheese there.'

'Don't be so sure,' said Emelynne, 'remember the high-born lady who ran off with the wraggle taggle gypsies?'

'Ah, but she was a romantic,' smiled Drew, 'not a snow queen like Lowena.'

Drew and Emelynne married in April and she trod lightly up the hill to the church on Gabriel Deverel's arm and there were white camellias in her bouquet from the gardens of Fosfelle and knots of primroses sprinkled the grassy mounds of the graves humped on either side of the path. Drew wore his Sunday suit, and it was warm enough to hold the wedding breakfast out of doors. Long trestle tables covered with spotless linen, jugs of cider and a cake baked in stages in the bakehouse oven along with the pies and pasties and Sunday roasts. Lowena was cool and elegant as chief bridesmaid, with a small, grave Cynthia on one side and smiling little Poggy - Tabby's younger daughter Margaret - on the other. After the bride and groom had driven away in Gabriel's pony and trap, bound for the station and an unknown destination, the feast continued far into the spring night. The women talked of the nuptials to come, the midsummer wedding of Lowena and George. Lowena, they said, would make a lovelier bride than Emelynne but never a more willing one. And Lowena herself had wandered down to the Vantage to stare above the roof tops and out over the harbour - the best view in all of Cornwall, according to Annabel, to where the lights of the fleet, strung out like a diamond necklace, glittered below the horizon.

'A penny for them, Miss Maddaver,' said Alfie O'Brien.

Lowena said nothing, only hunched her shoulder away from him. But he continued doggedly, 'I've had enough now, a surfeit of cakes and ale. I'm going walking to try and clear my head. All this getting together and jollification today - it really set me thinking about my own folk....'

Lowena did not even glance toward him. 'There are no O'Briens in this village, there never were. You're an impostor, everyone knows that.' Alfie shrugged, 'Very well, I'll admit it, but only in taking a name that never really was mine - and that's not an uncommon act where I hail from. Alfie T. O'Brien, that's me and you could ask what the T stands for.'

'No,' said Lowena 'because it doesn't interest me in the slightest.'

'Toller,' said Alfie and knew he had her attention, saw her stiffen, saw the red head jerk upwards. 'I'm Jack Toller's son.'

'No,' said Lowena, 'he died when the Mohegan went down; his name is there, at St. Keverne. There's a mass grave.'

Alfie said gently, 'there's another man there, a nob he was, a rich man with a beautiful daughter, returning to America. They'll be side by side and no doubt she knows her own father. There was a murder hanging over my father, so he changed places - he got to be in the right place at the right time. He never killed anyone but he blamed himself for the death and they would have hung him, so he had to disappear. It may not suit your ladyship but my roots are as deep here as your own. Tabby's house, that was where they lived, wasn't it, Granfer

Toller and the boys, Frank and Jack? He could hardly remember his mother, died when he was a scrap of a lad but I promised if I ever got to England, which didn't seem likely at the time, I would seek her out.'

Lowena was studying him then, as if she was seeing every feature for the very first time; the very blond hair, the golden skin he had brought with him from the southern continent and which refused to dull even in the dark mud of France, the mobile mouth, the grey eyes. She said, 'Janniper Boswell lies in the churchyard - a grassy mound on the very fringe of the burial ground, a little distant from the worthy families of Boase, Denbow and Combellack, humped below the dry stone wall and showered with pear blossom when the time is right - old Granfer did that for her - for he did love her. But I doubt she sleeps as well as your drowned American. The Boswells were gypsies, down from the moors. He met her at a fair, over to Liskeard. She never really liked it down in the village, she preferred the bracken of the cliff tops and the old standing stones at Castle Du. That's where she went to get away from all the wagging tongues. That's where you want to go isn't it? I often go up there on summer evenings. When I was a child I thought it was the top of the world.'

'You would show me the way?' said Alfie, humbly for him, eyes demure and downcast. Lowena gave him a long, searching look and then nodded. 'I'll call in at home for a shawl and meet you where the cliff track forks.'

'We'll need a lamp?' hazarded O'Brien.

'Not with the moon at full - we'll manage.' She turned away from the Vantage and he watched her move down through the terraces of the garden. He gave her three minutes and set off after her. There were already lights in the window at Chy an Lor. Annabel was home. She did not glance up as he went whistling by, or query Lowena's passing comment that she was going out for a breath of air and would not be long. The girl did not hurry herself and O'Brien, pacing there at the fork in the path, believed that she had thought better of this escapade. He grinned at her. She motioned ahead, where the path snaked up the cliff side between furze and flower, swept past him, like a white moon moth in her wedding finery, and strode on ahead, confident that he was following her. It was he who staggered breathless at the cliff top. She was laughing at him, her young, high bosom hardly heaving at all. In summer, the fields that topped the cliffs would be waist high with crops, golden and whispering, full of poppies and the scurrying of harvest mice. Tonight, they were dark and silent.

Lowena took the path inland with its gentle undulations and unsuspected rise, she said nothing and for once something inborn told O'Brien to keep his silence too. And then they were at the Stones, on high ground somewhere between the dark backdrop of the distant moors with the menace of their tors and the soundless, invisible sea. As stone circles go, Castel Du was unimpressive; half a dozen drunken stones and a crazy arch, lurching like the lintel for a gingerbread house. O'Brien, about to laugh and dismiss the whole scene, caught his breath as the moon came up and sent dark shadows across the short grass. Somewhere, a dog fox gave a short, abrupt bark and there were owls away towards the river valley.

Lowena spread her shawl upon a fallen giant and sat down, knees drawn up. The breeze was quite strong here and caught at her hair. She withdrew the pins and shook it out about her shoulders. In the cold light flooding down from the moon it had no colour of its own; she might have been blonde, redheaded or gypsy-dark like Janniper Boswell. O'Brien ventured to sit beside her. He thought of the young Granfer Toller, bewitched by the gypsy. Perhaps she had lit fires and sat combing out her long hair. Perhaps she came here, basket over arm, for the herbs that must be gathered at full moon. Perhaps she danced for Toller, weaving about amongst the stones.

'I think you are Janniper tonight,' he said, and put out a hand to touch the rippling hair.

And Lowena, who was to marry a man she supposed she loved but did not desire, was happy enough to believe that this fair young Australian, this dead man's child, was Jem Toller, come to claim Janniper from Castel Du. It was a speedy, rough wooing but if O'Brien had given her time to think she would have drawn back from the edge of madness. Covered with his hot kisses and half divested of her wedding finery he had carried her to the soft grass below the arch stones, pressing her down into the green April darkness. And there was no holding back with the respect he had felt for kind and cozened Lady Jacquie. He made love to her fiercely and she did not shrink from it. Always the thought was there that this would be the last time a man would make love to her with such ardour - that George would be kind and considerate. Or anyway, whatever kind of lover he proved to be, this young man's heat and desire would always come between them.

O'Brien slid away from her to lie staring up at the risen moon and its bright star accomplice. Not even the owl cried out.

'*Night and silence* -,' said Lowena. 'What are we going to do?'

'What should we do?' asked Alfie. 'Take up life as it was meant to be. You'll marry George and become mistress of Fosfelle. I shall roam the world, eventually, at any rate, but I shall remember tonight. You must remember too, when you're sitting in your summer house, embroidering tablecloths. Wait, I'll give you a keepsake, something tangible to prove that tonight actually happened.' He still had the little bag at his neck. He drew it over his head and extracted the jet earring and placed its trembling droplet on her white palm.

'Only one?' said Lowena. He shrugged:

'The other went to a good cause. You could have it made into a pendant, I suppose. I should not have parted so lightly with its fellow. It seemed a good idea at the time.'

Lowena said, 'a beggar - you gave it away to a beggar man!'

'A beggar maid - she felt the better for its reassurance,' he smiled, thinking of Lady Jacquie but perhaps it was the last thought he ever gave her.

Lowena moved slowly to her feet, her moon-white dress in disarray, and her hair in knots. Alfie pulled her towards him and kissed her violently, and then she pushed him away and stood back a little. It's time to put Janniper and Jem back into the chest. You must never speak of tonight.'

He grinned, 'if you say so, m'lady, but it will always be there, won't it?'

She nodded, deftly pinning up her hair. 'When we get to the fork in the path let me go home alone.' She turned once as they left the stones but the moon was in cloud and they had melted into the hillside. They did not hold hands as they threaded their way very cautiously down the Cliffside again and, by the time they reached the fork in the path, they had forgotten how to speak to each other again. Lowena slipped away and left him in the darkness with the murmur of the sea for company. There was only the sea to master now, thought Alfie. He had taken the girl, had what he wanted from her. That she was George's betrothed did not figure at all, that she was Drew's sister only tugged at his conscience momentarily.

CHAPTER ELEVEN

As the days grew longer and the seas took on a kindlier, more gentle aspect, Alfie took to accompanying Drew on the Waterwitch. If it was all a game to him, to give him his due he worked hard. Esco Cluett was still with them, staunch as ever, and Colan Denbow who had grown into a passable mariner whilst Drew was away. It was like old times again except that Esco and Alfie openly disliked each other. 'He'll get over it,' said Denbow, 'when he realises that Alfie has no wish to take his place.' But Drew knew there was something more, something instinctive in the older man's dislike of O'Brien and, because he would have trusted Esco with his life, he knew that there was a warning here for himself if only he could define it. But Alfie was the same as he had always been, chirpy, alive and interested, and skies were blue and it was good to be alive, good to come home to Emelynne. They had rented a cottage on the far side of the harbour. From their bedroom window they could look out across to Chy an Lor, peeping between the eaves on the far side of The Strand, and up to the terraced garden of Fosfelle where sometimes George would wave from the Vantage or they could follow Gabriel and Hetty's slow progress through the flowers. Hetty was not to see the year out but she lived long enough to be sure that she would have at least one grandchild. Emlynne's baby was due in January and from the moment she was certain of its advent she walked on the lightest of clouds, cocooned in contentment. She would sit on her step through the hot summer days, watching the world go by, exchanging news and greetings with everyman and his wife. Tabby's children loved her and would stop by for lemonade and fairy cakes and grave little Cynthia would offer to go to the shops whilst Poggy examined the baby clothes or chased Tristan up and down the quay. And, if Esco's intuition warned him about O'Brien then Emelynne, lapped by her own contentment, was not too removed from the real world to fail to notice that all was not well with Lowena.

She rarely ventured voluntarily about the village, complaining of the summer heat but she would disappear up onto the cliffs for long hours at a time and, because Emelynne had seen the signs in her own body she knew that the girl was pregnant. She followed her one afternoon, up onto the cliff to one of the old hewers' shelters where women and boys and old men used to rest, waiting for the pilchard shoals before beginning a wild series of semaphore signals to point out their whereabouts to the men at the seine boats.

'It's no good, Lowena, I know what's happened. You're pregnant.'

Lowena said, 'Isn't it cosy, we can swap stories, perhaps you'll teach me to knit - I never had the patience. I'm confused, Emmy, do I concentrate on the layette before I finish the wedding dress? Would it be cheaper to wait a while and combine the two ceremonies? It would save keeping a tier of the cake!'

'Oh, Lowena, what's happened to you? I know what the doctors said about George but doctors can be wrong!'

'You know it isn't George's getting. Your saintly brother is afraid to touch me!'

'That's unfair. George worships you. I shouldn't ask who the father is or where or why but Lowena, you have to tell George, call off the wedding and marry this man!'

'I have to and shall do neither,' said Lowena, a flash of the old defiance in her eyes. 'I have no wish to marry him or he me. It would never work; it would be disastrous. I shall go ahead as planned. George will keep silent rather than let the whole world know his bride made a cuckold of him before the wedding night. Perhaps he may even believe in miracles!'

'You can't do this to him, I won't let you!' flared Emelynne. 'Why can't you marry the father? You mean he's married already?'

'Lord no! But he's a waster; he'll make nothing of his life. Besides, there's Fosfelle.'

Emelynne said, 'A good woman can do much to change a man. You owe it to the child....'

Lowena smiled crookedly, 'I never was a good woman, was I, Emmy? Besides, he'll go back home one day. Can you see me on a sheep farm or stuck out in the red heat of the Outback, perched in a rocking chair on my shabby, peeling verandah?'

'Alfie!' said Emelynne. 'You let Alfie - Oh, Lowena, it was a moment of madness surely. Oh darling, did he force you?'

Lowena began to laugh, a wild look in her eyes. 'Madness. Yes that was the word for it, Emmy, a night of madness. It was the wildest night of my life but I never want to see him again. I don't expect you to understand. George would not.'

'No,' said Emelynne, 'he would not understand but he might, perhaps, forgive.'

'Emelynne, I want you to swear to say nothing of this, not to my mother or yours, not to George, not even to my precious brother. I have to have your promise!'

Emelynne shrugged, 'Very well, but please, please think about it. It's a terrible thing you're doing to George; he doesn't deserve it.'

'Do you think I don't know that? Oh please go, Emmy, I can't take any more of your mournful glances.'

So the July wedding, planned for so long because there were Deverels to invite from up and down the Duchy, and some from north of the Tamar, grew nearer. And there were those, misty eyed with wedding dreams, who thought that the bride grew lovelier and more ethereal.

They were to be wed on a Saturday morning. The day before had been very hot and there was a hint of thunder in the air. By the evening the sky had taken on a strange opalescence, mocked by the sea, so that it was impossible to see where one merged into the other and the gulls, instead of winging out to their cliffside ledges, wheeled incessantly, mournfully, over the village as if the world had gone mad and they were disorientated.

It was a night for decision, for rocking the foundations of life and three Maddavers stood at their doors and looked up at the wheeling gulls and made resolutions and stuck to them and altered lives for ever.

Emelynne went down to the boat where Drew was preparing for the night's trip. He was alone. Esco had dislocated his arm in the last of the summer's storms to precede these few days of calm, and Colan Denbow would no doubt be taking a quick tea with his widowed mother before coming down; they were alone.

'Drew, I have to talk. Can we go below for a while?' She smiled as he helped her through the hatch, she was not so clumsy yet that it presented any problems for her. She was as light on her feet as ever.

She sat down on his bunk in the darkness; only the sunlight through the hatch lit the gloom with a bright shaft, full of dust motes.

'Drew, I made a promise to your sister but I have to break it. I have to tell someone.'

Drew smiled 'Don't look so woe-begone, Emmy, we're husband and wife, one flesh, and it's not a mortal sin. Lowena shouldn't force an oath to drive man and wife apart. Don't let it worry your head. You know how dramatic she likes to be. Now tell me all about it.'

Emelynne said, 'I don't know how.'

'Take a deep breath and just come out with it!'

'Emelynne concentrated on the darkest corner of the cabin. It smelt of fish and bilge water, oil, bacon and old socks.

'Lowena marries George tomorrow with Alfie O'Brien's child inside her. I told her she mustn't do it. I've told her she must marry Alfie; she has no choice.'

'No,' said Drew, 'she can't marry him.' But whether he was referring to George or to Alfie he did not qualify the words. Instead, he put an arm round her and kissed her, put a finger under her chin and turned her face toward him. 'Don't say another word, Emmy, not to a living soul. It'll be sorted out somehow. Go home and try not to fret. All will be well.'

And because she loved him and trusted him implicitly and because she was tired of the thoughts going round in her head, she let it rest and walked slowly back to the cottage. 'And tomorrow will take care of the thoughts of itself' was a text the Rev. Trefusis might well have taken for last Sunday's sermon.

Lowena climbed the path from The Strand, up through the gardens of Fosfelle, bright with summer flowers; the tall spires of delphiniums, soft purple foxgloves and the pink of shirley poppies. Here and there she was glad of the small patches of shade from the ancient pines or the bowers of weeping fuchsias. George was at the Vantage, where he always was at this time in the evening, pipe in hand, hair burnished to a healthy bronze by the summer sun. He had seen her long before she emerged and his face, still with its battle honours of hollows and lines, lit up as it always did. Solid, dependable, kind, boring George, firm as Cornish granite – '*steel true and blade straight*' as Stevenson so aptly put it. He held out a hand for hers and drew her to his side.

The Vantage was a most spectacular view-point, a tiny walled area dedicated to its own goddess, Aphrodite. Her dark eyes were hard as agates; the lips too lush, too wide for beauty; the golden curls piled high, brassy and perilous above her broad forehead; the snub, flat-tipped nose adding a weird incongruity to the most beautiful woman in this world or out of it. She had been the goddess figurehead of the Aphrodite in the golden days of Nelson and the Nile and Dr Boase had found her in a barn, supporting a cow-byre, had bought her for shillings and placed her at the Vantage, buttressing a dry stone wall and sheltered by the tamarisks. Now she looked down upon a toy fleet, huddled in the curved arm of Trevander Bay, and smiled her enigmatic, Mona Lisa smile. The Vantage was positioned at the elbow bend of the path which dropped from Fosfelle to the Strand. A small paved area in the crook of the wall, furnished with a white wrought-iron bench where Jane Boase had bought her embroidery on hot afternoons and Hetty Deverel tattled with her neighbours over the tea cups.

The view from the Vantage was almost unparalleled in Trevander. The blue of the bay, where sky met sea, the dancing points of light upon the fret of the waves, the white froth of the first crests on a breezy day, the green arches of the breakers when the force-eighters roared in from the South East. Now, the soft fronds of the tamarisks dipped and swayed, pink tasselled and full of whispers.

Hetty had withdrawn indoors long ago for the light was going and the Vantage was left to George and Lowena, leaning over the wall and watching the squalls shafting down along the horizon. The gardens of Fosfelle were woven into both their lives. George had been born in the house and Lowena, as Annabel's daughter, had grown up with stories of her girlhood among the bird-haunted, flower-filled terraces; a lonely child's tales of make-believe. George was tapping his pipe out on Aphrodite's battered head – Hetty disapproved of the habit – sucking at the old briar he was like a babe with a comforter. But it had only ever been a blind, the constant tut-tutting over George's peccadilloes. He was the favourite, the only son, the bright hope for a mother's secure old age, not like his scapegrace sister Emelynne, a mother's bane if ever there was one!

He said quietly. 'You have come to tell me that you cannot marry me tomorrow.' He watched her pretty jaw drop and the guilt flash into her eyes. 'No, don't answer me. Because I have something to say first and I don't want to be interrupted - just this once.'

She nodded, lost for words. He did not look at her then; he leant over the Vantage watching the fleet preparing to sail on the ebb tide. The Waterwitch was quite plain in her distinctive colours, green and gold. Drew was there, plainly having an argument with Colan Denbow - their voices batted backwards and forwards about the bowl of the harbour, words indistinguishable. George said. 'I know you are having another man's child. Do you think I do not know every glance, every movement, and every mood by now? Lowena, I have loved you, oh so long. I have grieved that we should have no children. I have agonised over my right to take this away from you. I think that God has found a way to give us a son....'

Lowena could not bear his reasonable words. She snapped, 'If God had wanted to give you sons he should have thought of that at Jutland!'

George smiled, 'That's my girl! I've missed that sharp tongue these last few weeks. Oh never believe that this has not crushed me, hurt me to my heart's core, but if you will take me still, you will be mistress of Fosfelle and my son will never need to know who fathered him. He will never need to be unsure because I shall love and cherish him for his mother's sake and his own.'

Lowena smiled at him bravely, she hoped with gratitude, but she saw the bars of a prison begin to descend on every side. There was no escape...

Down in the harbour Denbow had stormed away and Alfie O'Brien was sauntering along the quay. He jumped lightly aboard the Waterwitch and Lowena heard his laughter as she turned, her arm through George's, and began the walk up to the house.

It was a calm night, the opalescence never leaving the milky sea until it was charged by the silver path of the moon. Drew and Alfie shot their nets beyond the Eddystone in the deep waters of the Ray Pits. Alfie was at his most chirpy and charming. He was once again the companion of Drew's escape, the man who had kept him going and seen him safe back in England. Drew had to shake himself into believing that he was also the man who had betrayed all their kindnesses; George and Emelynne and himself. They made tea in the cosy fug of the cabin and later tossed for first watch on deck.

'Heads I win,' grinned Alfie and knew that he would, he always did. Drew took a whisky bottle from the box under his bunk and slopped a measure into his tea mug. He stoppered it and tossed it after Alfie.

'A toast to my sister, why not?'

Alfie caught it and looked at him enquiringly. 'That's generous of you, my son. Like brother, like sister, I suppose. She's a generous girl.'

It was then that Drew knew that he hated him. Knew that there would be no compunction in doing what must be done.

Up on deck O'Brien leant against the engine house, unstoppering the bottle with his teeth. The sea was as calm as a millpond and there was no-one else near to them, just the silhouettes of two or three other boats out on the horizon, nothing more.

'Somewhere,' mused Alfie, 'on the other side of the world, several oceans away, lies Australia, eternally warm and filled with sunshine.' There was nothing now to keep him here. He squinted up at the stars and tilted the bottle. 'Here's to the Southern Cross! I'm going home.'

There was quite a little gathering on the quayside when the four stragglers came in on the flood. They began to unload their catches. Somehow, there was a sombre air about the whole proceedings. They worked as if there was a heaviness in their hearts.

Annabel, watching her son from the harbour wall, said nothing until the last of the maunds was filled and carted away.

'What happened? Emelynne was fretting, she came round to us.' Drew took her aside out of earshot of the workers on the quay.

'This must go no further yet, I don't want Emmy upset and Lowena must get through tomorrow. We have all greed on silence for a day or two.' His hand waved to encompass the other three skippers.

'Drew, you're infuriating. What has happened?'

'Alfie - he's gone overboard. We searched for hours. There's really no hope. He wasn't a swimmer.'

The blood drained from Annabel's face. 'It was a calm night. Dear God, could there have been a flatter sea?'

Drew wasn't looking at her; his eyes were on the horizon. 'He took first watch. I think he had been drinking; there was an empty bottle in the bilges when we came to look about. He must have been larking about, playing sailors in that silly way he had. He'd unleashed the jigger boom. Just a sudden cat's paw catching her must have been enough to unbalance him and he went over. I cast about for ages then I fired off the maroon and that got the others to my aid when they could. We searched until there was no longer any hope left. Ask Nankivell, he'll tell you we did all we could.'

Annabel said, 'To come half way round the world and through the fighting to end on a calm night. You're right though, we must let Lowena have her day tomorrow. We'll make excuses; let them go off on honeymoon. I doubt she'll even miss him.'

But she knew that they would all miss him; that for a long time there would be a silence where he had been. Jack had come back to them all only to disappear again so soon. There would be no resurrection for Alfie O'Brien. When he came ashore finally it would not be on these shores; he would find himself in an unmarked grave. Sometimes life seemed so pointless. She went back to Chy an Lor to dress her daughter in her wedding finery but her mind was on an afternoon long ago in Nankivell's sail loft when a red-headed girl gave herself to handsome Jack Toller. She could not know that the blushing bride had dreams of her own; moonlight on the standing stones and Jack Toller's son.

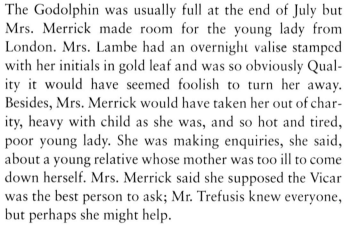

The Godolphin was usually full at the end of July but Mrs. Merrick made room for the young lady from London. Mrs. Lambe had an overnight valise stamped with her initials in gold leaf and was so obviously Quality it would have seemed foolish to turn her away. Besides, Mrs. Merrick would have taken her out of charity, heavy with child as she was, and so hot and tired, poor young lady. She was making enquiries, she said, about a young relative whose mother was too ill to come down herself. Mrs. Merrick said she supposed the Vicar was the best person to ask; Mr. Trefusis knew everyone, but perhaps she might help.

Mrs. Lambe supped her tea with her feet on a tapestry stool. He was an Australian serviceman; she didn't suppose they had many such finding their way down here. His mother was so worried, if only there was a scrap of news about his whereabouts. O'Brien was the name, Alfred. His mother called him Alfie.'

Mrs. Merrick wished that the Vicar wasn't over to Penherrit with Jenna Varco's ailing father; he would have known how to prepare the lady for such a shock. She took a deep breath and plunged in.

'The sea took him. He be drowned, my lover, three weeks ago.'

Later, the Vicar did talk to her, even suggested that she might speak to Drew Maddaver who had been aboard the Waterwitch that fatal night but the young woman shook her head. No, she couldn't stay, she had to get back to London; things to do. She would go tonight. Perhaps they could arrange transport to the station?

Fortified with hot, strong tea, she went slowly along The Strand and up the path towards the cliffs, pausing at the gate to Penolva. There was a woman sweeping the path, resigned and careworn, once she must have been very pretty; her black skirts were dusty. Mrs. Lambe stood at the cliff's edge, watching the creaming line of the water a long way below. But that wasn't the way. They always said she was a game girl, Lady Jacqueline Lambe. It was time to get on with the rest of her life.

PART III

The Cut Throat Sons of Cain

It's the old old road and the old old quest
Of the cut-throat sons of Cain,
South by west and a quarter west,
And hey for the Spanish Main.

— John Masefield

CHAPTER TWELVE

1931

Gina Deverel had been initiated into the Sea-Beggars on the day that she had discovered the Golden Hoard pushed to the back of Kitto's Cavern. Gina was a solitary child, a solitude enforced by a deformed foot and a left leg which was shorter than its fellow by a good two inches and needed a stout, built-up shoe to get her about. It was a problem keeping up with the other children with their light, rubber-soled plimsolls and sand shoes. She made her own way about the cliff-top paths and knew the bird-nesting sites and the rocks where the cormorants gathered and the necklace of tiny hidden coves below the cliffs to the east, and every cave for miles about.

Oh, she did well enough, lame though she was, and they weren't unkind. Her cousins, the Maddaver boys, belonged to a secret society named the Sea-Beggars after an obscure episode of Dutch history, discovered in a dusty tome in Shrimpy Varco's attic one rainy Friday in November. The Beggars were a patriotic band of free-booters terrorising the high seas in the name of Dutch Independence, led by the rascally Admiral Van Der Marck. No one had quite understood the politics of it all but there were wonderful pictures and Laurence Maddaver (Lanty to anyone who mattered) had become Van Der Marck and only the brightest and the best and the fleet of foot had been allowed to join the Sea-Beggars and to take part in piratical exploits.

Until, that is, that typical April day of bright spurts of sunshine and brief drenching downpours. Gina had scrambled down to the sands of Spanish Cove - named for the raiders of an early and mercifully unsuccessful invasion - and, sitting on Cuddy's Rock, had taken off shoes and socks to dabble her toes in the making tide. There was no-one in sight, the sky was forget-me-not blue with fleecy clouds coming and going, and there was a cuckoo up above the cliff. Then the rain came down again and she gathered up her shoes and made for Kitto's Cavern and the adequate shelter of its wide mouth.

Gina had a torch, bulging and ungainly in the pocket of her green dress. She flashed it over the accumulated flotsam and jetsam of the last spring tide - the heaped pebbles, abandoned floats and splintered driftwood. When you went back as far as you thought you could go, the cave suddenly doglegged and ran parallel to the cliff above it and there she found it - a large tea-chest almost as tall as she was, its top stove in with a hearty blow from an axe, so that the wood was splintered. Inside, no gold bars, no barrels of indigo, no ivory, not an ape or peacock in sight, but straw, tinder dry. She stood on tiptoe, reaching gingerly into this bran tub of mysterious delights. Her hand closed over the smooth chill of a bottle and she drew it out by the neck, stoppered and sealed and full of glinting amber liquid. Brandy from France? Rum from Jamaica? The prosaic label proclaimed good old Scots Whisky from distilleries nearer to home than the Caribbean, but there was a chest of it and spirits weren't cheap. And then a hand came down and twisted the torch from her grasp and a voice from the smothering darkness said:

You realise we're never going to be able to let you go - you've seen too much. We may even have to kill you!'

'Tim Maddaver!' said Gina. 'And more fool you to leave it unguarded!'

'We only went back for the Teddy Donkey,' said Pawley Cluett laconically. The Teddy Donkey spent its existence ferrying potatoes and turnips from cliff top allotments to the stalls of Trevander's Wednesday Market. It was a wayward creature who knew its own worth. It could be cozened but not coerced. Gina had always had a way with it.

It was Lanty's voice which said peremptorily. 'Bring her out here!' And Tim prodded her out of the cave and into the full sunlight; a sturdy little girl in a grubby flow-ered dress, wild red-gold hair about a smudged face, eyes as green as beryls. Cuddy's Rock steamed and the sea was blue again. She smiled a secret smile which lifted the corners of a mouth too wide for prettiness, and looked her cousin straight in the eye.

Lanty Maddaver was her own age - they had been born within days of each other - Lanty was already shoot-ing up, with the dark hair and blue eyes of the true Celt and too much of swaggering insolence for a boy of ten.

'She's found the Golden Hoard!' said Tim. What do we do with her?'

'She'll have to swear an oath,' said Lanty, standing legs apart, hands on hips like the engraving of Van Der Marck.

'No,' said Georgina, 'and you can't make me, Lanty Maddaver. And if you touch me I'll tell them all, the whole of Trevander, and they'll take it away and -'

'What do you want, everyone has their price? We'll get you a doll, one that opens and shuts its eyes.'

'The one in Mrs. Pascoe's shop in Plymouth, with the real hair and silk knickers?'

'If you like, but you'll have to swear.'

'I don't want it; I'm too old for dolls. Besides, Pamela Denbow is having one next birthday. I wouldn't want one that looked the same, would I?'

'Name your price, princess.'

Gina looked about her, at Lanty, the Pirate King, scout knife stuck in his belt at a jaunty angle, and his fellow buccaneers: brother Tim, nine years old, smaller, slighter, Pawley Cluett, Esco's grandson belligerent, tossing back the thick, brown thatch of his hair, Cecil Denbow, the oldest amongst them, twelve and already shooting up like a runaway bean, and Shrimpy Varco with his shirt torn, bramble scratches on his knees and a patch on his seat. She thrust her chin forward, 'I'm going to be a Sea Beggar!'

'I suppose she could be the mascot,' said Cecil, anxious for a compromise.

'Mascots aren't girls,' said Tim, 'they're goats or black cats or wolf hounds or -'

'All right,' said Lanty, 'we know what you mean!'

'Not a mascot,' said Georgina, 'fully fledged and signed up and sealed in blood.'

'There aren't any girls in the Sea Beggars,' said Lanty, 'it's a dangerous life and, besides -' his blue eyes travelled down to the twisted foot. Unconsciously she had buried it in the sand at her feet.

'Long John Silver,' said Georgina 'had a wooden one. I think he managed very well.' She was smaller than Tim, she would never be a beauty; a little podge her mother called her (not like Pamela Denbow who always looked like a fairy ready for the Christmas Tree, who never got her sleek black hair into tangles or soaked her socks jumping into rock-pools). If she was desperate, Gina did not intend to show it, but there was determination in the small square face, the lips slightly parted now to reveal perfect white teeth.

'Done!' said Lanty, spat on his palm and held it out to her. Georgina, who had a good aim with prune stones, reciprocated.

'Vivent les Gueux!' said Lanty loudly. It was the cry of the Beggars, according to the history book. No-one was learning French, no-one had any idea what it meant and you couldn't ask an adult and let the side down, but it sounded good.

'Vivent les Gueux!' shrieked the Sea-Beggars in unison and Gina's small face split from ear to ear.

'Now, lead me to the Teddy Donkey,' she said 'he'll come all the way down for me, that way you won't have to stagger up the cliff with all those bottles. Will that stuff keep till Wednesday Market?'

Lanty tossed back his head and laughed in a very superior way. 'That 'stuff' is whisky, it'll keep for ever. You *are* a baby. This is an undercover operation - can't sell on the open market but we've got contacts who'll take it off our hands and give us a good price.' There spoke the true Cornishman, right heir to the free-traders. Slowly they panted away up the cliff path to where the Teddy Donkey, head in the hedge, pulled at the new lush tuffets of grass in total disregard for the world about it.

Gina undid her faded green sash and wound it about her head, in the best pirate tradition, tucked her dress into her knickers and stood hands on hips. At her feet were knots of pale, rain-drenched primroses, overhead the gulls wheeled and called in frenzy, dazzling against the blue sky. 'This is the best day of my life,' she said, rubbing noses with the Teddy Donkey, 'the very, very best!'

⤐

'*Soft is the note, and sad the lay*
  That mourns the lovely Rosabelle'

It was doubtful if 'lovely' had ever been a word to describe the Rosabelle. At best a 'dirty British Coaster' and now a well-known rust bucket. Her crew were a pathetic bunch, gleaned from the stews of the world. Only one spoke English but they managed to jabber away to each other in a mixture of patois and a kind of bastard Spanish.

And so it was that faulty navigation, a still, calm night and a dense fog bank had stranded them on the rocks off Hannafore Point. They were near enough in their white silence to hear the waters fretting at the shore-line and, in spite of their Captain's entreaties had insisted on launching the boat and bumping, slithering their way among the rocks until they could walk to dry land.

The Seamen's Mission in Looe had taken them in, given them a bed and fed them, and no cajolements could make them return to the Rosabelle in the hope of floating her off on the high tide. The Captain solaced himself in the Jolly Sailor on the West Quay.

The fog bank persisted and, sometime after the flood set her free from the reef which held her, the Rosabelle, a mist-wraith herself, slipped out on the ebb tide. When an easterly wind dissipated the fog at last, she was nowhere to be seen. Someday, thought the captain disconsolately, nursing his hangover, she would be marked upon the wreck maps of the South West Peninsular, fated to be reproduced on table-mats in the best chippies in Cornwall.

Gina Deverel and her cousin, Tim, had a string of lobster pots off Pellancarva Point. When it suited them they checked them over and re-baited them. Gina woke to the clearest of mornings. From her bedroom window beneath the eaves she could look out through the trees which clung to the terraces of Fosfelle and see the tiny coruscating points of light upon the sea at the harbour mouth. The houses, clinging to the cleft of the coombe, half in sunshine, half in deep shadow, slept on. Just a handful of fishermen, voices thrown back and forward across the harbour, to disturb the sleeping village, only they, and a colony of gulls, abandoning their cliff-side ledges and sweeping in with the dawn.

It was the best kind of day, thought Gina, the clearest light of all; the painters' light which drew hungry young artists down to the south-west; the light for holidaymakers, who occasionally drifted in clutching their Box Brownies; the adventurers' light, carrying its strong enchantments to lure the laziest from comfortable beds.

It was a Thursday, it was school but between soft summer dawn and Mr. Combellack's maths lesson there was time for the greatest of escapades. Gina scrambled into a summer frock, apple green and sprigged with violets, and crept awkwardly downstairs, carrying her shoes. She sat under the tamarisks fastening them on, and threaded her way lightly, in spite of her lameness, through flowers and shrubs until she reached the little gate which opened onto The Strand. A short walk brought her to Drew Maddaver's house.

The boys' bedroom overlooked the street and a shower of pebbles brought Tim to the window, rubbing his eyes. He knew what she wanted. Even with his curtains pulled close, he smelt the kind of day it was. They would take the 'Watersprite', the Waterwitch's tender, and row out to the pots. Lanty had his own string of pots, half a mile in the opposite direction, he preferred to work independently. Tim was soon dressed and they made for the slip, unhitching the 'Sprite' and climbing aboard.

You only needed strong arms to row, the feet didn't matter. Gina, a sturdy fourteen now, excelled at it. Tim, a year younger, was still small and slender for his age. Even so, they took it in turns, moving out through the wheeling gulls, pulling strongly until they were beyond the mouth of the harbour and out of sight of the clustering houses. Trevander Light, a stunted white finger, rose above them, still winking in the brightness. The gulls quietened down and the lap of the water and the dull clunk of the rowlocks sent them both into trances.

They had reached Pellancarva now, Tim searching for their markers, tattered flags which had seen better days, bobbing on the water like abandoned bunting.

The Rosabelle lay on her side at the mouth of the bay, a beached leviathan, pocked and patched and limpet-crusted. Tim caught his breath and Gina, leaning on an oar, turned to glance behind her. For a little while, they shipped oars and stared, neither saying a word. At last, Tim broke the silence. 'Our own shipwreck! Come on, let's take a look!'

'There could be people, still on board ....,' faltered Gina.

'Corpses?' said Tim, bright eyed. He was still young enough to have a predilection for the macabre. They were pulling for the wreck now, but not too strongly, not quite so sure what they were likely to find.

'The boat's gone!' said Gina with relief. 'I hope they got away. We'd better search the shore-line.'

They nosed under the stern where the name was quite clear, pretty and romantic and totally alien to her looks.

'*But sea-caves rung, and the wild winds sung*
The dirge of lovely Rosabelle,' quoted Gina, an avid devourer of the romantic epic

The wreck was lying on her beam-ends, partly submerged, and even the die-hard Sea-Beggars realised the danger she presented. They moored up to the rocks and quartered the shoreline between them, looking for signs of castaways but the silver sands above the high tide mark at the head of the tiny bay were soft and footless.

'There's no-one here,' said Gina when they met up together again. 'There never was anyone here. They abandoned her long before she reached Pellancarva.' But Tim had passed beyond the stage of beaching corpses with a bill-hook or succouring starving maroons.

'Cargo? I expect she was making for Plymouth. It will be just our luck if she's in ballast!'

But Gina, scrambling over the rocks, was pointing toward a couple of boxes, bobbing a little way out. 'Get the boathook; we've got to be going. Hurry, Tim!'

He obeyed her as he always did and they fished a small crate out of the tide, levered off the top and stared down at the contents. There was a golden gleam from the nest of damp straw.....

'Ducats ...' hazarded Tim hopefully.

'Idiot, they're copper kettles! There must be a dozen in this box alone!'

Tim screwed up his nose. 'How many kettles can you get through in a lifetime? Say we give them away as Christmas presents and sell a few.... Gina, we can't flog a shipfull of kettles!'

Gina was watching another crate bobbing in and out of the wreckage, flat and long. 'They can't all be kettles,' she said. 'My guess is they're an assortment; household and luxury goods for the shops and markets of Plymouth. If we can get at it perhaps we can re-direct it. They'd buy this sort of thing at market and up-country at Penherrit, even perhaps as far as Fowey. We must get back and find Lanty, summon the Sea-Beggars. But it's our find, remember, our claim!'

'Vivent les Gueux!' shouted Tim excitedly, so that the cliffs echoed back his unbroken voice. 'Vivent les Gueux!' Then he slipped on a patch sea-weed, his feet shooting from beneath him, and ended up sitting in a rock-pool. Gina had to row all the way home so that, lying on his face in the bows, the sun could dry the wet patch on his school shorts.

'It's a man's life!' thought Gina.

They found Lanty at the old net loft up on the West Cliff. It was black in there with the shutters closed; dark as the lining of a cow's stomach!

'Shall I call the Beggars together?' asked Tim, his voice echoing about the rafters.

'No!' Lanty put out a hand to stop him. 'We can't wait until school's over and we can't all play hooky. They're burying Great Aunt Deverel today, over to Penherrit, aren't they?'

'How will that help?' shrugged Gina. 'Has she asked to be buried at sea?'

'No, idiot, but we might be expected to pay our last respects, mightn't we?'

'Dad says she was a belligerent old tyrant and should have gone long ago,' said Tim.

'Yes, but old Combellack doesn't know that. A letter slipped in to school asking for the morning off for us two, well If he does twig it it'll be too late by the time we get back.'

'And what about me?' said Gina.

'Well, we can't all go....'

'She was my great aunt as well, wasn't she? I don't see why not. You can't expect me to keep quiet. With the greatest will in the world, being a girl, I'm bound to let something out!'

Lanty couldn't see her face. He said, 'Well, yes, there is that, I suppose. She could ruin it all. I'll put her name in the note, push it through the door and we'll get what we need. We'll stash the cargo in the old look-out hut above Pellancarva. I'll take a padlock. It'll be safe there till we can move it. A morning's work should fetch us a nice income. Get the boat ready, Tim, everything we may need; boat hook, block and tackle. Gina, it'll be thirsty work, we'll need bottles of ginger beer and bread and cheese - well, whatever you can lay hands on.'

Gina sighed, 'A woman's work is never done.'

'The commissariat is vital to a well-planned operation and you're so good at it,' said Lanty patronisingly.

'Oh, hurrah for the Pirate King!' Gina thumbed a nose at his departing back and followed the brothers out into the morning sunshine. All Trevander was bathed in light and cleansed with dew, hushed and waiting for the day's adventure, still nestling in the Never Never world of childhood.

They made a fine morning of it, ferrying cargo from ship to shore, dipping in and out of the blue waters, sunning themselves from time to time on the rocks at the water's edge, hauling their spoils from a tiny sandy landing strip up thirty foot of cliff face by pulley. Sometimes it was tense, serious work, at others they laughed until they had to flop on their backs, reaching for the ginger-beer and Tizer. There was the time a flimsy wooden crate smashed against the rock face so that a score of kettles clattered their way seawards again, setting up cacophonous echoes, sending the gulls wheeling high in frenzy.

In the noontide sun they settled to their purloined repast, filched from the kitchen at Fosfelle; hunks of bread, chunks of mature cheddar, sweating in the heat, a jar of pickled onions, home grown tomatoes and peaches from the south wall. Gina opened a leather case, crammed with rings and chains and ropes of pearl - a true pirates' hoard. Lanty reckoned that Woolworth would have scorned to display them but Gina wound them about her neck and wrist and ankles and hopped about comically treating them to her Dance of the Seven Veils whilst Tim played a sand dance on his harmonica and Lanty clapped in time to the jingle and sparkle of the gewgaws. Lying on his stomach, chin in hand, he watched from beneath long fringed lashes. It was strange how little one noticed the lame foot - her awkwardness was eclipsed by the wild tangle of her hair and the laughter in her green eyes.

Below them lay the Rosabelle, lapped by a gentle summer tide. It was Tim who said suddenly, 'I shall remember today for the rest of my life! Even when I'm old and huddled on the quay in my darned Guernsey, deaf and half-blind and waiting for the last flood tide to carry me away. I shall think about today and smile a bit.'

Gina dropped to the ground in a jangle of chains. 'How morbid, you talk as if this was the last voyage of the Sea Beggars but it isn't. It can't be. Where's the Tizer? We'll pour a libation to the sea-god, to mighty Neptune, and ask for just one more adventure.'

'Yes,' said Lanty, 'the greatest of them all!'

They stood, all three, before Nathan Combellack, the Reverend Mr. Combellack.

'Mrs. Varco,' said he 'brought me news back from Penherrit way, from the coast-path up by the old look-out. Yesterday afternoon, she identified all three of you. She was sure, she said. She would admit of no possibility that there might have been a mistake. Were you there? Laurence Maddaver?'

'Yes, sir.'

'Timothy?'

'Yes, sir.'

'Georgina Deverel?'

'Yes, sir.'

'And this letter, signed by a parent, your parent Laurence Maddaver, this attendance at Eleanor Deverel's funeral, do I take it that it was not supplied by Mr. Maddaver?'

Lanty swallowed, 'Not by that Mr. Maddaver, sir.'

'Don't be obstructive, boy. Which Mr. Maddaver then?'

'Me, sir.' He drew breath.' My father knew nothing about it, or Georgina's parents. It was my idea.'

'You were not then to have attended this family funeral?'

'No, sir. It seemed a good excuse at the time, something different, sir.'

'Indeed, a masterly ruse.'

'Thank you, sir.'

'Mr. Maddaver, are you being insolent?'

'No, sir! On my honour, sir!'

'So, I am to understand that you were sole instigator in this escapade. Your idea to play truant, your idea to forge the letter from your parents, your idea to use the sacred funeral service as an instrument for your lies! All your ideas, Mr. Maddaver?'

'Yes, sir. I persuaded these two along.'

'Oh, Lanty,' muttered Georgina between her teeth, 'do shut up. Forget about 'alone stood brave Horatius'!'

'I went of my own free will,' said Tim aloud.

'And you, Georgina Deverel?' boomed Combellack, 'Don't you have a tongue in your head?'

'Yes, sir, I'm sorry sir, I wanted to go, sir, I did really!'

Lanty, out of the corner of his mouth, said, 'if you cry now, I'll never take you anywhere again!'

'You have something to say, Mr. Maddaver?'

'No, sir. Thinking aloud, sir.'

'So, I am to see my way clearly through this pack of lies and deceptions. Well, I will write to your parents and let them know of your antics, my own displeasure will be obvious to them.' He paused for the effect his words were having but the three faces were impassive. The Deverels were fairly liberal and Drew Maddaver hardly the man to strike fear and dread into his young offspring. He tried again. 'Tonight you will remain behind for an hour, more if need. You will write an essay for me on the follies of your conduct. If it is not done well it will be done again on Monday night. Is that clear?'

'Yes, Mr. Combellack,' they chorused demurely.

'Oh, no, Mr. Maddaver, not you. I have a greater honour in store for our leader of men, our man of ideas. Whilst these two miscreants are engaged in writing a catalogue of their sins, yours will be indelibly inscribed elsewhere. You are following my drift, Mr. Maddaver?'

'I believe so, sir.'

'Come, it is unlike you to be reticent! Speak out, boy.'

Lanty looked him in the eye. 'I think you mean the cane, sir.'

'Exactly so. You will be here as soon as the bell has gone for the end of school. It will be inadvisable to be late. Now you may go.'

Lanty hesitated. 'Sir?'

'Well, Mr. Maddaver?'

'Sir, couldn't I, couldn't we get it over with now, sir. I'd much rather.' It was like Oliver Twist daring to ask for more. Combellack walked round him in a circle, scratching his chin.

'Couldn't we? Well, yes, I expect we could. Shall we? No, I think not. Have you not heard it said that it is better to travel hopefully than to arrive? I should think that in your case arrival would be better postponed permanently but then, we cannot have all our wishes granted on this earth. Have you never heard of anticipation? Anticipate then, Laurence. Until 4 p.m.'

'Come on, Lanty!' hissed Tim. He was still hovering in the doorway.

'Sir?' murmured Lanty.

'Still here, boy? Well?'

'You forgot, sir, that is - you didn't tell me - how many, sir?' Combellack's mouth lifted in a smile at the corners like a little-used cloth pegged out to dry.

'My dear boy, I thought you'd never ask me. Six. I could not, after all, insult a young man of your calibre with less, could I?'

The question was not answered. Lanty had disappeared.

He only told Tim but by dinner break it was all round the school. They sat at tables with their packed lunches.

Shrimpy Varco, eyes wide, said, 'Six, that could half kill a man!'

'Thanks,' said Lanty dryly 'you're a great comfort.'

'No-one ever gets six these days, I mean, Jim Pascoe passed out after two.'

'He would,' said Georgina.

'You could pack your pants with newspapers,' said Tim.

'What about the National Geographic,' said Pawley Cluett, 'I could let you have a couple if you like - two pence each.'

'No, thanks!'

Shrimpy said, 'you wouldn't get away with that trick. It wouldn't sound right would it? I mean, flesh has a different ring to it.'

Pawley said, 'don't you want your sandwiches?'

'Not much.'

'What are they?'

'Tomato.'

'Don't you like tomatoes?'

'You can have them.'

'You should eat, you know. Keep your strength up. You might lose a lot of blood. Now where's he off to. I was talking to him!'

'I should think,' said Tim 'that he's going to be sick. He's got that greenish look.'

'D'you think I can keep the sandwich box?'

'I shouldn't think so; he'll need it on Monday.'

'Perhaps he won't be here on Monday. You know, men died of flogging on The Bounty. I bet Combellack's old enough to have served on The Bounty - I bet –' His voice died away into the distance as Georgina went in search of Maddaver.

He was leaning over the gate, looking out across the fields to the sea. He didn't acknowledge her, only said, 'Can I borrow your lucky pig?'

'Of course you can.' She looped it over her head and settled it about his own neck. 'They don't mean to be such ghouls. It's just that they think you're the bravest of the brave, they're just testing.'

'And you?'

Georgina took one of his hands. 'Your nails are newly bitten to the quick. Don't let Combellack see them; they give you away.'

Lanty grinned, 'All right, Sherlock, but he isn't going to be concentrating on that part of my anatomy. I'll let you have the pig back tomorrow, will that do? Has Pawley eaten my sandwiches?'

'Fraid so. You can have one of mine. Cheese and pickle, will that do? And Lanty, I'm pretty sure Van Der Marck bit his nails - in fact, I'm quite certain of it.'

Georgina was leaning over the wrought iron gate where Fosfelle's path wound up from The Strand, talking to Pamela Denbow. The dark girl melted away with a laugh when Maddaver hovered uncertainly a yard or so away. He came up to the gate.

'Gina, were you in trouble at home?'

She shrugged her shoulders. 'Father looked pained like he always does and said how disappointed he was with me, and then he went back to his newspaper. Mother was rather forthright. Did I think before I encouraged others into mischief? Did I consider what it would mean for you because you were a boy? I suppose she's right, I didn't think. Was it very dreadful? Did it hurt a lot?'

'No,' said Lanty. 'I enjoyed every minute. I'm a sado-masochist, didn't I ever tell you?'

'You'd better come in,' said Gina 'and tell me all about it.' The grass was long and cool beside the pool, it badly needed scything. Maddaver flopped down on his stomach.

'I don't want to talk about it. Why does everyone think I do? It's finished. Over, done with, oh, but I'm so bloody sore!' he finished in desperation.

'Poor Lanty,' said Georgina, stretched out beside him. 'I'm really very sorry. Would you like me to kiss you, to make it up to you?'

He moved tentatively onto his side. 'Yes, yes, I think I would.'

Her legs were brown below her faded sun frock; her hair whispered about his face as she leant over and placed a quick kiss upon his lips. She tried again, a slow and lingering movie style cinch, one hand moving down his side until she found his stripes, his gasp covered by the kiss. Her nearness, her touch exited him in a way he hardly understood, and something was happening, something wonderful but terrible at the same time.

He didn't know what to do next. Down at the boat on a Saturday morning, he'd often heard the lads calling back and forth, ribbing each other over their Friday night conquests, 'Did you get a leg over then?' 'Did you get a hand up her skirt?' He found her knee and ventured the thigh above it. It was warm and so very soft and he no longer had any control over what was happening to him. Georgina, in fourteen year old maidenly outrage, knocked the hand away and flailed at him with both fists.

'How could you, oh, how could you? She sprang to her feet and ran as quickly as her crippled foot would let her, up the path towards Fosfelle.

Maddaver lay on his stomach and closed his eyes. Girls!

'Young man, Lanty isn't it?' He opened them again and focussed on a sensible pair of brown brogues. Raising his sights he squinted up at Cousin Cynthia, Mathew Toller's eldest daughter, standing there with a full basket of strawberries, ripe for jam making.

'What are you doing here? You can make yourself useful. Carry this up the hill for me. Where are your manners? You shouldn't need asking!'

'I can't,' he said.

'Why on earth not?'

Lanty cast about him for any excuse. 'I don't feel well. I feel sick.'

'Then you'd best come with me anyway. We'll get you dosed up.'

'No, I can't.'

'Do as you're told. I'm waiting!'

There was dread finality in her tone. He got up stiffly, trying to turn away from her, trying to tug down his Guernsey but it was his old one, shrunk from too many washes, and his efforts only drew attention to the stain he was trying to hide. Cynthia Toller was the archetypal spinster. It was feared she would never marry.

'You unspeakable little devil, so that's what you were at!' But there was an excited gleam in her eye that he did not like.

'I'm surprised you knew!' he retorted insolently, deserving the crack of her right hand across his face. Her ring tore his cheekbone. It didn't stop her clouting him again.

'Cynthia, whatever is going on!' Margaret Toller, likewise laden with a large basket was panting up the path behind them.

'There in the grass,' said Cynthia 'this beastly brat - it'll be his ruin! By all accounts you've had a day to remember. When I've seen your father you'll get another whipping!' She swung away from them, panting along the path toward the house.

Margaret Toller set down her basket. Lanty had fled to the old apple tree, his face against one arm. The tears he hadn't shed for Combellack were hot against his sleeve. Pog Toller waited for several minutes, put an arm round him then said. 'It's not your week, is it, my lamb? If you've just about finished I've a three point plan. Do you want to hear it?' Pog was the plainer of two plain sisters. Their young brother was a devastatingly hand-some boy.

'What?' sniffed Lanty.

'Firstly,' Pog was rummaging in her capacious hand-bag. She produced a large plain handkerchief. 'Blow your nose and wipe your eyes - well, preferably the other way about – more hygienic.' She waited whilst he did as he was told. 'Point two; that's a nasty cut, we need the

Elastoplast.' Another delve into the shadowy depths of the handbag. She was still a little taller than he. She dabbed at the cut with another hankie and applied the dressing carefully. 'You'll have a scar for a while, give you quite a satanic air, I shouldn't wonder. You'll live.'

'And the third point?' asked Lanty.

'You carry the basket. Oh, not up to Fosfelle, I've changed my mind. We'll go back along The Strand until we reach Chy an Lor. I'll leave you there. I can manage the last few yards on my own. There'll be no-one at home when you get back?'

He shook his head.

'Then you can get -' she paused 'tidied up, and none the wiser.'

'Cousin Cynthia, she's going to speak to father.'

Pog tutted. 'Not she, she'd be far too embarrassed, I promise you and anyway, I shouldn't worry about Drew. Come along.' She chivvied him out of the gate and chattering all the time walked the short way to Chy an Lor. They stood on the doorstep, the basket between them. Suddenly he put it down, flung his arms about her and gave her a smacking kiss:

'You're a wonderful person, Pog, you've saved my life.'

Pog said. 'Nonsense! I've got a young brother, remember, growing up isn't easy. Now go inside while the goings good.'

'It wasn't like she thought, really it wasn't, it just happened.'

'I don't need an inquest. Any more revelations and you won't want to sit opposite me for Ludo at Christmas. I always enjoy our games of Ludo.' Pog in a print summer frock stood on one leg and clasped the other behind her in a ludicrous attempt at Long John Silver. 'Whatever happened to the Pirate King?'

'Silver was a sea cook,' said Lanty 'I can't even boil an egg!'

But he was smiling. The sun had come out of the clouds again.

Pog lugged her basket along The Strand again, back to Penolva. She had a serenity which transcended beauty. God, she supposed, had put her on this earth to be useful. The jam could wait.

CHAPTER THIRTEEN

The summer of '39 was a golden time. Afterwards, looking back, no-one could remember any rain clouds and
the storm brewing over the channel was light years away.
The days drifted by with opalescent skies, a merge of
rainbow colours from horizon to zenith, waters scat-
tered with the multicoloured sails of the rich and
famous, golden beaches swarming with little girls in sand
shoes and pink babies in giant sun bonnets.

Trevander was rather off the beaten track for the
holiday trade and summer was still their own. Catches
were plentiful and Drew skippered the Waterwitch
with Tim and Lanty and Colan Denbow. Sometimes
Mathey's son accompanied them, the dreamy-eyed Tristan Toller. Come August Bank Holiday Lanty and Tim
sailed the Waterwitch into Fowey with a noisy crowd of
youngsters aboard, all eager to see the start of the latest
regatta. Gina Deverel was with them and her friend and
foil, Pamela Denbow. Pamela's father was the local doctor which put her a class above the rest of them but it
was the way Pamela like it. She was slim and dark and
long-legged. It seemed that Tim had worshipped her
from afar all his days but she blew hot and cold and
flirted with every man who came her way, discarding
them as quickly. Standing in the prow of the Waterwitch
in brief white shorts and a figure-moulding Breton

jersey she knew she contrasted well with Gina - red-blonde and freckled, a long, floating dress hiding her feet - her favourite green, her hat clamped to the back of her neck, trailing its satin ribbons. The Sea-Beggars were growing up, growing apart or growing together. Like Tim, Gina had loved from afar but this summer had wrought miracles for the lame-duckling. Lanty had confessed, half shy, half bantering that he loved her, wanted them to get engaged. They had chosen a ring at the jeweller's up country in Liskeard - an emerald, surrounded by tiny diamonds. This morning, he was to have picked it up from the shop. Today, somewhere amidst the laughter and the bunting and the proud hulls of the ocean-going yachts he would find a moment to present it to her.

The Waterwitch rounded the Washing Rocks where, legend said, Christ had alighted with Joseph of Arimathea. St. Catherine's Castle sat, grey and old, atop the cliff on the other side of the harbour. Then the whole panorama began to open out before them; the river mouth with its terraces of Victorian houses and Edwardian Hotels; Polruan on the east bank, cluttered about its boat yards and, between the two, hundreds of rocking masts, needle sharp against the soft back drop of green woods and blue-grey waters.

They alighted at the Town Quay leaving Tim to find a mooring.

'Let's get away,' said Lanty, seizing her hand. So they strolled through the town, through forests of bronzed limbs and a bright selection of fashionable hats, past the sleeping church, through the maze of chandlers' shops, past open alleyways with their jewelled glimpses of the Fowey River, to join the promenade along the

Esplanade, the perambulation of the smart set from the hotels and the blazer-clad crews from the yachts, brass buttons agleam. Eventually, they climbed out onto the coastal path that snaked its way past a necklace of bright bays. The crowd were far behind them now and there was only the silence of the sea which is no silence at all; the breathing of the water, fretting at the rocks, the whispering of golden grasses in the fields behind them, laced with the rust spires of dock and sorrel, pricked with white daisies; the bleating of sheep far along the coombes; the screaming of gulls circling the far cliff; the laughter of an invisible woodpecker, mocking their words.

Lanty helped her climb the rocks as if suddenly she had become precious cargo and someone beyond their old friendship. Standing above her, shirt open at the neck, bronzed and clear-eyed he was suddenly so heart-stoppingly handsome that her breath caught in her throat. The legacy of Cornish interbreeding had left him with more than one man's share of good looks, from the tousled dark hair of a latter-day Heathcliffe to the sea blue of his eyes, the determined line of his jaw and the polish of high-set cheekbones, honed by the south-westerlies. He knelt on one knee as even pirate kings have to do and slid the ring onto her finger.

'I'd like,' said Gina, 'to be a June bride. I would like white satin and orange-blossom.' She lay on her back, waving her fingers in the air about her so that fire shafted from the diamonds and a magic green ray darted from the heart of the emerald.

'Don't you think June is a long way away?' Lanty lay beside her, propped on one elbow, amused by her enthusiasm.

'Oh, it's worlds away but I want to savour every minute till then, every shining hour. But you, I never asked, what do you want?'

Lanty grabbed for the waving hand and imprisoned the ring against his own palm. He began to kiss her. 'I want this every night and morning.' Suddenly, he rose and pulled her to her feet. She stumbled a little as she had taken off the heavy shoes and hidden them in a little hollow in the rocks but Lanty only lifted her into his arms, leapt lightly from the rocks and carried her up the little beach into the green shade of the coombe with its short, lush grasses and the sound of a trickling stream, fighting its way through rushes and bog-cotton. 'I'm rehearsing,' he murmured, panting a little, 'for that step across the threshold. But this is softer than any bed and I will never want you more than I want you now!' His kisses had changed; there was a wildness that was alien to the sunny day, alien to the shy suitor who had led her by the hand through the crowds, the ring burning in his pocket. Perhaps he was Henry Morgan, stretched out in the heat of a coral atoll, an eager, dark-skinned beauty beneath him, hot for his love-making. Gina was Cornish and twenty and these were the northern latitudes and for the first time in her life she had this wild dark boy completely under her spell, wholly in her power. She pushed him away.

'I mean to go to my wedding a virgin bride,' she said demurely from the weeds of her hair and the tumble of the green dress.

'Christ!' said Lanty, coming out of shock.

'I don't want whispers and tittle-tattle and sly looks as I take the path to St. Petroc's.'

Lanty was laughing. 'Mrs. Nankevill and Mrs. Varco, heads together behind the family graves, 'I hear that hussy is no better than she should be - left her knickers on Coombe Hawne beach, so they say.' Gina, how do you think anyone in this world is going to know?'

'They all knew Mary Colquite spent all too long in the lambing pens, it went round the pews like a whispering game.'

'Only because she was eight months pregnant! Gina, I love you more than truth or life or honour!'

Gina was on her feet, dusting down her dress. 'That was Ronald Coleman in the Prisoner of Zenda. When Madeline Carroll said 'no' he knew she meant it. I mean it, Lanty!'

The chin was jutting out as of old; there would be no moving her. He went down to the beach and retrieved her shoes. The sun was dipping low behind the Gribbin, its landmark finger a stalwart silhouette. They walked all the way back to the boat then he kissed her and swung her aboard and soon she was sitting in the stern with Pamela Denbow, heads bent over the ring.

'Only one bridesmaid?' said Pamela. 'I mean to have at least three.'

It was May 1940 and the situation was grave. Not the war although, of course, that was serious in itself, with the BEF fleeing toward the channel ports in disarray but that wasn't common knowledge, not yet.

Lanty had arrived home on embarkation leave from HMS Daedalus to find that the Waterwitch had taken off for Ramsgate with one good engine, a set of sails in the forward cuddy, brother Tim as skipper and with a motley crew consisting of Gina Deverel and Pamela Denbow. Old Esco Cluett greeted him sheepishly as he strode down the quay. Lanty looked alarmingly handsome in his uniform, still carrying his kit bag.

'Ramsgate! Why Ramsgate, of all the godforsaken corners of the Empire?'

'The Missus liked Ramsgate; us all liked Ramsgate,' said Esco defensively.

'But there's a war on, hasn't anyone down here noticed?'

'They've only got the auxiliary ...' Esco began 'engine, I mean.'

'Dear god, it gets worse! Ramsgate!'

'Don't 'ee keep saying Ramsgate as if it was Sodom and Gomorrah. Miss Denbow's uncle lives over to Ramsgate.'

'A social visit, is it? I'll wring dear little Pammy's neck!'

'You don't understand,' said Esco stating the obvious. 'The Kelvin went, totally scuppered, nobody could do anything, everyone tried ...'

'I can imagine,' said Lanty dryly.

'We even went over to Polruan. Swallowed our pride and tried the yards but no one could help. Then Miss Denbow came down to the quay and said her uncle had one – hardly used - and it be ours for the taking. Well, fetching rather than taking. So that's where they've gone. He'll fit it for them, make sure it's firing well and titivate the auxiliary up too. They'll be fine. They took on a full set of working sails just in case.'

'It'll be like the last voyage of Magellan! Oh, I suppose you're right, they'll get there and it'll be an outing for the girls. I'd better start straight away.'

'But you haven't been home! You've got a father and a grandmother all ready to kill the fatted calf. You can't put the boat before the entire Maddaver clan!'

'Why ever not,' grinned Lanty, 'I always did!' and he was away down the quay, light of foot.

'At least,' murmured Esco to himself ''un'll be out of the way for a few days. There's nothing much can happen to a man in Ramsgate in May, not even to a madcap Maddaver. Naturally, he was wrong.

'It has to be fate,' said Gina Deverel. 'All four of us in the right place at the right time for once. And something we can do to help out. Oh how I've longed to be useful. You two in the Navy, well Tim almost in and Pamela….'

'Oh, yes,' said Lanty 'congratulations Pam, a Wren officer, I didn't know you had an uncle at the Admiralty.'

'But I don't.' Pamela Denbow flashed a puzzled look up at him.

They were all sitting down about the stove in the fo'c'sle, drinking cocoa from cracked mugs.

'Really?' grinned Lanty. 'I thought you had uncles strategically placed all over the kingdom!'

Pamela put out the tip of a very pink tongue. 'I *was* worried about the Interview Board but the Admiral knew Daddy, he was such a sweetie.'

Lanty caught Gina's eye and choked over his cocoa.

Tim said, 'we must make ready. We'll need to check the first aid kit, take on water, some iron rations…'

Gina laughed. 'You have the queen of the commissariat with you, don't forget. It's already seen too.'

'Are they going to arm us?' Lanty was addressing Tim. It was strange how easy it was to cut the girls out of the line of vision when it came to real man's talk.

'Some hope,' said Tim ruefully. 'A record of the 1812 Overture might help. I think we get an escort with a few popguns, be thankful for small mercies. I don't like the idea of the girls coming; it could be pretty hairy. No-one knows what its like over there.'

'Just try and stop us, little cousin, and you'll end in Trevander Bay with a mill-stone tied to your feet!' Gina was ready to defend herself. There was a wildcat gleam in her green eyes, known and suffered as of old.

Lanty was not even bothering to remonstrate. Besides, they had had this argument out half an hour ago. A little later, when he and Tim had their heads bent over the Kelvin, he murmured, 'the whole aspect of crewing may be taken entirely out of our hands. I think they'll send the girls ashore before they let us move out; they can't keep out of sight below decks for ever.' They smiled conspiratorially at each other.

Lanty had arrived in Ramsgate earlier that morning to find the Waterwitch down at Vellacott's Boatyard, already rejuvenated and practically purring. Tim had greeted him with a wild story of night-time channel crossings and a vast and stranded army to collect from the beaches of France.

'They want everything that will move and they want it now! I've got details of the assembly point. I think they mean us to leave tonight. We've to pick up charts and take on enough fuel and water!'

On the quay they met up with their fellow seamen, a motley gathering of the young and old; the tense ones smoking too much, others covering their boyish excitement with back-slapping and bonhomie and terrible jokes. There was the crew of the Margate Lifeboat and men of the East Coast cockle fleets but there were solicitors and bankers, actors and musicians too; an army of weekend sailors, many with a dubious knowledge of the idiosyncrasies of their engines and knowing less about lining off the route on the supplied charts. About the Waterwitch were an amazing array of small craft; fishing vessels like herself alongside the pride of a dozen yacht clubs, paintwork gleaming; little cabin cruisers; excursion boats and ferries; the graceful sprit-sailed barges from the mouth of the Thames; dredgers....

A final speedy check and brief word of encouragement for the two young Cornishmen failed, or perhaps did not wish, to spot the two figures in the darkness of the fo'c'sle; the young man in the oversized Guernsey with the peak of his cap pulled down low and a nervous grin on his smooth-cheeked face and the slim lad, surely no more than eighteen, with the comical woollen hat stretched over his ears and the collar of his reefer jacket up against the night chills.

Lanty and Tim turned in surprise to find that their companions had not been ousted from the shadows. The girls emerged in slacks and deck shoes.

'You devious little...' Lanty said admiringly. There was no doubt that both looked well in their disguises. Pamela cut a slim, boyish figure in spite of her perfect heart-shaped face and dark-fringed violet-blue eyes, whilst Gina, far too shapely, was flushed with excitement, green eyes sparkling.

'I didn't think ...' said Lanty.

'That they would be so desperate?' smiled Gina. 'Adversity, my lad, makes strange bed-fellows.'

'Is that an invitation?' grinned Lanty, a louche look in his blue eyes.

'Certainly not! I thought you were skippering this outfit. The Sea Beggars all together again – and Pammy of course. Let's get under way. We've an army to find!'

They set off in convoy, tagged on to a small flotilla of motor-boats: The Blue Bird, The Nelson, The Pride of Folkestone, The Girl Nancy... Waiting outside Ramsgate Breakwater was their escort, the motorboat Triton. That night the sea was kind to them, its surface flat as a millpond and, over all, the protective aegis of a heavy mist and a low cloud base to hide them from the marauding Luftwaffe. The Second Stuka Squadron did try stooging about for all of ten minutes, then returned to base.

But the seriousness of the adventure which had started with almost a party atmosphere was brought home to them as they steered past the returning troop ships, loaded to the gunwales with weary fugitives from the beaches of France and Belgium. Pamela Denbow caused consternation on all sides. Taking a turn crouching in the bows as look-out she screamed out. 'Lanty, hard-a-port! Submarine, port bow!'

But it proved to be the top six feet of foremast of the Lucy Vanning, darling of her owners and jewel of Salcome Harbour. There was nothing else to be seen but the rainbow colours of a light oil slick caught in the glow from a storm lamp as they passed.

As dawn approached and with it the Belgian coast, the excitement of it all died to a gnawing in the stomach, a fear of what they must face, what they must see. The sun was rising when they anchored off La Panne and waited for Triton to gather her chicks and issue orders. When the mist lifted they knew what they had to do; took in the enormity of the task ahead of them all.

At La Panne they had kept the guns going to the last, whilst bombs rained down upon them. Now, the men of II Corps crowded the beaches, once the holiday playground of the Belgian middle classes. But from La Panne westwards to Dunkirk the beaches shelved gradually for a mile to seawards and the first destroyers on the scene had stood by virtually helpless, unable to close the beach for fear of grounding themselves. Until the arrival of the little ships they were relying upon their own boats to ferry troops out. As Tim put it 'like emptying Dozmary Pool with a limpet shell!' All along the coast the fires of the oil-refineries of Dunkirk and the systematic destruction of the French and Belgian countryside, left a pall of black smoke as far as the eye could see, with an angry glow too far south to be confused with the rising sun, its face obscured by heavy cloud mass. Over the sands and out into the sea snaked endless columns of men, hardly seeming to move.

Lanty and his crew were all on deck. They had taken it in turns resting below on the journey over. Now they stood amidships, clinging to each other in silent awe. The enormity of their task threatened to overwhelm them all. Gina would have liked to cry and caught Pamela wiping away a furtive tear. They knew that the shelving of the beach would not allow them far inshore and that, unlike the Thames barges and the Dutch Schuits with their shallow draughts, the Waterwitch was not designed for boarding from the sea bed. South Cornish luggers were craft of rocky inlets and narrow, high-walled harbours. For a time they found a niche for themselves, towing small craft – punts and tenders, life rafts and dinghies - out to the destroyers and the larger vessels anchored in the offing, occasionally managing to pick up men from the sea. But it was hard work hauling them over the gunwales with the aid of boat hooks and drapes of netting, for the girls and Tim were slightly built. Their muscles ached with the effort; their eyes were smarting with the acridity of the drifting smoke haze, heads aching with the pounding of distant guns as pockets of the rearguard made desperate efforts to keep the enemy from the shore. They went on till dusk, till Lanty could see they were all flagging, then they made for one of the hotchpotch of jetties cobbled together from lines of lorries roofed with duckboard to make bailey bridges. Here it was possible to moor alongside and let the men embark from deck level.

The first time the Stukas came it took them all by surprise. They did not understand the screaming from the skies as the terror fliers in the dreaded bombers dived upon the waiting lines of men. Lanty pulled Gina down into the dubious shelter of the wheel-house and they lay in sticky pools of water from the bilges, hearts beating fast, breath ragged. The men, where they could, flung themselves down. Some dived for the water; others were tipped from the precarious crocodile on the makeshift bridge as the deadly fire cut a swathe through the line. When they had vanished, as swiftly as they had appeared, there was a rush to scramble into the boats, to get away from this hell, out to the open sea and the solid bulk of the nearest destroyer.

For a moment there was panic. Pamela Denbow, trying to regulate the numbers climbing aboard lest they should be swamped, was pushed over the fish hold coamings by a sudden rush of terror-stricken bodies. A burly sergeant, six foot or more of pure muscle, lifted her up as if she weighed no more than a puppy, set her on her feet and exclaimed. 'Why, it's a little lass!' Then he began to take charge of his men; when Lanty decided that they were full, barring the way to further boarders, standing at the gunwales, hands on hips.

'Like a mighty colossus,' thought Gina. They did several trips out to the nearest of the destroyers and he stayed aboard. His name was Tom Harris.

At last Lanty said, 'One more boat load and we'll steam for home, take on more fuel, then we'll be back.'

'England,' breathed Gina who had given up her male pretence and whose red-gold hair clung stickily about her face. 'England – but you're right, we have to come back….'

Wearily, they took on another load, explaining that those who boarded risked crossing the channel in an unprotected fishing boat built for a crew of five. But the men were all so pleased to be getting away that they would have boarded the Flying Dutchman and been glad of it. The Waterwitch left La Panne in the last of the dying light, Tim at the wheel with Pamela squeezed beside him. Gina and Lanty and Tom were sitting on the edge of the open hatch above the net hold, itself home to several men. Gina, aching with tiredness, lulled by the lapping of a sea remarkably well-behaved, watching Lanty from beneath the curtain of the red hair. He looked fine in his dark Guernsey; he always did, though he was dog-tired with violet circles beneath the louche blue eyes that gave a sense of vulnerability to his usually brash exterior. She had never loved him more than she loved him now. They had asked for a last adventure before maturity laid the Sea-Beggars finally to rest. God, she supposed, had sent them Dunkirk. And then, out of the blue, a lone aircraft, stooging about looking for trade, found a cloud-break and spied the Waterwitch. Perhaps he was almost out of fuel for he made only one descent before rising again and making off toward the French coast and the lines of men digging themselves into the dunes. He made one pass and in those seconds stitched the Waterwitch amidships.

Three men were killed outright. Lanty was pitched to the deck with a hole in his back. He lay there spread-eagled amid the screams and cries of the wounded, Gina at his head, calling his name, half in shock. It was then that Tom Harris took charge again. The dead had to go overboard; there was no time for sentiment, just a quick snatch of an I.D. disc before they went over the side. The Sea-Beggars crowded about Lanty, relieved to see that he was conscious.

'Tim,' Gina said 'the destroyer, there'll be a doctor on board, he'll help us; he must!' She was kneeling on the blood-soaked deck. Her eyes met Tom Harris's. They were deep-set, honest grey eyes. He shook his head slowly and she knew that he was right. There was no hope. Someone had fastened a dressing onto that horrific wound but they dared not move him.

'How long?' Gina's lips formed the words silently.

Harris shrugged, 'Hours maybe.'

'Then we make all speed,' said Gina. 'Tim, shortest route back. We must take him home.'

Pamela, singled-minded as ever said, 'We must come back. We can't abandon those men. Not if, not if....' Her eyes went to Lanty. He wouldn't want it.' The tears were coursing down her lovely, stubborn face.

Gina said, 'Did you hear me, Tim? Shortest route! I'll make you a promise, Pammy. We'll re-fuel and we'll come back. I swear it!' La Panne and its stricken beaches were already receding.

Tim, white-faced with shock but still unbelieving, kept telling himself that they would get Lanty back to Ramsgate. It would be all right then, of course it would. Gina knelt beside the man she was to have married, shivering in the night wind until Tom found her a battle-dress top to put round her shoulders. He liked her, this tough little Cornish girl with the gammy leg.

Pamela roused herself to try to find blankets and anything she could rustle up from the galley. For Gina it was the longest journey of her life. The men who had stayed with them, happy to chance the English Channel, melted into the shadows to give her space as she lay down beside Lanty, holding his head, talking, talking through the endless hours; of inconsequential things; of Trevander and Fosfelle; of the Waterwitch and the last fishing season; of the old adventures of the Sea-Beggars, and as she saw the deathly pallor of his face and the light dying in his eyes, she talked of their future and her love for him. But as the English shoreline drew nearer she knew she was losing him.

'Where are we?' his voice was almost indistinguishable.

'We're almost home.' She tried to keep her voice steady.

'Home? Trevander?' he hazarded.

'Yes, of course, Trevander.' She flashed a warning glance at Tom Harris. 'We're closing the bay now.'

'Trevander Light ?'

'No, its out, remember? The war....'

'Of course. It's dark, too dark.'

'Close your eyes, we're under the cliff. Your father will be there and Aunt Pog. They'll have hot soup ready and a brick in the bed. You can hear the gulls, the last late roosts. Tomorrow it will be fine and Trevander will look as it's always looked and – '

'Sweetheart,' said Tom 'I'm afraid he's gone.' He took her in his arms.

'The ebb tide,' said Pamela Denbow 'they always go out on the ebb tide – the spirits of the dead. Poor Tim, he'll miss Lanty sorely.'

'That is the end then,' said Tim in the deck-house, hands gripping the wheel, 'the end of all the adventures. I lose a brother and gain the Waterwitch, I suppose. What will I do without him, Pammy, what will Gina do?'

'You still have me,' said Pamela. 'You have me for always and Gina will manage, she always does. We'll take him back to Trevander, back to rest at St. Petroc's, looking out to the bay. We'll take him home on the Waterwitch like a Viking funeral. He would be proud of that.'

Gina could only remember a sunlit afternoon in the long grass behind Coombe Hawn Beach and the love she had denied him, and imagined the empty years ahead. Tim and Pamela would have the Navy and the War, she would be left behind. 'Oh, why not me too! I just don't think that I can bear it,' she murmured to Tom Harris. He plied her with a nip from his brandy flask.

'It won't' said Tom, who had lost his wife seven years before, 'it won't always be like this. That's all I can promise. Can you take the wheel, the boy's very tired?' He motioned toward Tim. Gina went into the wheel-house then and sent Tim out onto the deck, glad to be on her own at last.

PART IV

Sea Interlude

Chapter Fourteen

1943

Hoping to appeal to a level higher than 'bread and circuses', the government had decreed that lonely young servicemen, let loose in the Capital, should be fed a diet of lunchtime recitals, hastily assembled in unlikelyvenues, ENSA concerts in dusty church halls and art exhibitions; dim havens for the tortured soul.

When Greville Lazenby had opened up his gallery on the south side of Kew Gardens, he was well known for his fine portraiture but the exhibitions that came and went through the war years were, in the main, a mixture of froth and whimsy with the occasional voice of modernism crying in the wilderness. That first collection, housed behind a nameless and uninspiring façade had driven Harry Colenso to stand back, hands on hips, and quip 'That's the stuff to give the troops!' and so a name was born – Stuffs. Stuffs became the place to visit in the spring of 43.

But in spite of honest intentions as an opiate for the masses it was mainly the upper classes who stumbled over its doorstep, drifting in from Mayfair and the West End. Sometimes a drunk tumbled in, fugitive from the English winter, or the occasional Wren officer, immaculately attired. But on that grey April day with showers that were downpours and sunshine pushed out of existence, it was a young naval rating, blank of gaze, a little shell-shocked perhaps.

Greville Lazenby, whose recent portrait of Princess Elizabeth, bright and eager in a frilly party dress, was sent to grace Windsor Castle and whose masterpieces, the twin paintings of society beauties Frances and Diana Faraday hung at opposite ends of the great hall at Larkholme, epitome of the English manor houses they were all trying to save, was not without appreciation for this lost young man with the finely chiselled features and the haunted eyes which searched the room, travelling over every offering, searching yet seeing nothing not until... He had stopped at the Toft landscape, all sea and sky with the island rising from the sea fret; an Avalon, a dream isle. He sat down on the padded bench supplied for the foot-weary and the connoisseur and never took his eyes from that grey, impressionistic sea.

Lazenby nudged Harry Colenso, 'Can't say I've seen that kind of interest in your offerings, Harry old boy!'

Colenso shrugged. He was on a roll at that moment; his portraits were selling like hot cakes. He didn't need to drum up interest amongst the clientele of Stuffs. He motioned toward the young man. 'Looks ill to me, very ill, gaga even, but what a profile! Hands off, Greville, the Navy might want him back!'

It was the young woman who detached herself from their group and moved slowly, gracefully across the floor to stand at the boy's side, staring at the landscape, trying to see in it what he was seeing. If he had turned for a while and looked at her, he would have seen a tall, slim blonde in her late thirties, satin shirt tucked into tailored trousers. Her skin was fair, her hair almost white, her eyes the colour of the tiny blue scabious which dotted the cliff tops all round Trevander Bay. She drew on a cigarette perched at the end of a long holder:

'I think you know the island. I think you know it well.' Her voice was melodious, accent less. He turned, startled, thinking he was still alone.

'Yes. Yes, I do – Enys Du, Trevander Bay. I camped there, trespassed there, swam – oh, everything, long ago now.' He was indeed striking, an almost Byzantine narrowness to his face and green eyes, long lashed. He was too young, too decorative to be obliterated by the war.

'Then you approve?' The woman sat easily beside him.

'Of the painting? Oh yes, of course. It's home really. The light is right, just right for an autumn mist. The fragility of the outline, as if the island was floating above the waves and the rocks; a living entity. Who is the artist?'

'Lillian Toft,' said Lillian Toft. 'I'm glad you approve.'

'Yours? I did not realise.'

'How could you and you flatter me? Are you on shore leave?'

'Sick leave, yes.'

'And battle weary. Do you have family still in the South West?'

'Trevander, yes, a mother and sisters.'

'And you will be going back, they've given you time?'

'Yes, plenty of time – for that – but no, I am not going to see them.'

'Oh, what a pity. I felt you loved the place.'

'I do. It would be heaven after what I've just been through but the family would just stifle me. I need space, time to think.' For the first time he put a hand to his head and she noticed bandages beneath his service cap. He looked white now, strained and tired.

'I'm going down to Marazion tomorrow. I have a cottage by the sea, not very grand but quiet. I'd like to do some sketches – real Cornish faces, that kind of thing. If you don't mind; if you need the peace. It isn't Trevander but it's beautiful there.'

'A portrait for posterity?' said the young man. 'Posterity isn't a word I have much use for.' He touched his head. 'It could happen at any time they tell me. I can't bring that on them at home. Oh, it's not a noble thought really, just that they would choke me with their love and kindnesses and I couldn't bear it….'

'Where are you staying?' asked Lillian. 'I have a car. I'll pick you up tomorrow. And no, you won't be a burden to me. What do I call you?'

'Tris,' he said 'Tristan Toller.'

It was a strange ménage a trois at Morlanow. Lillian's cottage lay back from the strand at the limits of the highest tide as its name suggested. It was old and grey without the benefit of pastel wash or white distemper. Its roof was golden with the lichens of years and the paint had long ago peeled from its window frames. Instead, its façade was enriched by the vines of old roses with names which had disappeared from the garden catalogues half a century ago. The garden was a shrubby wilderness fighting for sunlight, over spilling poppies and columbine and lavender onto the crazed path which wound its way to the shore-line where it picked up sea pinks and campions before losing itself in the drifting sand at the tide's edge.

Here Lillian had her studio, here she shed her bored, woman-about-town image and went bare-foot in a faded blue gown which would have shamed a gypsy, and a broad-brimmed straw hat wreathed in silk Albertines, trailing ribbons in its wake. She wore no make-up and her hair was bleached to bone whiteness.

Harry Colenso visited most days, teasing them both, filling the cottage with his rollicking , salty laugh, calling her Morvoren, his Cornish mermaid, producing coq au vin from scrawny chickens he had run over in his old roadster. One night they had jugged hare and sat out under the stars and talked into the early hours. Harry was in love with Lillian, of course he was who could help it. Tristan could see them together even unto old age; each with separate studios; meeting for meals; walking hand in hand along the tide's edge on summer nights; sharing the firelight on winter's evenings. He wondered if they would, either of them, remember him and this brief interruption to their easy lives.

But when Harry went home and they could hear him singing as he drove away toward Marazion or, when petrol was absolutely unobtainable, walking all the way, singing old capstan shanties, because it was right and proper to do so, then he had her all to himself. He would sit out in the old tumbledown arbour, wreathed with the scented vines of Felicite roses, and the night wind would bring with it the salt taste of the sea, to be obliterated by the scent of herbs, crushed under foot as she made her way barefoot down the path to join him. He dared not ask if she made love to him out of pity for the life he was losing, but he thought not for she took everything easily as she wanted it and did not question her desires. And she did want him, of that he was certain, lying there amongst the fallen roses with her mermaid's hair about her lovely face.

He died in the October storms, taken at the ebb as was fitting. He was standing at the cottage door, watching her come down the path, wrapped in a paisley shawl, more gypsy-like than ever. She was laughing as he lifted a hand to greet her. Then he was gone.

She wrote to them all in Trevander; Tabby Cluett that was and Cynthia and Pog Toller, his sisters, but they did not understand why he had chosen to spend his last months with a total stranger. She had not expected them to understand but she saw to it that his body went home to the grey church on the hill, to lie with Granfer and Janniper and Frank; young company for the bones of his cousin, Lanty Maddaver.

Three weeks later, Lillian Toft married Harry Colenso and they were always to talk about Tris Toller as if he were their son. But, of course, they had a son. He had his mother's blonde hair and Harry's laugh, though some thought he had little else of his vagabond father. Lillian was in London when Hitler loosed the Doodlebugs. Her body was not identified. Harry never returned to Morlanow and eventually the roses claimed it for themselves, forcing their way through the broken windows, pushing healthy shoots up between the flags of the kitchen hearth. The path disappeared and the arbour disintegrated. Harry took his son to London to a rambling Edwardian semi which had seen prouder days. There, after a fashion, they settled down together....

PART V

Minions of the Moon

*Let us be Diana's foresters, gentlemen
of the shade, minions of the moon.*

King Henry IV, Part I

— William Shakespeare

CHAPTER FIFTEEN

December 1942

They had left Stanton Cleveley at 20.35 hours, circling once before heading south for the Channel. Essex was bright with snow-light and below them, the trees and hedgerows, already furred with the night's hoar frost, became Christmas Card scenes. At their Dispersal they had stamped up and down, clapping their hands, whilst cat-ice crackled beneath their feet; a thin topping to the puddles briefly thawed by the midday sun.

But now, inside the cockpit of K-King, all was warm and snug, purring with the steady vibration which was the sign of two healthy Merlin engines. Outside, the fields of England were a glittering counterpane of white and silver, velvet black and dark purple shadow. Within the cockpit, vision was telescoped to contain the pale glow of the instrument panel, the luminosity of a collection of twitching dials and the varied shapes of a multitude of knobs and levers.

Pilot and Navigator turned to glance one at the other, thumbs up in acknowledgement of a near perfect take-off. K-King, Mosquito Night-Fighter, crossed the channel flying low, hugging the winter sea, clinging to its slatey, grey face to escape the German radar net. They had a roving commission, these two. Group put in the occasional desultory suggestion as to where they should patrol but they knew their way by now, they had a job to do and they were good at it. Well, they were still alive, weren't they?

Flight Sergeant Archie Lorimer had his head bent low over his charts, flashlight in hand. He traced the outline of the Brest peninsular with a long forefinger, singing a strange, unintelligible song, undeniably flat. Rob Ashley, his skipper, turned his head slightly, glanced over his right shoulder and grinned at the bent head. He flipped the Mossie viciously onto her port side in a half-roll. The sea came up on their left side and subsided again as he righted her. Lorimer swore, the narrow beam from the flashlight flicked about them as he searched for his pencil.

'That was bloody childish!' He mouthed.

'You are still with us then?' said Ashley over the inter-com. 'Sorry Arch.' But there was no trace of contrition in his voice. Undistorted by static it was a light, pleasant, accent less, middle-class voice.

Over Brittany they began climbing again; Brest, Lori-ent, La Rochelle, were all centres of U-Boat activity. The two-man crew of K-King were making for the Brittany railway system, supply lifeline of the garrisons of St. Nazaire.

Lorimer glanced at his watch: almost 21.15. It was time they started looking about them for trade. They were cruising now at 180 mph, on the look-out for the tell-tale puffs of smoke which would betray an engine, all the time searching the bright skies for enemy fighters. It was Lorimer who spotted the approaching train and proceeded to deafen his skipper with a loud hoot.

'Three O'clock, Ash, Go!'

Flt.Sgt. Ashley put the Mossie into a shallow dive, setting his sights on the engine. They were down to 1,000 feet, Lorimer with eyes on the rear of the snaking procession of trucks and hoppers, searching for a flack-car, so often attached to freight-carriers as defence against air-attack. K-King was diving now and Ashley gave the chugging engine a long burst from his combined armament - the four machine guns in the nose and the cannon in the Mossie's belly. His Navigator was yelling excitedly, cheering as the target dissolved into a ball of steam and smoke.

'Let's get the hell out of here!' He shouted as K-King lost speed with the recoil of her guns. Christ! That's not a hopper, weave for gawd's sake!' But Ashley was already accelerating into a tight, climbing turn to port, one hand thrown up against the glare of the red-hot bursts of tracer, fanning out from the rear truck. He winced as they heard the thud of shells striking home and glanced apprehensively to starboard; there were sparks coming from the engine cowling. Ashley fought off the slashing patterns of light that still hindered his sight and peered at the oil-temperature gauge. Off the clock! He depressed the button which activated the fire extinguisher and feathered the starboard engine.

'We're on our way home, Archie!'

They turned for the coast again, barely managing to maintain height. The clear, moonlit skies of the outward journey had bunched up into cloud and, over the Channel; they hit a sudden squall, reducing visibility, rocking the lame Mosquito.

Ashley's hazel eyes flickered over the dials. The Mosquito flew happily enough on one good engine but there was an unhealthy juddering coming from the port motor and they were already low on fuel with the main tanks holed. The state of the outer tanks was healthy but they needed to conserve the juice for landing.

Rain and hail spun off the port propeller and the inherent charge of static transformed it into a giant Catherine Wheel, a glowing arc against the night sky. They could hear the chink and clatter of ice against the fuselage. Pilot and Navigator turned and looked at each other, blue eyes met brown.

'Go on then, find me an airfield!' said Ashley. 'And not the far side of the Wash either. I'm serious, Archie, any port in a storm.'

'That bad, is it?' Lorimer was squinting at his charts. 'It's got to be St. Keyne; Hobson's choice really.'

'Okay, as long as we can maintain height over the South Cornish cliffs, I suppose we'll make it. What d'you know about St. Keyne?'

Lorimer shrugged broad shoulders: '1939 it housed Ansons for Coastal Command. After the fall of France they got Spits and Hurris. The Luftwaffe scored a direct hit on the main hanger; summer of forty, and again the following January. Recently, the USAAF used it for their Liberators - anti shipping patrols, I suppose and -'

'Archie, I don't want a bloody history lesson! I want to know the layout. How many runways?'

'Three. How many d'you want? And we're not there yet, don't panic.'

'Why not? I can't see a darn thing. God, how I hate these Cornish fogs. We're lost!'

'Impossible!'

'Don't argue. I'll get a QDM.'

Lorimer shot him a withering look. 'Such faith is touching! A storm like this and you wouldn't raise the control tower if you were sitting on top of it!'

Ashley narrowed his aching eyes. 'What's that, a light of sorts?' He was trying to pierce the shifting fog bank,

to make some sort of sense of the dark, humped landscape below them.

'I told you, we can't be there yet. It could be Nanvallock.'

'What's that?'

'Care & Maintenance Depot.'

'But we could make a let-down?'

'I'm telling you, it's practically derelict.'

'Have they ploughed up the runway?'

'Why should they? They'll need all these forward
stations for the big push. This bit of England will be a
thriving hive of activity any day now. Ash, what are we
doing?'

'Going in for a recce.'

'You can't land at Nanvallack, it's an awful place!'
But Ashley appeared not to have heard him. He was
carrying out a circuit of the deserted airfield. The mists
had parted but the rain still lashed at them. They could
rouse nothing more than a barrage of static on the R.T.
Ashley flashed a letter K in Morse from the indicator
light in the Mossie's nose.

'Sure this isn't a Q Site?' He fell silent, thinking of
those decoy airfields, designed to lead enemy raiders
astray; ghost stations.

Nanvallack was perched perilously on top of the
Cornish cliffs. It had three good runways, a couple of 'D'
Type hangars, a huddle of admin buildings grouped
about a squat control tower - the only light appeared to
come from a storm lantern crossing a ploughed field
beyond the east-west runway. Ashley began making his
final checks, beginning an anti-clockwise circuit in
preparation for a landing with the starboard motor out
of commission: radiators open, brakes off, wheels down

and locked - flaps were useless, needing firm control of the airspeed -115 knots, they needed a long landing run. Storm force winds had directed the choice of runway, rain and sleet had succeeded in masking its length; unfinished, it petered out into a muddy track.

K-King, unperturbed, trundled on and on, Ashley fighting to keep her head to wind. Pilot and Navigator were buffeted about in their straps as the Mossie bucked and kicked and struggled to perform a spectacular ground-loop. When she at last came to a halt and the whirr of the single prop had died away, the night seemed silent at last, the wind and rain far beyond the perspex of the cockpit canopy. Lorimer wiped the sweat from his forehead and glanced at Ashley, crouched over the stick.

'Don't you ever do that to me again, chum, too much strain on the old ticker is that kind of a landing!'

Ashley lifted his head and just at that moment, a sudden gust of wind butted at the Mossie, and a sheet of rain struck them, head-on, rattling against the windscreen like a fist-full of shingle tossed up the beach by an angry tide. Grey-faced, he turned, caught Lorimer's eyes and they both began to laugh until they were bent double, leaning against each other for support, tears of mirth channelling their sweat-soaked faces.

They were both good-looking young men. Archie Lorimer was six foot two, big boned and long limbed with a square face and light blue eyes. The cropped hair, entirely hidden by his helmet was mid-brown. A pronounced Yorkshire accent left no doubts as to his tough, northern stock. Archie came from Bradford, from streets of back-to-back houses with outdoor loos. Archie had brains and had used them to get to the grammar school, to get into the R.A.F. Rob Ashley hailed from the

Midlands, from Marcher Country. There were no satanic mills on the banks of the Severn, only the silent wheels which once churned Belloc's 'rough water brown' to grind the flour for the villages beneath Breiddin. Ashley's had been a comfortable, middle-class existence until the school cadet corps tumbled him out into the Alice-in-Wonderland world of the R.A.F. He was twenty two, a couple of inches shorter than his Navigator perhaps, with a head of bronze hair and steady hazel eyes, heavy lidded, either side of a face slashed by a regular, straight nose, a straight mouth - a face which in repose gave little away but hinted at some secret amusement not to be shared. Somewhere beneath the middle-class conventional exterior there was a tougher, wilder streak, which had homed in upon Archie Lorimer within hours of their meeting up at the Operational Training Unit. Pilots and Navigators were thrown together with the object of pairing up to form workable partnerships. Ashley and Lorimer had recognised in each other a soul-mate, a twin being against whom there was no need to strive, to match up to, or to surpass. No need now to fight fear, the dark enchanter. If Ashley was scared to hell then Archie was in like case and they had only to turn and read their own feelings in each other's eyes to sigh with relief and laugh in the face of whatever came.

For Ashley, it was a re-birth. United, they could stand up against the wiles of insistent Intelligence Officers and dapper Adjutants, sarcastic M.O.'s and irate Station Commanders. Their successes in the few weeks that they had flown their Mossie on 'Intruder' sorties or 'Ranger' patrols had prompted their Station Commander to put their names forward to the War Office Selection Board for commissions. The old Lorimer would have ridiculed the suggestion as totally alien to his own leftwing leanings but, ever the Thespian, he had warmed to the idea of exchanging chevrons for stripes and they had both decided to play the game for all it was worth.

They shared everything; their work and leisure hours, billet and meals, possessions and thoughts and even, at times, their women. As Archie said: 'When we go down to hell, we'll go together. That way, we can carry on where we left off!' And they had shaken on it. Now they were both aware that hell had crept a little nearer and the relief at their narrow escape made them both light-headed.

Along the muddy track, into their rain-spotted field of vision, a lantern wavered and the sickly beam of a torch penetrated the darkness as three figures slithered toward them. Ashley opened a window and put out his head. He was relieved to find that the approaching trio were service personnel rather than a collection of yokels returning, tanked-up, from a spree at the local hostelry. They struggled forward, the wind at their backs, great-coats thrown over their pyjamas.

'This isn't going to be your most popular land-fall,' said Lorimer. He opened the hatch in the starboard side and put down the ladder; then he sat back and waited. Both men were realising how tired they really were - and how hungry!

The arm that hauled its owner above the door-sill bore sergeant's stripes.

'You can't stay here; you'll have to have it moved at once!' It was a familiar cry to the instigators of unorthodox landings and Ashley had made plenty of those. But the two young men appeared dumb-struck for a moment. If the words held no surprises, their owner had more of

an impact. The hair beneath the service cap was mud
brown and straight and wringing wet. It clung about its
owner's collar. It was undoubtedly a woman, if a plain
one, but Lorimer had to acknowledge that even Carol
Lombard would have looked plain in a force nine gale,
clinging to the top of a boarding ladder whilst the heavens tipped down all they had. The woman tried again.

'You'll be in mud up to the props by morning.'

'Can we report in somewhere, miss?' asked Archie.

'Sgt. Douglas,' snapped the young woman. 'Yes. Pilot
Officer Todd should be camped out in the Watch Office.
You could go and wake him up, I suppose.'

Ashley was weary; the thought that P.O. Todd had his
head down whilst he and Archie were battling through
the skies irked him. 'Don't you even maintain a listening
watch? We could have done with some help getting
down! It's not my idea of a happy despatch, being cata-
pulted off the Cornish cliffs like the last act of Swan
Lake! If you'll let us get out, Sergeant, we'll ring up our
home base.'

The woman pushed back her wet hair. 'Where are you
from, if it's not a state secret?' There were no prizes to be
had for guessing where she hailed from. She might as
well have worn a sprig of heather behind one ear. Her
rear retreated through the hatch again and her head
disappeared as it had come.

'Stanton Cleveley,' said Lorimer.

'You are poor wee lost lambs,' mocked Sgt. Douglas.

'Ba, ba, ba!' came a chorus from the foot of the ladder.

Lorimer stuck his head out of the hatch, Ashley
behind him. They looked down into two more rain-
streaked faces. One with two red pig-tails sticking out
incongruously from beneath her service cap, the other

with a corona of rag curlers clustered about her head, pyjama trousers stuffed into the tops of an enormous pair of gum boots.

'You have WAAFs here?' said Ashley in amazement.

'No, we're officers' comforts,' said the one with the rags and winked at him.

'That's enough, Nesbit,' snapped Jean Douglas. 'Go and start up the Fordson, we'll tow them away. Corporal Paget, take this pair over to Mr. Todd in the Watch Office.'

'Righto,' said the red-head with the pig-tails.

'Steady on!' said Ashley 'I mean, have you done this sort of thing before?'

Sgt. Douglas gave him a look of withering, flesh-searing contempt. 'At Treligga - you'll have heard of Treligga, no doubt - the entire field is manned by Wrens, hence the high incidence of emergency landings by the Yanks. We happy few can't compete in numbers, but here at Nanvallack, Flight Sergeant, you will find that we are all things to all men. So, if you will take yourself off to the Watch Office we shall remove this obstruction forthwith!'

Lorimer nudged his skipper. 'That's cut you down to size, chum. Lead on Cpl. Paget, we'll follow in the very sod!'

They set off across the field toward the square tower of Control. Cpl. Paget was petite. Above the storm lantern her eyes were large and blue. At every step the mud sucked at her Wellingtons. She spoke breathily when addressed.

'You're a Care & Maintenance unit?' asked Lorimer.

'Oh, no, we're really an O.T.U. but the birds have flown. I suppose we're Rest & Recuperation now. People fly in and out; a flight of this or a flight of that for the odd kipper patrol. We had a month of Beaufighters on anti-sub; that was a hairy time for all concerned.'

'Who's your C.O.?' yelled Ashley through the Force Niner.

'What? The C.O. isn't at home, we hardly ever see him these days. Do you want me to put through a call to Stanton Cleveley?

Lorimer nodded, 'they'll be thinking we've popped our clogs, like as not.' Cpl. Paget looked startled. 'Oh, you're a Yorkshire man!'

'Reet, lass,' he grinned as she pushed open the door at the foot of the Watch Tower and led the way upstairs. They clumped after her, dripping rainwater, leaving huge muddy prints in their wake, like a pair of latter day yetis. Ashley thought that the snowy wastes of East Anglia would be infinitely preferable to the delights of the milder south-west peninsular. Cpl. Paget knocked on the Control Room door and marched briskly in. The duty officer, alone in the room, lay stretched out on a camp bed, dead to the wide. There was an aura of whisky about him. The light from a shaded lamp haloed his blond hair. Cpl. Paget hung over him. 'Mr. Todd, will you wake up please, Sir?' She shrugged her shoulders.

'Heavy night was it?' queried Ashley.

'Oh, no, Sgt. He's not been off the Station. He's always like this. It's Nanvallack. It gets to everyone in time. If you want to phone Group use the red phone, that's the scrambler. You can phone your base on the black one. I'll make us all a nice cup of tea. See if you can get a bit more life out of the stove.'

Whilst they made their phone calls she clattered about and appeared with four mugs and a real china teapot.

They pulled up chairs and huddled about the stove. P.O. Todd surfaced and held onto his head.

'I've made a nice brew. Do you good, Sir,' said Cpl. Paget. 'And we've got visitors. Sgt. Douglas is having them towed off the runway now.'

'Good old Dougie. Are they badly smashed up?'

'No, Sir, they're here, Sir.'

'Oh, so they are. Expect you'd like to use the blower.' Lorimer and Ashley exchanged glances.

'Are you in charge, Sir?'

'Fraid so. You'll have to stay the night. You can catch the train tomorrow. At least, I think you can. What day is it, Peggy? Tomorrow, that is?' The girl said, 'It's already tomorrow, by five minutes. There's no train on a Friday. Can't they borrow the Oxford and fly out, Sir?'

'Good idea, Corporal, well thought out. Add another bar to your DFM. That's the second this week, isn't it? Good show.' P.O. Todd smiled from the depths of a bibulous haze. He was only about twenty, square-jawed and handsome with a mop of thick blond hair and blue-grey eyes. Peggy Paget gave him a mothering smile. He addressed the new comers. 'You'll be relieved to get out of this hell-hole, I shouldn't wonder. You'll have to doss down here for tonight; there are no billets on site. Can't even offer you a bath. Cpl. Paget will cut you a sandwich and find you some blankets.'

'Sorry to deprive you of your beauty-sleep, lass,' said Lorimer. 'What I can't fathom is what all these pyjama-clad lovelies are doing roaming about the cliff-tops round the midnight hour.'

'Lovelies?' said Ashley with a lift of one eyebrow, and added ungallantly, 'you need your eyes testing, Archie. Did you take a shuftie at Sgt. Douglas?

P.O. Todd grinned, 'Our Bonnie Jean can out valkyrie the Hitler Madchen. This sounds like her slippered tread, gliding up the grand staircase now!'

All four turned expectantly toward the door which crashed back to reveal Sgt. Douglas, soaked through, hair in rats' tails. She shook herself rather spectacularly, like a big St. Bernard dog and made for the stove; behind her panted LACW Nesbit, mud up to the haunches, streaking her face, oozing from the top of her ten-league gum boots. The rag curlers, unbound, hung about her small, sharp face like the ribbons of an abandoned maypole. She squeezed the water out of her handkerchief before blowing her nose.

'That's your baby all tucked up for the night, Flight Sergeant. We've got a tarpaulin over the starboard engine. You made a mess of her didn't you!' she admonished.

Ashley did not take kindly to being hauled over the coals by a snotty little female Erk who probably stood four foot nothing in her stockinged feet. He said. 'You didn't have to prostrate yourself in the mud and let her roll over you, did you, girl?'

Lorimer, bent on keeping the peace, said, 'You've done a grand job, ladies. Can we escort you back to your billets, perhaps?'

'Certainly not!' said Sgt. Douglas. 'We couldn't hear of it. Come along, girls!'

Peggy Paget deposited a bundle of blankets in Archie's lap and they trekked out again into the night.

'I like the big, blue-eyed one,' said Peggy wistfully.

Jean Douglas snorted, 'Not your type at all, Paget!'

'Are you sure, Sarge? He had such marvellous, dreamy eyes.'

'Quite sure. What about Susan, she's remarkably quiet.'

LACW Nesbit, battling against the wind said, 'I can't bear to see them like that!' and wiped her nose on the sleeve of her great coat.

Jean Douglas slid her a sidelong glance, 'Oh, they'll be as right as rain tomorrow. It's extraordinary, the resilience of some of these young men, you see it all the time. A good night's sleep and ...'

LACW Nesbit let out a howl of anguish, 'Sarge, I'm talking about the starboard motor - a miracle of engineering - pounded to bits!'

Peggy and Jean exchanged exasperated glances. 'That,' said Peggy 'is a typical Nesbit utterance; only the two best-looking characters to set foot on this island of mud since Robinson Crusoe and she's worrying about their spark plugs!'

'Well,' retorted LACW Nesbit, with a toss of the rag curlers 'someone has to. Who's for cocoa?'

Rob Ashley awoke in the pre-dawn darkness, cold and very stiff, aware that the stove had gone out and that there was a thick pasting of ice on the inside of the window. He pulled his blanket tighter about his ears.

'You awake, Arch?' It was a stage whisper.

Lorimer gave a little snort and switched onto consciousness. 'I wasn't. Christ, its cold as the icicles on ...'

'Yeah, I was just looking at the frost ferns, pretty really. I bet they never get those out in Bir Hakim.'

'Lucky them! Is that what you wanted to say? Is that why I was woken up?' Ashley turned onto his back, put out a hand and felt about the floor for a packet of cigarettes.

'It's too cold for sleep, I just wanted the company.'

'Stupid sod! Should I be flattered? You'd think Prince Charming over there would have given up the bed to his house guests, wouldn't you?'

'Officers!' scoffed Ashley, rubbing at the stubble on his chin and feeling horribly disreputable.

'Any day now and that'll be us,' said Lorimer 'and the world our oyster, boy. We'll be hob-nobbing with WAAF officers, dining out with Dukes' daughters.'

'Muffins at the Ritz?' said Ashley sarcastically. 'You fancy yourself, Arch.' He lit two cigarettes and passed one to his Navigator. 'The WAAF officers at Stanton Cleveley never have forgiven us for the red light we fixed up over their billet - just cause they got no takers. I wonder what they've got here. You can't have WAAFs without WAAF officers. Remember that little girl we picked up in Debden? She had nice legs. She was an Assistant Section Officer.'

'Well, she seemed only too happy to assist us,' said Lorimer with a grin, blowing on his finger ends. 'I'll bring a friend,' she says and turns up on her own. What stamina!'

P.O. Todd stirred on his camp bed. 'What happened? Did you toss for her?'

'Lord luv us, no,' said Lorimer. 'We booked the bridal suite, all complete with Elizabethan four-poster, blue brocade and moths. There was room for all three in that!'

'It sounds pretty disgusting,' said the blond boy jealously, sitting up and swinging his feet to the floor, blindly feeling about the lino for his shoes. Lorimer had wandered to the window and was rubbing a hole in the ice. Todd said. 'The Old Man will be back at first light. You don't get out of here until he flies in in the Oxford.'

'Suits us.' Lorimer was swathed in his blanket and was pacing the floor like Geronimo on his way to a war council. 'Can we get breakfast? No, don't tell me, there's no cookhouse on site either! What is there on this station? Its like the end of the world without even benefit of a fiery furnace!'

Todd shrugged his shoulders, 'Mrs. Pellymounter down at the Moonraker does a lovely bacon brunch, as much as you can cram down. I don't know how she does it but the Black Market is nothing to the Cornish after centuries of cheating the revenue men!'

Ashley had sprung into life, 'Is it far?'

'Two miles over the headland, three by road,' said Todd with a grin. 'Will you settle for tea and jam slabs?'

Lorimer had his eye to the ice-hole again, 'I can hear trade of some sort. D'you get raiders over here now?'

'Not at this time in the morning. But if it isn't in 'Every Boy's Book of Aircraft Recognition' you'll hear the Bofors gun on Mellin Rock opening up, then its time for the panic bowlers!'

'It's your Oxford,' said Lorimer.

'Bloody hell!' said Todd. 'I never told them to man the Chance Light. If it was a good enough Jolly last night to induce double vision this morning then the Old Man'll be out in the bay by now!' They all stood still and listened as the splutter of an engine died away to silence.

'He's down!' reported Lorimer.

'Right,' said Ashley, 'just let's have her refuelled and we'll be on our way.' His teeth chattered against a mug of tea which had suddenly appeared from an alcove, born aloft by a sleepy Erk. Very shortly afterwards the door crashed back theatrically and Group Captain O'Neill appeared on the threshold, feet astride, arms akimbo, goggles perched atop his forehead, a bright orange scarf knotted about his throat.

'Morning, Toddy. That was well worth the jaunt but the Pongos don't feed you like the Navy does. Ah, I heard we had guests - orphans of the storm.'

Michael O'Neill was a big man, somewhere round the forty mark with a craggy face and an aggressively jutting jaw. With his helmet removed his thick bronze hair sprang to new life. Swaggering there in full flying regalia he was reminiscent of the pirates of old; Long John Silver in the doorway of the Admiral Benbow.

'Tip me the Black Spot!' murmured Lorimer behind his hand, his imagination running riot. Beside him Ashley stiffened, saying nothing.

'What was that? Where did you say you came from?' bellowed O'Neill, knuckling his ears and swallowing hard. 'That's better.' He beamed at them both, standing there silhouetted against the dawn light from the window like two cardboard cut-outs.

'Stanton Cleveley, Sir,' said Lorimer at last, and cast a quick sidelong glance at his skipper, who appeared stony faced, body taut. O'Neill took two steps nearer, thrust out an arm and grabbed for the lamp on the Controller's desk, flicking it on and swinging the beam up into Ashley's face. The young man did not flinch; his eyes were cold and dark.

'Good God!' said O'Neill. if it isn't the Shropshire Lad!' The lampless hand waved towards the chevrons on the boy's sleeve. 'Flight Sergeant, I see, so you took the King's shilling after all. What are you flying?'

'Mossie - Night-Fighter.' There was a kind of defiance in the words.

O'Neill only said. 'We mustn't forget the civilities – 'Night-Fighter, Sir'. And how are Diana and your sainted father?'

'Well, the family are all well. If you'll excuse me, I'm leaving as soon as the Oxford's refuelled - Sir.

O'Neill frowned. 'Don't push your luck. Our one link with civilisation is that Ox-Box - the liberty boat, you might say. If it comes back with one scratch on the hull, the tiniest dent and I'll string you up from the highest vane this side of Clee. Now scram! Both of you!'

'Come on,' said Lorimer 'before he changes his mind and we're stuck in this hole. Race you out!' Once down the stairs he began to run toward the waiting Oxford, Ashley on his heels. They reached it breathless, to find that the ground crew, emerging from the morning mist, had done a quick turn round and she was ready to fly out again.

Once airborne the mists closed in again and Nanvallack disappeared beneath the wraith-like layer. Up above the sky was blue and the sun on the canopy began to thaw out their young bones.

'What's between you and the Crimson Pirate?' asked Lorimer. Their only communication from front to rear was by Gosport Tube. After the Mossie it was like flying a box-kite. 'We might have been treated to breakfast at his groaning board. He seemed affable enough until he recognised you!'

Ashley said, 'a spectre from the past, that's all, a figure from another world, Archie. Forget all about it. Now, it's Essex, home and beauty! Hold tight, let's see if this coffin can reach 200 m.p.h.'

CHAPTER SIXTEEN

St. Keyne, the station on the Cornish moors which had
remained elusive, lost in the Celtic mists on the night
that Ashley and Lorimer made landfall at Nanvallock,
was still destined to feature in their lives. At the end of
March their Mosquito Squadron was seconded to the
South-West, to be based at St. Keyne as part of a new
strike wing created to attack specified targets in northern France.

St. Keyne was a rambling place, a far cry now from
the early days of 1940 when fighter operations had been
master-minded from tented offices and the new Spitfires
had stood out among the heather. The site had mush-
roomed, with vast hangars and storerooms, fuel
compounds, armoury and villages of nissen huts in neat,
camouflaged rows. There were bays for the ambulances
and fire-tenders, control tower, equipment stores,
NAAFI and sick-quarters. As far as the eye could see this
purpose-built, dreary town covered the moor, grey
beneath a greyer sky; corrugated iron, brick and
maycrete. Even Lorimer from the land of mill chimneys
looked about him in dismay as they stepped from their
Mossie on arrival.

Ashley was unmoved; he had spent a year in
Lincolnshire before moving on for flying training and
experienced the joys of such varied centres as Marham,

Bicester and Dyce. Stanton Cleveley had seemed a haven indeed and the penguins who ordered such things were unlikely to allow them to become soft by posting them off to the orchards of Kent or the sands of sunny Sussex.

'There is a war on, Arch,' said Ashley. 'At least, the messing facilities should be good and there'll be a cinema and ENSA concerts. A couple of weeks to get the low-down on the place and we'll never remember we were anywhere else.' But they were not to be given those two weeks....

'B' Flight, Fairfax Squadron - they were all code named after Civil War generals - were ordered up on a 'Special'. Six Mossies acting in pairs were to attack a strategic airfield - St.Remy sur Somme - to render it inoperable - all part of the allied plan to immobilise communication centres ready for the much-heralded invasion. It was to be a high-speed, low-level onslaught and K-King, paired off with Flying Officer Partington and his navigator in F-Freddie, took off at noon into a cloudless sky.

The journey out had been eventless, suspiciously so. The midday sun on the windscreen had turned the cockpit into a glasshouse. Ashley flew in his shirtsleeves. A trickle of sweat slid over the notches of his spine as they found the field, a model drome with its neat row of pens holding toy fighters, blotched with camouflage. He turned to glance at Lorimer and raised both thumbs from the stick. 'Here goes!' He put K-King into a shallow dive and held his fire until they were fifty yards from the first fighter. There was a burst of light flak from across the field but it was too far away to worry about. Then, with a shout, Lorimer pointed to a Focke-Wulf 190 on finals, undercarriage already down, making for the runway.

He gave the enemy fighter a two second burst from his combined armament - cannon and machine gun, it burst into flames and spiralled to the ground. F-Freddie had caught another Focke-Wulf on the circuit. The Pilot had managed to raise his undercart and was attempting to climb again. Partington had her in his sights.

'Another flamer!' They heard him yell as the fighter exploded into an orange ball from which fell shards of shrapnel, spinning to earth as if in slow motion.

'Let's get out of here, Rob,' said Partington, calling up Ashley. 'We've done our whack and the natives are getting restless!'

Ashley flicked on his mike. 'Sure. Peter, after you. I want one more burst at those fighter pens.' He banked and came in again, striking home. Lorimer watched in fascination as whole sections of fabric seemed to sheer off the wings below them and the roar of exploding fuel tanks in their wake caused the Mossie to rock like a fairground horse as they climbed away. Then Lorimer was yelling:

'Christ! Behind and below, BF110!' It was the feared Zerstorer, the twin-engined Destroyer, its speed no match for a Mossie at full throttle, but K-King was still climbing. The hairs prickled on the back of Ashley's neck. The BF110 had upward-firing cannon and they heard it, the dreaded schrager musick - slanting music - as it was translated, striking into the vulnerable underside of the Mossie.

The port engine was in flames which rippled back along the wing. Lorimer saw that the enemy had left them, probably low on fuel and satisfied that they would never make the English coast. She banked and made to return to St. Remy. Ashley had feathered the burning engine and turned out over the coast but the flames had too strong a hold and were already licking at the fuselage; they only had to penetrate the inner fuel tanks......

'Get your chute, Archie, I'll feather the starboard prop and you can jump.'

'What about you?' Lorimer dragged his parachute out of its storage place in the nose.

'I'll bring her in on a glide if I can.' Neither had ever 'taken to their umbrella', the thought filled them both with dread.

'I'll stay aboard,' said Lorimer suddenly.

'Don't be bloody daft, you've got a good chance from this height. Stop arguing! I'll get out a Mayday. Strewth, this is getting too hot for comfort. We can't be too far off the Lizard, are you ready?'

'I can't, Ash, I'd rather take my chance with the crate.' Ashley had a hand in front of his face, shielding it from the heat. He feathered the remaining engine and waited for the windmilling prop to stutter into silence. To evacuate a Mosquito from the starboard door with the engine in operation meant certain decapitation.

Lorimer had a mutinous expression in his blue eyes; he wiped the sweat from his forehead.

'No.'

'It's an order, Archie, it's the first order I ever gave you as skipper. Now move!'

Lorimer struggled into his parachute harness and opened the door. A welcome blast of cool air hit him. He turned once and gripped Ashley's wrist. 'So long, Rob.' Then he pitched forward through the hatch. Ashley only waited to see the billowing silk of his parachute before starting the glide toward the grey mesh of the channel. It looked deceptively calm from 5,000 feet but when

K-King hit the water in a cloud of hissing steam, there was a swell on.

Ashley was thrown forward in his straps and hit his head on the instrument panel as K-King sheered along the tops of the waves. He did not see that the flames were doused or that the damaged port main-plane had sheared away from the fuselage.

He awoke in bed with a splitting headache and remembered Tony Garnet's twenty-first birthday thrash. The world was out of focus, someone was shining a light into his eyes and he felt distinctly queasy. He closed his eyes again and tried to move into a more comfortable position, his feet seemed too heavy to move. He lay for a long time listening to the rhythmic slapping of the waves. His boots were heavy because they were full of water and if his boots were wet he could hardly be in bed in their billet! He opened his eyes again. That coruscating needle of light was the afternoon sun, focused upon the shattered perspex of the windscreen. K-King was still attempting to float in rather a desultory fashion. Ashley sat up carefully and winced as he lifted his head from the instrument panel. His ribs ached from contact with the stick. He put up a hand and found that the cut upon his head was already drying. How long had he been out? An hour or so? It was almost four o'clock. He unfastened the safety straps and managed to open the escape hatch in the ceiling above his head. He checked his mae-west, grabbed his charts and stuck them in an inside pocket, slipped on his battledress top and kicked off the waterlogged boots. Then he heaved himself up and out onto the fuselage.

Somewhere, to the north-west, was a faint blur of the mainland. Elsewhere was only the sea, mile after unrelenting mile of water, green and inhospitable, waiting for the right moment to turn capricious and seize K-King, to suck her below.

'*Never was isle so little, never was sea so lone,*

But over the scud and the palm-trees an English flag was flown.' He remembered the village school at Uppington Magna, with its dark green walls and the cracked bell in the gable. How Miss Kendon had loved to recite Kipling, her eyes a shine with tears of pride as she forged through 'The English Flag', and that had been her favourite verse because it was the South Seas and the southern isles and Miss Kendon had been weaned on Robinson Crusoe. '*Never was isle so little, never was sea so lone.*' The words set up a chant in his tired brain. But the seas were cold and hostile, no warm golden beaches, no parrot islands. The distant shoreline had vanished in sea-fret. He thought of Archie without even the shattered hull of the Mossie to cling to and hoped that he had been found and was already on his way home.

The wreck was gradually filling with water, it was surprising how long the wooden fuselage had stayed afloat, but the wind was rising, the sun was blotted out and Ashley hunched on his perch, was bitterly cold. The constant searching of the horizon for a rescue launch made his eyes ache and the rhythm of the swell was making him sea-sick. He put his head down on his folded arms and tried to blot his surroundings out of his mind. When the end came for K-King he had the presence of mind to jump for it and strike out away from the wreck to avoid the undertow.

The Mossie seemed happy to go, almost serene. The green-grey waters closed over the fuselage and Ashley, feeling incredibly alone, took out the faith he remembered on Sundays, High Days and selected Saints, dusted it down and prayed for deliverance for himself and for Archie. God was not letting him have things too easily for it was almost dark when the Waterwitch out of Trevander, found him. Colan Denbow had caught the yellow glow of Ashley's mae-west and the skipper turned the bows toward him. The four man crew had set out with the Fowey lifeboat after Nanvallack had received the Mayday call. Trevander had no lifeboat of its own but there was a rota and always men on call for such an emergency. Ashley would not be the first flier to be taken from the waves by the Waterwitch.

Drew Maddaver nosed about the man in the water and cut the engine. A slim-wristed youngster put out an oar and Ashley clung to it with numbing fingers until two older men reached out and, hooking a hand under his armpits, pulled him inboard without ceremony. He lay on the duckboards, retching cruelly, back arched. 'He be alive then,' said Denbow unnecessarily and restarted the engine.

'It's orlright, boy, soon 'ave 'ee back on dry land,' said Esco Cluett, slapping Ashley between the shoulders so heavily that he choked afresh. The old man took off his glasses and rubbed them on his navy jersey so that he could better see what sort of fish they had landed.

Colan Denbow was a roly-poly man in bright yellow oilskins; he knelt over Ashley with a dry blanket. Through another bout of retching Ashley managed to say. 'My Nav, parachuted out, got to pick him up.'

'Don't fret,' said the young man who had pushed out the oar. 'Fowey lifeboat is out now, we're only a back-up and we're low on fuel. We'll get you ashore at Trevander. The Fowey crew won't give up; they'll find your Navigator.' He put out a hand for his sou-wester which went bobbing backward into the bilges. His red-gold hair, dulled by the flung spray, streamed out, crusted with salt. It had not been a young man after all; it was a woman, quite a pretty one, with green eyes.

'Strewth!' spluttered Ashley, 'Grace Darling!' She helped him to the side, away from the stench of fish in the bilges and he hung gratefully over the gunwales until the waves of sickness subsided.

The three men were huddled together in the deck-house, chuntering in that rich, round accent which seemed almost a foreign tongue to Ashley. The woman could look after the boy, which was her proper station after all. Peacetime would never have found a female crewing the Waterwitch but war had imposed many hardships and Gina Deverel had proved her determination and her courage on the sands of Dunkirk.

'Not long now, Flight Sergeant, just around the next headland and at least we're in calmer waters. You're obviously not a natural sailor. I've a flask of brandy if you think you can keep some down.'

Ashley found the words humiliating. He dragged himself up from his ignominious position, draped over the side, and ran his fingers through his bronze hair.

'Thanks Miss, Mrs.? The name's Rob, by the way.'

'You'd better call me Gina, the names Georgina - daughter of George - I was his one big production, hence the name.' She handed him a silver flask. He realised then that she was not the vision of Grace Darling, red hair rippling down about her shoulders, which he had glimpsed during his unceremonious arrival. She was flesh and blood and modern; mid-twenties perhaps and the hair was now twisted back and gathered into a snood on the nape of her neck. She had a square, healthy, country face with a wide mouth and clear green eyes. For Grace Darling he might have made an effort at conversation, for this relaxed young woman with the emerald of her engagement ring winking against the silver of the flask he felt disinclined. He huddled closer into his blanket, spurning the offer of a bed below, and drifted off into semi-consciousness.

'*Never was isle so little, never was sea so lone.*' He came too with his head on Miss Kendon's knee.

'*But over the scud and the palm trees an English flag was flown.*' But Miss Kendon never spoke in that light, beautifully modulated voice with its underlying Cornish sing song.

'*I have chased it north to the Lizard, ribboned and rolled and torn.*

I have spread its fold o'er the dying, adrift in a hopeless sea,' she finished for him.

'Archie,' began Ashley 'it's too cold out there, I was nearly finished when you found me. We've got to go back!'

'Lie still, your mind was wandering. Look, we're home. We're into the bay and they'll have seen us from the cliff. They'll be getting a room ready at the Moonraker. Dr. Denbow can have a look at you and Mrs Pellymounter will be happy to fuss over you; her own boy is at sea. She hasn't seen him in months.'

Ashley sat up suddenly, pulling away from her, 'I'm twenty-four, skipper of a Mossie, well, up till recently. I don't need a doctor, I don't need fussing over. I'll wait to collect my navigator and then we'll get out of your hair!'

Grace Darling smiled. Her eyes really were a rather incredible green. 'I've ruffled your feathers, I'm sorry.' No doubt, smartened up in his Best Blue, hair smoothed down, he would be quite a personable young man and believably the pilot of a fighter-bomber. Just now, wet and bedraggled, face grey with sea-sickness, lashes stuck together with salt, he looked younger than the years he claimed and as vulnerable as a child.

He was saying, 'No, it's my fault, that was very rude of me but I feel so bloody queasy; I'm going to be bloody well sick again!' He hung over the gunwales as the Waterwitch stealthily slipped into the harbour, the houses of Trevander, grey in the dusk, clinging tenaciously to the cliffs, tier upon tier, like a crazy wedding cake. Not a light showed and the only sounds were the wind and the rain and the tide slapping at the harbour wall. Gina Deverel's fingers lightly touched the nape of his neck.

'We're home. Can you manage the steps?' But Ashley was hauling himself to uncertain feet and turning to Drew, face grave.

'Thanks, I don't think I'd have held out much longer.' All words were inadequate as he stood there with his hand in that of this sturdy, dark Cornishman. Colan Denbow, making fast the stern rope, beamed at him, round brown face creased like a walnut and old Esco clapped him on the shoulder. Gina Deverel, holding the boat against the slippery wooden ladder up to the quay, waiting for him to alight said. 'Words will do for later. I think we'd all better make for the Moonraker.'

It had not changed in the years since Annabel had held the 'Share Out' in the back parlour. Rob Ashley, looking about him for the first time was conscious of grey stone walls, low beams and gleaming brass. It was an etching from all those boyhood classics; a haven for the émigrés of 'Tale of Two Cities', a coaching inn on the road to York where the locals would sprawl about their tables, mulling over Dick Turpin's latest transgressions. The heat from a log-fire hit them as they opened the door; the malty smells met them as they stepped over the threshold; tobacco smoke cocooned them as they crossed the floor. All conversation ceased abruptly, all eyes turned to stare at the intrepid flier, the man the Waterwitch had taken from the sea. Ashley stood damply, still in his mae-west. He ought to have looked like a recruiting poster but instead he was making small pools on the uneven stone floor and his teeth were chattering.

'Any news from Fowey, Mrs Pellymounter?' asked Gina.

The Landlord's wife shook her head, 'Boat's still out.'

'He's my Navigator,' said Ashley.

Mrs Pellymounter looked him over; saw the droop of the dark-fringed eyelids over the hazel eyes. 'You be standing there looking like a dying swallick. What about a bath, Flight Sergeant? Water be piping hot.'

'Yes, please, if it's no trouble.'

Gina smiled at Mrs Pellymounter. Clearly it would be no trouble for this nice-looking boy from some re-mote corner of England. He could have had a red car-pet it the Moonraker boasted such a thing. He would probably get clotted cream on his porridge in the morning, war or no war.

The call came in from Fowey at seven o'clock. Mrs Pellymounter handed the receiver to her husband. He listened intently, grunting and nodding every now and again, aware that the whole taproom had focused silently upon him. You could have heard a pin drop. At last he put down the receiver and turned to face his audience.

'Lifeboat be back. They've brought 'un in. Dead he be.' Then, 'Who be going to tell the boy?' His eyes slid toward Gina, sitting in the inglenook, cradling a mug of soup. She got up without a word and opened the door onto the narrow staircase.

Mrs Pellymounter had lit a fire in the guest room. The faded and flowery curtains were drawn tight against the storm. The bedspread, crocheted in squares by Molly Pellymounter and her sisters before the days of the Great War, was folded neatly back. Ashley was asleep in the chair by the fire, the empty soup mug hanging from one square-tipped finger. Gina stopped to take it from him and touched him lightly on the shoulder.

'Flight Sergeant, Rob, its Gina.' She went over to poke at the fire. She had her back to him as she said, 'the boat's back.'

'No luck then?' He was wide awake now and she knew that she must turn to face him.

'They've found him, your navigator. I'm sorry; there was nothing they could do – the intense cold.'

In one violent movement that all but overturned his chair, Ashley was on his feet and wrenching open the door.

Gina started to say, 'Its no use, he's not here. They landed at Fowey.' But he was down the stairs, across the taproom and out into the storm again. Gina followed slowly. All the men at the bar stared at her, faces blank. 'You handled that very badly,' she said to herself. Then, 'which way did he go, Jim?'

'Up along. Toward Drumgarrow,' said Pellymounter. 'Tes not a night for up-country folk to be larking about on the headland.'

'I'd better go after him.' Gina struggled into her oilskins and made for the door.

'Want one of us along with 'ee, maid?' Colan Denbow rested his elbow and set down his tankard resignedly. The storm was not abating. Rain lashed at the windows, emphasising the snugness inside.

Gina said, 'you know there isn't a path up there I wouldn't know with a sack over my head!' She smiled at him briefly and went out into a force-eighter, tearing in from the sea; the door crashed too behind her.

The road became a pathway; the pathway petered out into a muddy track and snaked its way over the headland. One path continued on toward The Burrows and Penherrit, the other clipped the edge of the great bluff of rock known as Drumgarrow. Here in spring there were banks of violets and primroses, clumps of wild daffodils, a splash of bright corn lilies and the wild, windswept hedgerows would be white with blackthorn, bright with gorse. Tonight they were treacherous byways, with rustling dark shapes threshed by the wind and rain-filled hollows where hidden paths shot off at a tangent down toward the rocks and the boiling sea.

Gina tried to imagine herself in the persona of a desperate young man, fleeing from the depths of his own misery and disbelief. She chose the cliff top path as the most dramatic setting on offer. The full force of the gale struck her in the face; the rain lashed her, streaming down her oilskins. It became a struggle, lame as she was, to keep her feet upon the slippery mud of the narrow track. Gorse clutched at her slacks and tried to hold her back. The path finally died out before the harbour beacon, lightless now for over four years. Beyond that was the sheer fall of rock known, rather predictably, as the Devil's Leap.

Head down into the teeth of the storm you could be over the top without being able to stop yourself. Gina steadied herself, one arm about the old light, feeling the roughness of the peeling paintwork beneath her fingers. Now she could see him. He was standing on the smooth flat ledge of rock above the leap, above the cauldron of threshing white water, hair plastered down, and shirt clinging to his body. He hadn't even had sense to grab his battle-dress top before he left the inn.

Gina was swiftly at his side. She had no need to mask her movements for he could not have heard her above the crash of the waves breaking below them. But all the same he sensed her presence and turned his head.

'You're running blind, Rob. This path leads nowhere.'

He managed a smile then. 'What you're saying is, there's no way out. Don't worry; it's not something I'm capable of. I just needed to get away, that's all. You shouldn't have come out in this. I suppose you don't have a cigarette?'

She nodded, 'Come away from the edge, there's a bench somewhere.' It was slippery with moss but in enough of a rocky hollow to afford them a little shelter. Ashley sat hunched forward, elbows resting on his knees, head bowed, for a long time. At last he said. 'We always thought, Archie and I, a mid-air explosion or plummeting to the ocean bed, straight in, vertical, snuffed out like a penny candle, but whatever way it came, we'd go together. We had a sort of pact, the kind kids make and seal with blood; it was that corny. He was the best mate I ever had was Archie Lorimer. We had something more than friendship, something very comfortable, more like a marriage as opposed to the steamy intimacy of a pick-up in a crowded bar and, strewth, I don't mean ...'

Gina, sitting beside him said, 'I know what you don't mean. That is, I know what you're trying to say, a friendship that comes once in a lifetime maybe, and until you lose it you never realise what little value you placed upon it. I lost a man to this war too.'

But he wasn't listening; he was making his own soliloquy. 'I killed him! I made him take to his chute when he begged to stay on board! I ordered him out! The only order I ever gave him. If he'd stayed with me he would have survived and we'd be down there at the Moonraker knocking back shorts and yarning with the old men. Christ, Gina, how do I live with that?' He choked on the words and turned his head away from her, hunching his shoulders in a gesture of futility. He was fighting a battle with loss and distress and guilt, a stranger in a strange land, for all up-country folk were strangers here. What had D. H. Lawrence said of Cornwall? 'It is not England, it is strange and bare and elemental.' Ashley was little older than Tim Maddaver, a little younger than Tris Toller would have been. She tried not to think of Lanty. Would there be anyone to comfort Tim, wrecked on a strange shore? There had been a woman there for Toller, they heard about it after his death. A beautiful woman who had arranged his funeral and come to the graveside and left without a word to any of them. Her thought touched a chord in her own enforced self-containment; the cocoon she had built about herself since Lanty's death. She slipped an arm about his shoulders; the flesh firm and warm in spite of the soaking, icy rain.

'I really don't see that you can reproach yourself, you gave him the best chance possible.'

He tried to pull himself together. 'God, what must you think of me? This isn't something I make a habit of!' He dashed a wrist across his face. 'I mean, pouring out my troubles on the nearest female breast. You shouldn't have followed me. I'd have come back when I'd thought things out.' He stood up and held out a hand to pull her to her feet.

She said, 'You don't know how treacherous these cliffs can prove. I was born here. No stranger ever appreciates the risks.'

He shrugged and said, 'Risks are a part of everyday life when you're flying. You think nothing of it when you've been in the game as long as I have!' He put a hand beneath her elbow and guided her back along the path. Gina had to smile at the chameleon change from despair to cocky assertiveness.

'We turn off here we don't want to take off into the hills!'

Ashley said, 'You're hurt, you're limping and you came all this way in such filthy weather! Gina, I'm sorry.'

She laughed then. 'Don't think about it. It's an old wound and I never talk about it. It's kept me out of the Services though, no room for the maimed, the halt and the blind, you know. So I bite my nails down here and wait for the flotsam of yet another raid. The Waterwitch belongs to my Uncle Drew and they're a little more accommodating about women on fishing boats than they used to be – but not much. Needs must, I suppose.'

Old Esco Cluett was puffing up the path toward them.

Gina said, 'The men and women of Trevander have long tongues, never likely to rust out from infrequent use. This is the vanguard!'

Ashley's eyebrows went up. 'One hour with me and your reputation's shot? Oh well, you wouldn't be the first.' He eyed her with a sideways flicker of the dark lashes.

'My, my, you do recover quickly!' thought Gina.

'Are 'ee orlright, maid?' Esco boomed into her pale face. They walked down together, backs to the storm. The Moonraker seemed doubly welcoming. Mrs Pellymounter showed visible relief.

'You look done-in, dearie; I've more soup on the range.' She persuaded Gina towards a chair. 'It's not but what we mind turning out to take a man from the sea but two rescues in one night!' she chided Ashley. 'Upstairs now and get out of those wet things and give yourself a good rub down. Properly now or I'll come and do it for ee!'

Jim Pellymounter winked at him, 'She do mean it. Mrs Pellymounter's word be law round 'ere.'

Ashley fled for the stairs.

'Did you get through to St Keyne?' Gina took the welcoming mug of soup.

'Yes, they'll be along to collect 'un in the morning. Did 'un take it badly, poor young man?'

'He'll be all right.'

Molly Pellymounter fluttered birdlike about the guest room, twitching at curtains, plumping pillows. Ashley finished his soup. His clothes were steaming by the fire. Robed in Jim's dressing gown he lay on the bed, arms behind his head, appreciating the fire, appreciating being alive.

'Mrs Pellymounter, what's Gina's other name, she never told me?'

'Then perhaps she thought you'd no reason to know it.'

'I don't see why not. Does she live down in the village?'

'It doesn't do to scatter folks' addresses about like confetti. Why should you be wanting to know?'

'I might want to thank her properly, maybe take her some flowers. You know.'

'Oh, I know. And that maid has enough to worry about with menfolk away at sea – doing some real fighting, not up having a flip in some wooden wonder!'

'That does cut me right down to size!' scoffed Ashley. 'Forget I was asking. I'll be away at first light.'

'Then I'll leave you to sleep off your adventures. I'm sorry about your friend. No use pretending 'tasn't happened, that won't help anyone. Now try to get a good night's sleep.'

But when she had gone he knew he would not sleep and when he closed his eyes, aching from the sting of the sea, Archie was there, talking and laughing as he had when they boarded K-King that morning. But Archie would laugh no more, unless men found something to laugh at down in hell. Archie would be lying in the Decontamination Centre at St. Keyne; that was where they'd put the chap who pranged on take-off last week – a desolate place even by St. Keyne standards. Ashley found he was shivering. The fire was almost out but it could not be that cold in the cosy little room. Perhaps it was wrong to try to sleep. He sat up, arms linked about his knees. Perhaps it was more fitting to keep a vigil with the dead.

CHAPTER SEVENTEEN

Rob Ashley took the train for Shrewsbury, sleeping most of the way, dozing on and off as they passed through Houseman's *Wild green woods of Wyre*, through Shropshire's gentle undulating hills, pricked with the grey spires of village steeples. Then he took the country bus out toward Uppington Magna and somehow enjoyed the jostling atmosphere, the gossip of market wives with their baskets crammed full of cabbages and beetroot, and ancient cronies hobbling back from even more ancient inns who nudged his shoulder and asked how the war was going, and pretty young girls susceptible to any young airman sporting a wings brevet. He could have phoned the vicarage and told them he was on leave but he preferred to walk the last two miles and to approach from the hill. Four years of war had done nothing to change that first view of St. Giles', its grey spire pointing heavenwards from the tree-lined valley where their own tributary of the Severn meandered through water-meadows dotted with buttercups and lady smocks. There, beside the stream, nestled the vicarage, mellow with age, wreathed in wisteria. The church clock was striking five as Ashley descended the hill by the path which crossed the stile and threaded its way through hollows where the sheep slept the summer nights away.

He slowed his step when he reached the wooden foot bridge and lingered awhile; gazing down into the brown stream where the watercress grew thickly and the yellow iris waded in the shallows, haunts of the brilliant damsel flies, blue as peacock wings. This was a favourite place from boyhood. Here he had come with Jenny-Jane, his mother, to play Pooh Sticks and fish for sticklebacks whilst Jenny-Jane set up her easel and quietly sketched away. But Jenny-Jane had left them both, Rob and his father, dying when he was ten years old. He had managed without a mother until Diana. He had been fifteen when Richard Ashley had brought her home. She had been Diana Faraday, society beauty and a friend of Jenny-Jane's sister. Perhaps it was his aunt who had brought the two together, mindful of Richard's loneliness and of Rob's need for a mother figure. But Diana was no Jenny-Jane to slip easily into the life of a country parson's wife. She had known she could never have taken up Jenny-Jane's mantle and wisely had determined to be herself, to make her mistakes and learn from them. And there had been mistakes. Befriending Rob perhaps had been one of them. She had never tried to be a mother figure, more an elder sister and willing confidante. It had been easy, for he was an attractive boy, but she had failed to see that at fifteen he was falling in love with her, with her blonde prettiness, her serene smile. Michael O'Neill had tried to warn her. Michael was a friend from way back and more than a little in love with her himself.

At sixteen the calf love had become an obsession and, one May afternoon, with the scent of wisteria tangible in the air, Rob Ashley had stammered out his love and longing for her and severed forever the special bond between them. It was not her startled rebuff which had cut him to the quick but her pouring out her heart to O'Neill which had hurt more. O'Neill, a frequent house-guest at the vicarage had cornered him in the summerhouse and given him a talking too which had begun man to man with sympathy and reason. But Rob could be obstinate and very unreasonable when he chose, and O'Neill had a temper, and voices were raised which could be heard as far as the bridge.

'What right have you to condemn me?' Rob stood his ground. 'You've lusted after her yourself years enough! You just can't bear the thought of a younger man finding his way into her bed!'

'Bed is it now?' roared Michael. 'I thought it was puppy love, pure and unsullied you had to offer, not adolescent gropings!'

'Better that than being pawed by a a....'

'Dirty old man might fit,' said O'Neill who was approaching thirty-five at the time. 'My dear little Oedipus, I think a sound thrashing might do you good!'

'She is not my mother. Father should never have married again. To imprison her here amongst his sermons and his books – it's a living hell!'

'How dramatic! I'm sorry to disappoint you but Diana was very much in love with your father when she married him. I believe she still is. You can't forgive Richard for not being the father you wanted, can you? Wasn't it Oscar Wilde who said that we rarely forgive our parents? Richard has been a darned sight better father to you than the wastrel who sired you. In his dry as dust way he does love you, he ....' O'Neill's voice trailed off. The boy was standing stock-still, his face drained of colour, blank with disbelief. 'Christ, boy, you didn't know. I never imagined that by this time he would not have told you. I am sorry and I think you'd better sit down!'

Rob shook off the hand he had placed on his shoulder but they moved to the weathered bench under the rhododendrons.

'This is not true! Mother would never, she couldn't! She was a vicar's wife. The Church and its teachings meant a lot to her. To have had an affaire...'

'No, no, not Jenny-Jane! God knows, the woman was a saint by all accounts. She wasn't able to have children – some medical reason. She and your father adopted you, they had you from birth. Don't ask me any more, boy. I shouldn't be the one to be telling you this and I curse my tongue. I had the story from Diana. In all honesty, I think the girl believed the same as I did, that you had been told and had disregarded the knowledge, accepted Richard and Jenny-Jane for the parents they were to you in all but name. Hang it all, you wretch, if we hadn't been having a set-to it would never have come out at all. Now I suppose I will have to confess to Richard.'

And, at last, Richard had called his son into the library, into his Holy of Holies, dark and cool and book-lined, smelling of calf leather bindings and worn leather chairs and the sweet mustiness of ancient tomes. Diana had placed a vase of white lilac on the desk and it was this scent and the white ghost-glow of the blooms which were to stay with her step-son for the rest of his life.

It was easier, after that day, to understand Richard. It was a relief for Rob to know that he was not flesh of his flesh. After that they stopped fighting and an easy friendship developed between them. Jenny-Jane was still his mother. It was easy to keep up that pretence. Visitors paused by the grand piano in the drawing room to pick

up a snapshot of the two of them, taken after school
Sports Day when he was eight. 'How like her you are!
How proud she would have been.' So, coming home was
still a refuge, St. Giles was the haven it had always been
and the peace of Uppington Magna was still the best
reason to fight a war, if reason there must be. He
dropped a stick into the fast flowing water, stayed to
watch it reappear on the other side of the bridge and go
sailing away amongst the petals of may blossom. Then
he took a deep breath, began to whistle and strode off
into the shrubbery. He was running by the time he
reached the path skirting the house and appeared at the
kitchen door. They had a cook, an unshapely Salopian
with the unlikely name of Pansy. He grabbed her round
the waist from behind and, amidst her shrieks of femi-
nine alarm, she said, 'How's Hitler?'

'A worried man, Pansy. Could we have drop scones
and how's the cat?'

After that, the Shropshire dusk closed in on them all,
soft and subtle, benighting lightless villages and farms.
But always there were dreams, and out of the horror of
the falling mosquito, surfaced the Waterwitch and Gina
Deverel with her tangled mane of red-gold hair.

Wing Commander North had known that this would be
a difficult interview; he was not disillusioned. Leader of
the St. Keyne Strike Wing he had always prided himself
on his consideration for the men under his command; had
tried where possible to equate their needs with the
demands made upon him by the RAF. Faced now with
this mutinous young man, he felt an abject failure. A few
days ago, Rob Ashley had been a happy-go-lucky young-

ster, possessed of a boundless energy, hardly masked by a studied indolence. He was also one of North's best pilots, well-suited to the Strike Wing. The death of his Navigator had shaken him up badly and on his return from survivor's leave North had decided that, for his own safety, he should be rested for a few weeks at a training unit – a desk job until he felt more his own self – was how North had put it. He did not expect rapturous approval of his plan but neither had he been prepared for the impassioned torrent of reasons Ashley put forward for staying with the Squadron. North was alarmed. Faced with authority, Ashley was never a man of many words and they were usually succinct and very much to the point. He was not an emotional young man but he had almost pleaded to be allowed to stay on flying duty.

'I've lost my Nav, my best mate, now you want to take me away from the only thing I've got left!' He fingered the cherished Wings Brevet, stitched above the pocket on his left breast. 'You can't do this to me, Sir. It's just relegating me to the scrap-heap!'

'It's for your own good,' North said calmly.

'That's not true, not if you think about it. I need to get back at something. Gerry is as good a target as any!'

North said. 'Up at Tarningwell you'll be carrying on the fight, perhaps in a less spectacular way. We can't all have glamour jobs. There is a great deal of satisfaction to be had from a job done conscientiously and.....'

Ashley's expletive was memorable. It was the first time North could remember it having been used to his face. 'Will you repeat that!' he thundered.

Ashley shook his bronze head with a ghost of the old light in the green-hazel eyes. 'Christ, Sir, it was enough of a gamble using it the first time!' he said and grinned then.

North grunted. 'Get out, Rob. You're on light flying duties for a week whilst your position is reviewed. In all conscience, I cannot inflict you upon Group Captain Alloway up at Tarningwell. He deserves better of me. You are temporarily reprieved.'

Ashley saluted, rather smartly for him, and got out whilst the going was good.

Now the seven days were up and they faced each other again. North shuffled through his paperwork.

'B Flight, Grayling Squadron, is sending a section on secondment to a forward station in preparation for the big push when it eventually comes. We have one pilot already on the station. You will fly out with Flight Lieutenant Partington. You will team up with your new Nav at your posting. Partington has had a hard time of it lately; it will give you both a chance to get your bearings again.'

'Where is it then, Sir, Baffin Island?'

North ignored the taunt. 'There will be coastal sorties, perhaps ground exercises, that sort of thing, but mainly you'll preserve yourselves for things to come.'

'Kipper Patrols!' said Ashley scornfully. 'The greatest indignity! Where in hell's name are we going, Sir?'

Wing Commander North had the grace to lower his eyes as he said. 'Nanvallock. No need to pack tropical kit.'

'Is this a joke, Sir? No it isn't, you're serious! That wilderness of mud! Have you ever flown in there, Sir? It's an awful place.' North was angry now. 'If you're so pernickety about what you do why did you volunteer for service? I've got no time for you. I've gone to great lengths to keep you flying – I may say against my better judgement. You fly out tomorrow. I hope that will give you time to get kitted out.'

'Kitted out, Sir? I don't understand. I can see we might need snorkels but...'

'Congratulations, Rob, your Commissions through. I shall expect a drink tonight – Pilot Officer Ashley.'

'Strewth, I didn't want that at all! It was Archie's idea. Archie liked the ring to it. How bloody ironic. He's gone and I've got to go it alone!'

North said. 'You understand now why some time away from St. Keyne is politic; a move from the Sergeants' Mess, new beginnings. At Nanvallock you'll be able to adjust.'

Ashley nodded uncertainly. 'I must have appeared an ungrateful sod lately. I just don't seem to have known how to handle things since – you know. At least I'll be out of your hair!'

'Good luck, Rob. You're still part of the Strike Wing, still under my aegis if I can be of any help......'

'Yes, Sir. Thank you, Sir.' He saluted and left the office.

The sun was going down, angry and red in the wind-torn sky. He strolled over to the Nissen hut that made up the air-crew billets and leant against the end wall. 'What will I do with a handle? It was going to be a game. D'you remember? Now I've got to go solo.' But there was no answer, not even Lorimer's mocking laugh.

'Talking to yourself, old chap? That will never do,' said Peter Partington. Hear you've got something to cele-brate.' So Ashley proceeded to get tanked up. They toasted his promotion. They toasted the move to Nanval-lock. They toasted the C.O. and the King and Winston Churchill and when there was no one left it didn't matter. But drinking was not proving the panacea it used to be and Ashley lay awake for a long while in the hut he was to share for the last time with the Sergeant Pilots and Navigators of St. Keyne. He wished he could bury his head in the pillow and howl like a child but the RAF billeting arrangements didn't allow for such luxuries, so he tried to focus particularly on the morning, on Nanvallock perched on its cliff top, on Station Commander Michael O'Neill, the Crimson Pirate, and nemesis of his boyhood, on the droopy, desultory P.O. Todd and the Amazonian Sgt. Douglas and her curious coven of WAAFS. 'Oh, brave new world that has such people in it!' Said Archie's voice in his head and Archie's laughter seemed to fill the hut. But the next bed was empty, its mattress and blankets stacked neatly, awaiting the next occupant.

Nanvallock on a wet afternoon in early June was little improvement upon the wild night a few weeks before when Ashley and Lorimer had made their emergency let-down and spent such an uncomfortable night in the Watch Office. The cloud base was low; the seas were mountainous and slate dark, the limestone cliffs jagged and inhospitable. Peter Partington with Flying Officer Hugh Daylesford, his Navigator, had arrived ahead of Ashley who had spent the morning assembling his new uniform and now felt distinctly uncomfortable and self-conscious as he stepped from the cockpit of V-Victor, assigned to him after the demise of K-King. V-Victor, he mused, had a lucky ring to it.

A corporal fitter saluted as Ashley stepped onto terra firma; a dark, curly-haired young man of his own age with a lugubrious face. But he offered to unload Ashley's kit and said. 'If you're reporting in to the Watch Office, Sir, you'll likely hit tea-break.'

Ashley thanked him and thought, 'tea! Could this be the high spot of their day?' He crossed the field, eventually forced to abandon the idea of circumnavigating mud, puddles and pot-holes. Perhaps it was going to be better for his image if his new uniform acquired a lived-in look as soon as possible. Half way up the stairs he met a young WAAF officer. She was of medium height and well-rounded, her blonde hair was brushed into an immaculate and shining bob which curled under at jaw-level. Her pink complexion deepened to a rosy red.

'Rob Ashley, ma'am. I guess I'm expected,' he said as they hedged about on the staircase.

'Oh gosh, yes, of course! Come and have a cuppa. The C.O.'s off the field; back this evening. Leslie's patrolling something vital and your chums are getting settled in. I expect you could do with putting your feet up.'

Ashley grinned. 'I've only flown in from St. Keyne, ma'am, not the North Pole!'

'Yes, of course, how silly of me! And you can't call me ma'am all the time. For the record, I'm Section Officer Felicity Hardy – as in Nelson.'

'Oh, yes, I see *Kiss me Hardy* and all that?'

'I'm not used to offers on such short acquaintance,' smiled Felicity. 'My chums call me Felix.'

Ashley wondered how chummy he was to become. He could see Miss Hardy on a spirited hunter, jacket buttoned tightly over her ample bosom, hard hat well down over the golden bob. She opened a door and motioned him inside. 'This is the de-briefing room; small and cosy after St. Keyne, isn't it? The chairs are more comfortable than those in the Watch Office next door. Here's the tea; shall I be mother?'

'Thank you. Two sugars. Are there many of you here?'

'Many of us?' Felicity looked at him blankly from round, china-blue eyes.

'WAAF officers.' Ashley stirred his tea.

'Oh, gracious me, no! I'm *the* WAAF officer. I also assist with de-briefing. Not that there's much activity just now. We all muck in here, Rob.'

Ashley thought mucking out might be more Miss Hardy's style. He had received two disappointments in one blow. There was to be no bevy of lissom young officers to flit about him and flying was the least thing that appeared to be of importance at Nanvallock. Felicity seemed to sense his disillusionment.

'You'll soon settle in. The C.O.'s rather a rum chap, takes a little getting used to. The Padre's a honey. The air crew you know, of course and, as for NCOs, we've got a grand bunch. Then there are my girls, the place would just wind up without Sergeant Douglas.'

'I can imagine,' said Ashley faintly. 'Thanks very much for the tea and the gen. I'd better sling my hammock. I take it aircrew billets are off the drome?'

'Oh gosh, you don't know, of course, you couldn't. It's not usual for these days, of course, we must be pretty unique, I suppose.'

'Miss Hardy, Felicity that is, could you spell it out with coloured bricks?'

She looked apologetic. 'Aircrew are all billeted on the station, have been since '41 when Jerry took out a flight of Spits with a stick of bombs because there was no-one near enough to get them off the ground.'

Ashley shrugged. 'Seems fair enough.'

'But you don't see. You have to bivouac, as it were; one tent per crew. Still you've missed the bad weather. Leslie Todd is a martyr to chilblains.'

'I don't believe this!' said Ashley. 'Isn't there anywhere in the village could put us up?'

'The NCOs and the Erks are in the village. It's not a very large village; they mess in the Methodist Hall. No, the C.O. thinks life under canvas will help simulate possible conditions on the Continent when the Invasion starts. He has a fairly low opinion of junior officers.'

'I can imagine,' said Ashley dryly.

'Oh, you'll like him. Cheer up, Rob. There're a couple of good pubs in Trevander, only a couple of miles over the headland, or if you fancy a trip into the village there's the Copper Kettle. Mrs Tregonza still manages to provide really scrummy cream teas.'

'Yes,' said Ashley 'after a morning on Kipper Patrol and an afternoon fighting with tent pegs in the middle of an ocean of mud, I'll be ready for a scrummy tea, I'll probably be ready to tell Mrs Bun the Baker's Wife where she can stuff her hot-buttered scones!'

'Oh, gosh,' said Felicity – this seemed to be her standard utterance, 'you really are down in the dumps, old man. Now, I've got to fly. Have a canter round, why not, get your bearings?' She left him quite suddenly at the gallop.

The future looked bleak. His worst fears were being surpassed. Life under canvas, he reflected gloomily, might have appealed to Rudolph Valentino, surrounded by thinly clad Turkish Delight, but what had Nanvallock to offer; the equine Felicity - and Sergeant Douglas. He doubted whether a whole bale of gauze and a tea chest of spangles would have transformed those two into husky-voiced houris.

He left the Control Tower and wandered toward a distant field where a third tent was mushrooming, encouraged no doubt by the damp in the atmosphere. The Corporal Fitter who had unloaded his kit from V-Victor stepped forward and saluted smartly again. 'Just putting up your bivvy now, Sir.'

'Thanks. I could have managed. Son of Hiawatha, that's me!'

The young man looked worried. 'Officers don't erect their own tents, Sir.'

'Don't they? Seems it'll be the only thing I do get erected round here!' Ashley retorted rather sulkily. There was a squeal of laughter from beneath the rising canvas and an overalled figure wriggled out backwards, clutching a large mallet.

'LACW Nesbit's a girl, Sir,' said the corporal in shocked tones.

'LACWs usually are, Duffy,' said the owner of the mallet getting to her feet and running a muddy hand through a head of short blonde curls. Ashley had a sudden flash back to rag curlers and outsize gumboots.

'I'm sorry,' he said lamely.

'That's all right, Sir, I'm not straight off the farm. Give me a hand, Duffy.'

'Officers and gentlemen!' scoffed Ian Duff from the shelter of the canvas. That one's not a proper officer, anyone can see.'

'Stop scowling, Duffy. He's got the DFC. That indicates deeds of daring-do at least.'

'It's the DFM.'

'Don't split hairs, now back off whilst I swing the hammer!'

'Susan, watch out!'

'I am watching out, there's nothing for miles,' said the blonde walking backwards into a guy rope and tottering precariously. The entire structure collapsed and she ended in a huddle amid the canvas. Ashley grinned and bent to haul her to her feet.

'Now perhaps I can take over.'

'Officers don't …' began Susan.

'Oh, this one does,' said Ashley. 'Perhaps you could rustle up some cha, Miss er…'

'Nesbit. I'm not on cookhouse duty, Sir.' She had a strong Cockney accent.

'What do you do then, apart from demolition jobs?'

Susan Nesbit gritted her teeth, tossed her head and marched off in the direction of the admin buildings. Ian Duff, puffing and panting on the other side of the deflated canvas said, with a hint of triumph in his voice, 'LACW Nesbit is your Flight Mechanic – Engine, Sir.'

'Bloody hell!' said Ashley. 'You're kidding. I know that women are acting as fitters at some training establishments but not on operational stations!'

Duff gave him a twisted smile, 'you forget, Sir, we were a training unit. Susan and I are left over, anachronisms you might say. They forgot us and we don't want anyone reminding them.'

'Nor anyone queering your pitch,' thought Ashley. 'But don't worry, Corporal. You've no competition for your grubby little blonde.' He set off toward the Watch Office, no happier about the Station and its strange occupants.

It was raining now and the mist was rolling in from the moors, imprisoning them for the night. He found Peter Partington, Leslie Todd and their two navigators and learnt that the officers messed at Tredega Farm and that there was a truck to take them back and forth. Supper was a tasty hotpot, followed by a huge slice of apple pie and cream. Ashley began to relax, lulled toward sleep by the warm meal and the scent of wood smoke curling out from the old brick grate.

Leslie Todd said, 'Would one of you chaps do Duty Officer for us tonight? Bill and I could do with a night on the town.' He looked across at the newcomers expectantly, like a spaniel that goes to fetch its lead in the hope of a walk.

'Shall we toss for it?' asked Hugh Daylesford? He was Partington's navigator, a likeable young man, tall and very fair, a foil for Peter's saturnine, dark looks, the side of his face badly scarred by burns gained in a dog-fight back in '40. Partington had had a long struggle to get back to flying.

They tossed twice. Ashley lost on the second throw. He had known he would. It was that kind of a day. They dropped him off at the Watch Office and he waved them away to the dubious delights of the fleshpots of Trevander. The darkness was complete now. He settled into a chair and let Peggy Pagett make him a cup of tea. Then they sat and chatted companionably enough for an hour or so whilst she took out a ball of wool and the front half of a sugar-pink jersey. There was no activity until the C.O. called them up and Peggy dropped the pink ball and became an efficient voice over the ether. She phoned down to the caravan near the end of Runway Two and had them light the flare path. Someone fired off a green Very cartridge as a signal to land and the old Oxford touched down and seemed to disappear into the mist. Peggy yawned and folded her knitting:

'I'm off duty now, Sir. I'll make another pot of tea and leave you to entertain the C.O.'

Ashley thanked her absently and leant back in his chair, hands clasped behind his head. He came to attention when Michael O'Neill appeared. The C.O. returned his salute and stomped the well-worn path to the stove. Today, swathed in an extra large sheepskin jacket, collar up, he was less of the Crimson Pirate, more Eskimo Nell.

'There's some tea in the pot, Sir,' suggested Ashley.

'Good show! Quiet night, is it?'

'Very quiet, Sir.'

'I suppose I should say 'Welcome aboard'.' O'Neill hooked a chair leg with the nearest flying boot and dragged it toward him. Then he let his eyes rove over the boy; over Diana's step-son. Gone was the slim, leggy schoolboy with the flop of hair which always fell forward over his forehead and provided him with the nervous mannerism of a toss of the head. He seemed sturdy enough, bright eyed and bushy tailed. He didn't want another one like Pilot Officer Todd. But it was to be remembered that here was one of Dick North's lame ducks. The boy wasn't showing signs of battle fatigue or whatever it had been. The square brown hand that poured Peggy's thick, dark brew from the big crock pot was steady enough. The boy had a handsome face; mouth styled for indolence; jaw for aggression; straight nose, clear brown eyes and too many freckles for a man of twenty four. He took the offered cup.

'I think you may find life here a trifle tame but that is not to say that I encourage slackness. What we perform I like to think we perform well. None of us takes kindly to passengers.'

'No, Sir. I hope there'll be a chance for some action. I was on Rangers.'

'Oh, I know all about you, laddie. O'Neill went over to his desk and pulled out a file from the middle of a skyscraper of paperwork. He flicked at the corner of a sheet:

'Your flying capabilities are not in doubt. A certain reputation seems to have preceded you.'

'Oh, thank you, Sir.' Ashley relaxed. O'Neill wandered back and sat down, legs stretched before him, head and neck sunk into his sheepskin collar. He raked his subordinate from head to foot. Ashley had the grace to look a little embarrassed. He put up his left hand and fingered the violet and white medal ribbon on his left breast. The C.O. gave him a twisted smile. 'Christ, not that! They're two-a-penny these days.' He had been leaning back in his chair, balanced upon the back legs. Suddenly, he shot forward, almost catapulting himself out. Ashley jumped violently.

'When I used the word 'reputation', laddie, I was never further from the clouds. I was very definitely at ground level, a certain earthiness creeping into my musings.'

Ashley thought: 'I don't understand a word he's jabbering about. Who called him Mad Michael? Perhaps he is mad.' He only said politely, 'I don't catch your drift, Sir.'

'Come a little closer and bend an ear.' O'Neill crooked a finger. 'A bit of a hell-raiser, are we?'

'I don't know, Sir, sometimes maybe.'

'Well, we'll not dwell on that as long as it's confined to off-the-field activities; as long as there's no dragging this station into disrepute. You have the King's Commission, just see you remember that and bear yourself accordingly.'

'Churchillian echoes,' though Ashley. 'Who does he think he is?' He was seething with resentment. 'Is that all for now – Sir?' But O'Neill appeared not to have heard him, he was rambling on:

'I have to consider my girls, Miss Hardy's girls. We are fortunate indeed to have these young ladies, banished as we are to this outpost of empire, this South-West Frontier. Miss Hardy's integrity is her own armour, but the others – Sergeant Douglas as Watch Keeper, Corporal Pagett as Radio Telegraphist are excellent workers; LACW Nesbit on the Flights – absolutely indispensable. I do not intend to have anyone rocking the boat, not even a dreamy Salopian with bedroom eyes and –'

'All right!' Said Ashley.

'Now we are through the formalities, a thousand welcomes! How are they all at Uppington Magna? Good god, boy, you're not going to take me seriously, are you? You're out of the thick of it for a while. Cornwall is to be enjoyed. It's halcyon days, laddie, halcyon days!'

CHAPTER EIGHTEEN

Ashley awoke to find a triangle of sunlight framed by his gaping tent-flap. Somewhere, a cow was lowing and there were birds singing their aftermath to the dawn chorus. A cock crowed from the direction of Nanvallock village. All the sounds of a country idyll assaulted his ears. He lay flat on his back, arms behind his head and sniffed at the spring air, stretching his limbs. This was a new day, the first day of a new life. It was the first time he had found himself coming out of the shadows cast by Archie's death. He would make the most of the country air, the village pubs, the cosy cafes and tucked away farmhouses. This was a corner of England only glimpsed from the air. Or was it England at all? The war had receded in the hours since V-Victor had landed on Runway Three. He had surely done his bit, why chafe at inactivity? But his blood was stirring as surely as sap in the misshapen hawthorn which sheltered their tents from the South Westerlies. He would have to be up and doing.

After breakfast at the farmhouse and the bumpy ride back down the long track to the Station, he decided to walk out to his dispersal and carry out some ground tests on V-Victor. LAC Duff and Susan Nesbit were pouring over a tattered diagram spread out on an old wooden crate and weighted at the corners with pieces of rock. Their conversation was low, earnest and very technical.

'Morning Duffy, morning Susan,' said Ashley cheerfully and slapped his engine mechanic on her round, overalled rear. The girl gave an undignified yelp. 'Oh, it's you, Sir!'

Ian Duff's face darkened with anger. 'Look here, Sir, LACW Nesbit is doing a fine job here, a man's job some might say, but that's no reason you shouldn't allow her the respect due to a lady!' They stood eyeing each other warily. Behind Duff, Susan was signalling that he should be silent and keep out of it.

Ashley shrugged his shoulders. 'Okay. You're quite right Corporal.' He turned to the girl. 'I'm sorry, Susan. No offence was meant.'

'Oh, none taken, Sir,' said the girl chirpily but when he had wandered away to prowl about V-Victor, making external checks, she ran to Duff and threw her arms about his neck:

'Duffy, you were wonderful sticking up for me to an officer, just like the knights of old. You don't know how good it makes a girl feel! You shall be dubbed my official champion!'

'I'll always be your champion, Susie,' said Duff rather gruffly. 'Now, let's get back to work, shall we?'

That afternoon, Ashley's Navigator arrived, ferried in from Kent. Geoffrey Blennerhasset was tall, fair and aristocratic. He seemed to have been born into the officer class. It would have been impossible to have imagined him in the ranks. His course through life could be plotted accurately without a glance at his Service Record; Prep School, Public School, Oxbridge. He introduced himself to Ashley as they walked across to their bivouacs.

'Geoffrey Blennerhasset, Geoff if you like though my friends call me 'Goofy'. It started at Prep School, the teeth, you know.' Ashley shot him a sidelong glance. 'I'm quite used to it now. Is this our bivvy? I didn't bargain for being under canvas but I shall enjoy it enormously; shades of all those Scout Camps at Ilfracombe.' He sat on his mattress and began bouncing like a child to get the feel of it.

'You outrank me,' said Ashley suddenly. 'I never thought of that happening.'

'Don't think about it now. Up aloft you're skipper. Down here you'd better not throw your weight around. We should get along all right; I'm the easy-going sort, line of least resistance and all that. I save my ardour for Gerry. What happened to your last Nav? How d'you get split up?'

Ashley said. 'I killed him,' and walked out into the sunlight.

With Nanvallack receding behind him and June sun above, Ashley set out to explore the coastline toward Trevander. Gone were the mists which had heralded his arrival, the sky was pure blue, deep as cornflowers, the sea, green at the cliff foot, spread out toward the horizon streaked with patches of Homer's wine darkness and, everywhere, the light coruscated on the ridges of tiny listless waves; a thousand scintillating points of sunshine.

The cliff path cut a sandy swathe through deep sweet-smelling banks of grasses, sewn with a living tapestry of flowers; campions, pink as raspberries and cream; tiny blue scabious like miniature pin cushions; the white stars of stitchwort; rambling purple vetches; the tall bell-towers of early foxgloves and, always before him, danced flights of June-happy butterflies, weaving a soundless song, mad with the delight of being. And Ashley was happy too. How could he not be? He followed a winding rabbit track down from the cliff, cutting through arched tunnels of gorse and brambles until he found himself on a tiny beach. The sand was the colour of ripe peaches and the ebbing tide was sucking its way out to sea, leaving a causeway of flat grey rocks steaming in the sun. Here there was no barbed wire, no reminder of the war, no fear of invasion.

Ashley stripped off his uniform and stretched out on one of the smooth warm slabs, head on arms, eyes half closed, squinting sideways at the wheeling gulls as their shadows criss-crossed his body. The retreating tide lulled him into sleep.

Gina Deverel came upon him quite unawares. She had taken the same path, slithering down through sand and shale, a loose robe over her green swimming costume. He had startled her, lying there, turning the blood in her veins to ice-water. For a moment she had feared that this was a man taken by the sea and as roughly rejected, spat up at the high tide. She stood over him uncertainly, glad that he was alive as she was to enjoy such a perfect day. And then with a second jolt of her heart she realised that she knew him, recognised the dark lashes lying lightly on the freckled cheeks. The breeze ruffled his bronzy hair but did not wake him so she dared to appraise his naked length. They still spoke of him down in Trevander, the 'boy from the sea' and went on wishing him well. For a tiny community they had lost so many sons and this one, snatched back from the jaws of hell, must stay alive, must prove a talisman for them all. She was miles away, watching the sand flies flicking about his bare toes. She did not know that he had woken and was watching her with amusement rather than embarrassment.

'And does Grace Darling approve what she sees?' he asked on a laugh. 'Does sea wrack bestow ownership on its retriever?'

'Oh, always,' said Gina 'and I'm sorry; it was rude of me to stare but I thought for a moment you had washed in on the making tide. Have you come for a swim? This is a wonderful spot. No one comes here. That is, no one did until…'

'And I can neither swim nor retreat,' grinned Ashley 'unless you turn your back. I shall have to lie here and grill in the noon sun like a saint on a griddle!'

Gina smiled. 'I shall close my eyes and count to ten. That will give you time to make for the sea but not time enough to scramble for your clothes.'

'La Belle Dame sans Merci. Then I shall lie here until I blister unless you promise to join me in the water of course.'

'That is what I came for,' said Gina. 'I can't trudge all the way up the cliff again without a dip.' She sat down on the edge of his rock, eyes tightly shut. 'One, two – I'm counting, Rob Ashley, three, four – Oh!' Her lids fluttered open to find that he was leaning over her, eyes narrowed, face faunlike in the sunshine.

'*And there I kissed her wild, wild eyes with kisses four!*' He had only touched her lightly on the forehead, a mere brush of his lips. Now his hands were upon her shoulders and he was kissing her half-closed lids, more assured now, before his lips slid down to hers and fastened hungrily upon them and he was kneeling on the warm rock, pulling her back against his nakedness before letting her go and sprinting for the waves. It was a long time before she plucked up courage to join him.

Halfway between the shore and the sea she stopped abruptly. 'Oh, he is not Lanty,' she thought and then 'neither do I wish him to be. He is Rob Ashley and I am falling in love with him.'

After that he became a familiar figure about the streets of Trevander; down on the harbour passing the time with the oldsters, carrying shopping for Aunt Pog, hastening through the gardens of Fosfelle, dusty with flower pollen, salt in his hair, the taste of it on his skin. Lowena was cool towards him. She did not know why. He was a bright, personable young man and Gina was very much in love. He came from a good, yet unpretentious country family. He was, by all accounts, a hero. But there was something about him which made her uneasy. She discussed it with George who told her they were middle-aged fancies and did she want Gina on the shelf? But the feeling would not go away and eventually Lowena took to avoiding the young airman. She wondered if Rob found it strange that so often as he and Gina, hand in hand, were making their way, lingering through the garden, stopping at every viewpoint to gaze across the harbour, she and George would be trudging down, bent on a long visit to Pog and Cynthia up at Penolva or off to call on the vicar, a visit that could not possibly be postponed! Lowena would fix the young man with a steely glint in her eye and George would shrug his shoulders apologetically and suck harder at his pipe. And so it was that they often had Fosfelle to themselves; the house, dark and cool with everywhere the scent of roses drifting in from the open windows.

Gina's room, nestling under the eaves, looked out over the harbour and beyond to the horizon. In Dr.

Boase's day this had been the nursery. Annabel's rocking horse, battered but unbowed, stood in a corner surrounded by the flotsam and jetsam of her grand-daughter's childhood; green witch balls - the floats from abandoned nets; boxes of shells and dusty boys' adventure books. Not for Gina 'Angela Brazil' and the laughing chums of cliff top boarding schools but gold tooled, leather bound copies of Kidnapped and Treasure Island, The Swiss Family Robinson and Moonfleet. But it was not a boy's room. The dressing table boasted a jumble of pots and potions, there was a healthy amount of lace on the pillowslips and the pretty patchwork quilt had been lovingly stitched by Aunt Pog from snippets of their combined rag bags. Gina had always thought that Margaret Toller's dreams were stitched up amongst the coloured squares. There had been a man at the beginning of this war, and they had exchanged promises before he went away to die in Africa, dashing the late flowering of Pog's hopes of marriage and family. She had turned to socks; they were safer. No-one ever dropped stitches of hope into a turned heel. She was good old Aunt Pog from now to eternity.

Gina smoothed out the quilt idly with a shiver. She had lost Lanty; she would not lose Rob too and end like Pog. She kicked off her shoes and sank down onto the bed, drawing him down beside her until he was tangled in the witchery of the red gold hair, seduced by the gleam of her white body. And round the tilted eaves the gulls wheeled and dipped, frenzied and disorientated, and far below the faint chug of an engine heralded the return of the fleet. Somewhere, the drone of a plane brought Ashley down to earth and reality.

'Marry me, Gina, marry me soon!'

'Oh, I'll think about it,' she teased him. 'I'll need a ring, of course. You'll need to go up country for a ring, Plymouth maybe.'

'Won't you settle for a kiss in earnest, just for today?' His lips had found her breasts again. She smiled into the darkness where the bright dust motes shafted in rainbow colours from the little window:

'Oh, kisses are two a penny, I must have a pledge!'

'This, then.' He had reached for his tunic and taken a small cardboard box from his inside pocket. The lid was broken at the corners and as he held it aloft the contents tumbled between them.

'An earring and only one? Queried Gina. 'Where is its fellow?'

'Who knows? Somewhere across the world, I imagine.'

'And you carry it with you. It's so beautiful; I've never seen anything so intricate.'

'It belonged to my mother, my real mother,' said Ashley 'she had it of my father. He promised to match it with its fellow but she never saw him again. He died at sea before they could marry, before I was born. I told you that I was adopted by my aunt and uncle? My mother thought she was doing the best she could in giving me up. She was a lady; she would have been an outcast. Richard and Jenny Jane couldn't have children of their own so they adopted me. So my mother became my aunt. I loved both of them, Jenny Jane and Aunt Jacquie. She never did marry; she stayed true to the memory of my father. He was an Australian, fought at Pozieres in the Great War. This is all I have to connect with him. Keep it until I have a ring.'

Gina nodded. 'I'll wear it round my neck. I'll keep it safe for you. But we are engaged, aren't we? I can at least tell mother and father?'

'Oh, tell the world. But I'll need to ask the C.O.'s permission so don't let it go any further than your parents for a few days.'

'Mum's the word then. I've no coupons for a wedding dress and what about the cake? All that sugar! You'd better go before the parents get back.'

'Shouldn't I see your father to ask for your hand in marriage or do the Cornish do things differently?'

'Its mother who needs placating in this family,' said Gina, dressing hurriedly. 'I do love you, Rob Ashley but will you go! I won't come down but I'll watch from the window, I promise.' They kissed again and he left, closing the door behind him. She watched him thread his way beneath the tamarisks until he was out of sight then sat down again and held her treasure up to the light so that the fires sprang from the tiny diamonds. There were no presentiments then to clutch at her heart. She only closed the window because the breeze was chilly.

Lowena stared down at the jet and diamond ear bob lying in her daughter's palm and she was not there at all, not sitting in the garden at Fosfelle under the tamarisks with Annabel's garden a waving sea of colour all about her. She was up at the old stones above the village with a brash young Australian who was dangling just such a jewel before her as he had proffered its fellow to Lady Jacqueline Lambe.

'Mam, what is it?' Gina used the term of endearment rarely. Lowena had never been the sort of parent other girls had, the comfortable shapeless sort of matron who laughed a lot, wore floral pinnies and answered to epithets like Mum and Mummy. She was as slim as she had been at twenty, just as beautiful and just as remote.

'God, Gina, how can I tell you? How do I explain after all these years? You cannot marry that boy. You have to believe me when I tell you it is impossible!'

'Because you dislike him so? Because you always have?'

'No, not that. He reminded me of someone, someone from another world almost. What can I do to make you see?'

'You could tell me the truth,' said Gina. 'It won't make an atom of difference, of course, but you could try.'

'Then go into the house and bring me my jewel box. The key is in the top drawer of my dressing table. Go now whilst your father is in his study. Oh, he knows what I must tell you but he has no need to hear the story again. He has blotted it out well enough all these years. Go quickly!'

She watched Gina climb the steps to the terrace, not as light of foot as when she had sought her out, fresh from the arms of her young lover. Oh yes, Lowena knew that they were lovers, Gina's eyes gave her secret away and the glow of her skin. She returned with an old wooden box. Johnny Fortnight had made it for his daughter for her sixteenth birthday and she would always treasure it. Lowena placed it beside her on the garden bench.

'I should have told you long ago but somehow it was never the right moment. Gina, George is not your father. I was pregnant when I married him. He knew and he accepted you and has loved you as his own. Your own father died, before you were born.'

Gina was silent for a long time. It was a shock, of course it was, but what difference could it make now to her and to Rob Ashley?

'Who was my father?' she asked simply. One of the boats had just come in and the gulls set up a mocking cacophony far below them in the harbour.

'He called himself Alfie O'Brien; he was a young Australian serviceman, demobbed from the Great War. He was your Uncle Drew's companion all through their wartime escapes. I didn't really love him and I was promised to your father but it happened. Alfie O'Brien was a Toller; his father was born here, up at Penolva, and was brother to Frank Toller, your grandmother's first husband, he who died of the typhus.'

Gina frowned, mentally composing a family tree. 'So this man, this Alfie, my real father, was your cousin?'

'Step cousin really.'

'But that's not blood related. What has he to do with Rob Ashley? You must tell me!'

Lowena was opening the jewel casket; a jumble of trinkets and her wedding pearls. She took out a small mother-of-pearl box and opened it. Lying on a square of white satin lay the fellow to Gina's gift from Ashley. She lifted it out and compared the two. They were identical.

'It's a coincidence, it has to be!' cried Gina.

Lowena shook her head. 'Ask him his father's name if he knows it. Then give him back his bauble and forget him.'

'Mother, I love him, I shall never love anyone else. I shan't get a third chance to snatch at happiness. What does it matter, it's all so long ago!'

'Girl, he's your brother – well, half brother. You can't marry your brother!'

'I don't care. I need not tell him. How can he find out if we both keep quiet?'

'You love him and would do that to him?'

'Then I will explain. I will tell him that it doesn't matter, that I don't care!'

'I will not let you do it.' Lowena retrieved her earring and locked the casket. 'I shall not keep silent for you. Who will marry the two of you?'

'We could go away after the war, somewhere where no one would ever know. Perhaps we won't marry at all.'

'You would be your brother's mistress. Gina, see sense. What will be left when the passion subsides – guilt and subterfuge? You cannot build a life on that!' But Gina was already fleeing down the path to the Strand and along past Penolva and up to the cliffs. Eventually, unknowingly, she found herself up at the Stones and flung herself down in the dark grasses, her mind in turmoil. She did not know the irony of coming to this place, the place of her own conceiving. The very stones must have been mocking her. Of course, being Gina, full of common sense and a decent honesty, she had to seek her lover out. She poured out the story down in the fo'c'sle of the Waterwitch, in the stifling heat of a July day. It took a long time for it to sink in, a long time before he said. 'My father's name was O'Brien, Alfred T. O'Brien. He drowned at sea, the Cornish sea.' And in that moment Gina knew she had lost him. The Shropshire Lad who had spent so many years fighting the vicar father who was not his father had after all absorbed too many Christian scruples, tucked away in the old grey vicarage at Uppington Magna. He was slipping away from her as he talked, even as, in her distress, he loved her more than he had ever loved her.

And afterwards, Consuela's earring back in his tunic pocket, he returned to Nanvallock. He spent the next few weeks wooing Susan Nesbit from Ian Duff, the man who really loved her. He married his little blonde engine mechanic that September by special licence. After that, the war hotted up again.

Susan stayed at Nanvallock when, in November, Ashley was posted to Woodhall Spa as part of the Mosquito Marker Force for the Lancasters of Conyngsby. Ashley and Goofy Blennerhasset were happy to work alone. The Lancasters left the base an hour before the lone Mosquito became airborne. It was to be a three hour sortie to drop red and yellow target indicators for the Lancaster force. Their target was the Mittelland Canal near Gravenhorst, close where it joined the Dortmund Ems Canal. Here they could wreak havoc on the arteries of Germany. The Dortmund Ems was a vast waterway running above the level of the surrounding countryside. Rivers meandered below its straight channel, roads passed beneath it. A strategic attack would flood the countryside and empty the canals, leaving the long barges stranded with their vital supplies for Hanover, Brunswick and Berlin.

The attack was successful if the loss of ten Lancasters and their crews could be deemed a success. It was several days later when Michael O'Neill, true to his word, drove down to Trevander to deliver Ashley's last letter to his half-sister. They sat in the parlour at Fosfelle whilst the rain lashed at the windows and the South Easterlies tore through the Coombes.

'Is there any hope, any hope at all?' asked Gina, hand shaking as she handed him a cup of tea; pretty china but not the comfortable mug of char he was used to, O'Neill reflected. He came to and said. 'I'm sorry, he dove straight in. There wouldn't be anything left.'

'And Goofy, did he get out?'

'No, they went in together.'

Gina did not ask if it was a quick death, to plunge burning to earthwards for such an eternity.

'He had a wife.'

'Oh, she'll get by; a plucky little thing.' He took his leave then, wondering why Ashley hadn't married her.

Gina stood for a long time at the window, looking out through the mist and the driving rain, gazing in the direction of Nanvallock. Oh why had they rescued him from the sea that day? Would it not have been better never to have known such pain? But she knew the answer. She saw a sunlit cove and Rob Ashley's young body naked on the rocks and felt his kisses on her upturned face; better to have loved and lost.... Having made such a decision Gina, who was after all a practical girl, set about building a future for herself.

PART VI

Magenta Minutes

Many a mad magenta minute
Lights the lavender of life.

— Sandys Wason

Chapter Nineteen

1962

There had never been a decade like the Sixties. Trevander had woken from post war austerity. She had slept through the gloom of its aftermath, endured rationing and boasted a thriving black market. Fishing had declined of course but there was still the pilchard fleet. Gone were the black bulwarks of the old luggers and the inner harbour boasted the bright hulls of crabbers and drifters in blues and greens and yellows, contrasting stripes on their rubbing strakes, blue and orange sails at their mizzens to keep them head to wind out in the bay. The old grey or white houses and cottages were being systematically given a lick of paint. Now they appeared in ice-cream colours; pinks and yellows and clotted creams. Along its length Fore Street sprouted new shop fronts; bright cafes; boutiques jam-packed with linen shift dresses – very Mary Quant - and figure moulding skinny-rib sweaters. There were gift shops, their racks crammed with picture postcards, spilling out buckets and spades and whirring windmills into the street outside. Down on the harbour, one enterprising young man had opened a stall, exuberant with looped garlands of coloured beads and cards of floral earrings; a must for sisters and cousins and aunts alike.

And through this heady, gaudy, noisy world strode David Maddaver. Pamela and Tim had married before the end of the war and David was their only child, a spoilt, handsome seventeen year old with exotic, Byronic good looks, whose inheritance was an elderly Cornish lugger and a taste for the dramatic.

Tim Maddaver had smoked himself into an early grave leaving Pamela, still as svelte and lovely as the day he had married her, to give her son everything he wanted and nothing that he really needed. It was David who organised the riotous summer bonfires on the beach and David, quiff a la Cliff Richard, who sat on the quay strumming moodily to a Spanish guitar, surrounded by an admiring string of teenage girls, all eager to become his backing group.

'The poor man's Adam Faith!' scoffed Shrimpy Varco. But if David had been cosseted and indulged by his bewitching mother, who had had him earmarked for a better life than the father who had lived out his own youth in brother Lanty's shadow, then others had seen to it that he at least learned his inherited trade at a young age.

Always in the background, waiting to pick up the pieces when Pammy's plans went awry, hovered Aunt George. Gina Deverel had never married. She had inherited Fosfelle when George and later Lowena died, had busied herself taking a full and active part in village life and had taken her cousin's son under her wing. Gina had lost two men to the war, one to die in her arms with a shell hole in his back, one to perish in flames in the immolation of a fighter bomber; a death even more cruel in her mind's eye because she was not there at the last to take some of his suffering onto herself. There would not be a third chance in life, not for happiness or, should it offer, she could not have brought herself to take the risk of jeopardising another man's life with the curse of her love. So the affection and the understanding she would have brought to a marriage with Lanty Maddaver or Rob Ashley had been transferred to Lanty's nephew, to Tim and Pamela's only son.

When he had been younger, David Maddaver had been keen to help crew the Waterwitch, to make up the lowliest fifth member of the crew; to brew the tea and singe the bacon; to hose fish scales from the deck; to pump the bilges; to spend hours with chapped fingers clearing the hooks when they went a long-lining. Maddaver was spared nothing in those early days and if Pamela had sought to rear a Little Lord Fauntleroy then Gina and the Cluetts had been determined that he would follow in the footsteps of Jim Hawkins and the boy heroes of their own childhood. When it rained – and it often rained, not the soft, silent Cornish rain of summer but chill winter downpours that seeped down the neck of the closest oilskins - they would go up to the attics at Fosfelle and rummage through old cabin trunks. Aunt George, as he always called her, would have to be Long John Silver on account of her gammy leg and he was usually Captain Hook, steering his way through a sea of crocodiles in search of parrot islands and palm trees. Between Aunt George and the Cluetts they made a competent Cornishman of Davey Maddaver with little he could not turn his hand to whether it was drifting for Pilchards in a stiff southerly, mackerel fishing in White-sand Bay, long-lining out beyond the Eddystone or dropping his strings of lobster pots amongst the rocks off Pellancarva. But David longed to spread his wings. He would stand on the cliffs beyond Penolva and sniff at the approaching spring and feel the life blood within him calling him to distant lands and far adventures. His companion in all his childhood escapades had been Alan Cluett, old Esco's great grandson, stolid, placid Alan, the hero-worshipping foil David badly needed in his life, though Alan's loyalty did not stop him giving sound advice or lecturing his friend when insanity threatened to pervade one of their ventures.

So the long hot summers drifted by and the fifties became the sixties. They were later to say that if you remembered the sixties you were not there. But the songs were always to be recalled; Frank Ifield's 'I remember You' bursting exuberantly from the doors of the Godolphin whilst, not to be outdone, Billy Fury's sultry tones assured all in hearing distance that 'Last Night was made for Love' as it drifted from the open windows of the Moonraker. Even sedate Mrs Tripconey at the Cosy Kettle allowed Perry Como's 'Caterina' and 'The March of the Siamese Children' to embellish the background to her Cornish teas. The Crabbers' Rest – drop in for drop outs as the locals called it – favoured Connie Francis spelling out V A C A T I O N; seemingly the limit of literacy amongst their clientele.

The beach parties went on until the autumn and 'Sealed with a Kiss' and 'Ginny Come Lately' were succeeded by 'It Might As Well Rain Until September'. But then it went on raining all through September and well into October.

David and Alan had helped to organize a folk evening at the Moonraker. It was to be the last such that season and had, in any case, been poorly attended but they still had to stay behind to clear up to worm another pint out of Dick Jerram, after which they grabbed leather jackets and, pulling their collars up against the onshore wind, took the steps up to the cliff to clear their heads and commiserate with each other over the dismal turn-out. Alan sat in one of the old huers' huts, legacy of seining days when a watch was set for the approaching pilchard shoals and a signal passed to the villagers below so that boats could be pushed off from the beach and the great seine nets stretched across the entrance to the outer harbour to trap the silver hoards.

David was pacing up and down in the rain giving one of his soliloquies. Alan had long ago learned to ignore these and to let him mutter and moan to his heart's content.

'I need to get away.' Maddaver stopped pacing and stood belligerently, framed in the hut entrance, a raging sea behind him. 'Nothing ever happens here any more.' And then, prophetically on cue, the maroons went off – a distress flare, its falling stars lighting the night sky. The two boys set off along the cliff path to find the best vantage point, peering vainly out to sea through the driving rain.

'Voices!' said Alan. 'I can actually hear voices! Come on!' But Maddaver had heard them too, far below them, words snatched away by the wind. Then the full moon tore a gap in the cloud mass and illuminated the battered hull of a once graceful sloop; mast severed and sail gone, a jagged hole in her superstructure just as if the rocks had already mauled her and cast her off again.

'Hello, anybody down there?' called Alan, cupping his hands and shouting at the boiling, frothing seas below him.

'Of course we're bloody well down here. Couldn't stay aboard that blasted sieve!' said a clear, angry young voice. 'Give us a hand will you!' And Alan came to, to see David already half way down the sloping cliff side, leaping from rocky outcrop to grassy hummock, agile as a mountain goat. Cluett was clumsier, slower.

The castaways were both young men around the thirty mark; the one dark and stocky, clinging to a rocky buttress, trying to keep upright, the other taller, fair-haired, wearing light coloured slacks and a sweater in Breton stripes, casually handsome. David put out a hand to help him across the foaming chasm between them, a lethal jump in the darkness.

'What took you so long?' asked Simon Bennetto.

Maddaver, irked by his tone said. 'Only a fool would sail so close to a lee shore. You're lucky you made it.'

'I couldn't agree more. But it's Charles' charter. Charles has already grovelled enough. Did you hear that Chas? The boy here thinks you're a fool. He is insured by the way. Is this a friend?' he glanced at Alan Cluett. 'Introductions can wait till later and is this really the best way up? All right, I'll keep quiet. I'd rather forgo another of those black-avised scowls of yours. Come along Charles, the pubs will be closed.'

'They are closed,' said Maddaver, triumph in his voice.

'Never mind. I have friends who will put me up and let me make free of their cellar. You won't need to offer me your sofa for the night. For God's sake Chas, keep up man!' At last they made the cliff top path and turned toward the lights of Trevander. 'We are enormously grateful in spite of the jibes,' said Bennetto. 'Without your help we'd still be down on those rocks. Dawn would have found us damp and somewhat chilly.'

'Dawn' said David ' would probably have found you somewhat dead, though it's surprising what a help the making tide is when you're stuck at the foot of a sheer cliff!'

'Then perhaps we owe you our lives. At least we owe you some civility. I'm Simon Bennetto,' he held out his hand. 'I'm in the process of buying Rosarrock. Impressed?'

'I might be,' said David, surprised by the firm handshake. Rosarrock was the largest house in Trevander in *the* prime spot; it had been built for a retired admiral who could never get used to life without a telescope clamped to one eye, so he built the house with perfect views both out to sea and across the village.

'Just a pied-a-terre really,' said Bennetto. 'The family home is outside St Mawes; it rambles rather. Mother – she was Romola Frayne by the way, *the* Romola Frayne – whilst perfectly divine, tends to cramp my style. Ah, I judge by your face that you have the same problem with yours. Now we have reached the parting of the ways, I see. I go up-along. Thank you once more, my young friend. No doubt we shall meet again before too long.' With a wave of his hand he was gone in the direction of Fore Street.

'What a prat!' said Alan. It was rather worrying that David did not reply at all!

And so Simon Bennetto came to Trevander and the Admiral's house was filled with rather arty furniture and a wide selection of Simon's friends. They were an eclectic bunch but all shared a desire to faun upon him, to hang on his every word, to accept the crumbs from his table. It had not taken Alan long to work out that whilst a number of beautiful women clung to his heels they never did so for long. His men friends were more constant. He was usually to be found propping up the bar in the Godolphin his entourage about him. And always, in the background, reluctantly spellbound by the laughter and the conversation, hovered David Maddaver. And sometimes Simon would deign to smile across at him or to wink conspiratorially and the boy would turn bright red and scowl back at him.

And then Simon, not content with the purchase of Rosarrock, bought a yacht. The Angel Clare was thirty foot long, thirty foot of gleaming, unflawed paintwork, two-masted and ketch-rigged; her streamlined hull was white, the coach roof a smart Oxford blue. Her name was emblazoned in bold letters on the canvas wind-breaks attached to the guardrails. When Simon first brought her into Trevander, sailing out of Fowey, they saw her from the cliffs, heeling to the wind, the light catching her shiny hull, bow lifting, sails leaning to the breeze. There was not a man or woman in Trevander who did not catch a breath. David Maddaver, used to the familiar comforting silhouette of the old Waterwitch with its scratched and peeling paintwork, fell head over heels in love with her on the spot.

Simon had a trip planned along the coast. He voiced his plans in the Godolphin. He would cruise around for a day or two, west to Falmouth and back taking in Fowey again, up to Plymouth and on to the South Hams to fashionable Salcombe, to Dartmouth with the Naval College clinging to the heights opposite dreamy Kingswear and up to Brixham. He rambled on and every place name he trotted out spilled forth a barrage of superlatives and made every harbour, every mooring sound as exiting as Valparaiso or Port au Prince. At the end, whilst he paused to reach out for a fresh glass pushed his way by another ardent fan, he said. 'Of course, I shall need a man to crew. I don't intend to do all the hard work myself. So dull, hauling on ropes and catting your own anchor. I'll need someone I can trust, of course, someone who knows the ropes very literally. I'm looking about me at the moment but don't pester me, any of you, I shall make my choice when I'm ready.' His eyes slid toward Maddaver. It was tantalising, perhaps it was cruel but from that day forward Maddaver had his mind set on the job. About the harbour more than ever, leaping from ship to shore, climbing a mast to replace a riding light, bronzed and half naked. Hauling down a bright blue mizzen sail, first to grab at a bow rope and hitch it to a capstan when the weekend sailors came in. No one in the world could have worked harder to catch at a dream than Davey Maddaver. Alan was worried and did not try to hide the fact.

Simon Bennetto, it was true, was tall, fair, tanned and athletic. He had all the attributes of a modern Apollo. He could turn the head of many a giddy girl or cause a flutter in the middle-aged breast, but most men would have steered clear of him from instinct. David Maddaver was not a man of the world, he was seventeen and impressionable and had been given to strong bouts of hero-worship at regular intervals throughout his young life.

Simon was an accomplished flatterer. The boy was eating out of his hand. Alan had said. 'You're not, you're not one of *them*, you're as normal as I am. I'd know. I've known you for years. I'd trust you anywhere!' But David wasn't so sure any more. Alan had said. 'You know what would happen; you know what he'd want you to do. If you take off in that boat you're a bigger fool than ever I thought you were!' But Maddaver had ignored Alan and, when Simon had smiled and crooked a finger and asked him to crew the Angel Clare, he had followed the siren song.

It was an idyllic summer, 1963, with Italianate skies they rarely saw in the gentle South-West and seas of every hue from translucent turquoise shallows to cool, dark ultramarine and exotic Lydian purple. Falmouth was bright with craft of every rig and every hue and they had a party on board with a host of Simon's arty friends. But when they left and moved out into the Carrick Roads and past St. Anthony's Point they had left them all behind. They sailed in silence the next afternoon past the sheathed teeth of the Manacles, grave of the Mohican, dipping through gentle seas, watching the long line of the ancient cliffs, the bright white houses where Mevagissey slept, tucked securely into the mouth of St. Austell Bay. They closed the red and white striped beacon which was the Gribbin, a tough, straight, uncompromising finger on a green hill, heralding the approach of the Fowey River. They lazed along past the holiday hotels and the strung fairy lights of the Esplanade, up to the deep water moorings where the clay boats, white with the dust of their cargoes, were berthed alongside the jetties, a listening watch on board; with narrow-eyed Chinese and nervous Russians keeping guard whilst their compatriots sought out the flesh pots of Fowey and Polruan. And on, anchoring in the shade of primeval oak woods, gnarled roots clinging to the very water's edge. Then back again past the Du Mauriers' Ferry House, with David at the taff rail, bronzed and healthy and happy. Simon, drawing on a slim panatela, watched him from eyes narrowed against the sun, and said very little.

They gave Trevander a wide birth this time and that night turned into the curve of Port Nadler Bay with its crescent moon of golden sand, its tall protective cliffs above which the sheep cropped short springy turf amongst buttercups and speedwells. It was one of Cornwall's loveliest bays and Maddaver thought that it could not have changed in all the centuries which had seen the upheavals of fish and tin and free-trading. They had dropped anchor in the silence of early evening. The sun disappearing below the protecting western arm of the bay, leaving the cliff top trees and stunted blackthorn hedges stark silhouettes against a sky of duck-egg blue, streaked the rippling tide with scarlet before plunging them into soft summer dusk. The salt tang of the ebbing tide brought with it the scents of the land, fresh and green, cool and earthy with the herby notes of upland thyme and samphire.

They had their evening meal on deck, watching the night close about them, holding in the day's warmth. The gulls were at rest and only the occasional bleating of sheep on the cliff and the slap of gentle waves along the Angel Clare's sleek, smooth sides punctuated the silence.

'Hearts at peace under an English heaven,' quoted Simon. 'Are you at peace, Davey?' Maddaver waved a forkful of Parma ham and shrugged his shoulders. 'You're right; there is no peace at seventeen. I'm pleased with her, the Angel Clare, she handles well; a real thoroughbred. What d'you think of the Muscadet? The 57 has the edge on the 59, I always say.' He knew Maddaver preferred bitter, whatever way it came. He was being purposefully annoying. David moved to the stern, leaning out over the rail, watching the waters brimming as a small shoal of pilchard passed on its way.

'What am I doing here?' he thought 'The Waterwitch will be out, making for the Eddystone with a scratch

crew.' There was something about bacon and beans on a
hot night that beat slivers of ham and fresh bread into a
cocked hat. They had a nightcap there under the stars
and he had gone below. Simon was smoking a panatela;
he seemed in no hurry to follow him.

'I'll be asleep before he comes down,' thought
Maddaver and then, 'Do I want to be? I can't, I have to
find out!'

He slipped naked between the sheets; dark blue satin,
at once nautical and wickedly sensuous. It had become
hot and airless on deck but here it felt as if a cool, silky
cocoon were lapping his body. He lay on his stomach,
reading a novel chosen at random from a box of paper-
backs under the empty bunk. He was listening for the
opening of the hatch.

At last, Simon came down, vaguely acknowledged
him, stripped to the skin unselfconsciously and wound
an outrageous scarlet kimono about his muscular body.
There was certainly nothing of the effete about him; he
seemed totally relaxed, even happy. He lay down on top
of his bunk and switched off his light, smoked another
panatela and left Maddaver illuminated in his own niche
on the other side of the cabin. The boy cast him occasional, sidelong glances from beneath the sweep of his
thick, dark lashes.

Simon stubbed out his cigar and, swinging his legs
to the floor, rose from his bunk, crossing to stand at
Maddaver's shoulder. The red silk of the kimono rus-
tled and hissed like a snake winding its way through
dry leaves; only a slight, rasping sound but the boy
found that his heart was beating much too fast. He
observed the phenomena with the detachment of a
stranger.

Bennetto put out a hand and jerked the novel from between his fingers. 'If you wanted me to believe you were reading you should have turned the occasional page,' he said quite pleasantly.

'Oh, I suppose I was miles away.'

'Then perhaps you could continue your odyssey with the light out?' He leant over and caught at the pull above the bunk, plunging them both into all but darkness. Just the ripple of the moonlit water reflected through the ports, the glint of gold flashed and coruscated on the alarming kimono. The boy's breath was ragged and audible now, seeming to him to fill the whole cabin.

Bennetto said easily, 'I'll say goodnight, David, we've an early start tomorrow; Plymouth, remember?' Disbelieving, the boy put out a hand for his wrist and fastened upon his arm.

'Simon, stay with me! I want you to.' He could not see that Bennetto was smiling and that it was a tight-lipped smile which twisted a little as he sat down upon the edge of the bunk.

'O *thou with whom I dallied*
Through all the hours of noon
Sweet water-boy more pallid
Than any watery moon....

Oh, you set the scene so well! That clean, lithe young body, naked beneath the sheets? The hair damp and more than a little tousled.... And do you buy your after-shave in bulk or just apply it with a fruit spray? What a little whore you are, Davey!'

Maddaver's breathing stopped then, as abruptly as if the man had thrown a bucket of icy water over him. Bennetto said into the darkness. 'If I'd wanted a fawning, compliant little catamite, would I have chosen a

Maddaver? Surely you would prefer a rougher wooing?'
He had the boy about the shoulders in an iron grip, until
the young, startled face was beneath his own, and then
he was kissing him full on the mouth; deliberately,
savagely, until Maddaver jerked his head away, shot
through with panic and undeniable revulsion.

'Simon, I can't, I really can't!'

The voice which, in the space of minutes, had moved
through a spectrum from bantering ease to icy sarcasm
became soft and silken and alien:

'Tch, tch, David, you are a little tease. Come now, its
what you've wanted all along, since before you ever set
foot aboard – all those languid poses in the rigging in the
briefest of trunks – those half glances shot from beneath
the fringe of those girl's lashes....' The voice was
hypnotic, the hands still had him firmly by the shoulders
without importuning further but Maddaver did not give
him time, he hit out blindly, turned away and retched
dryly into the pillow.

Bennetto suddenly reached for the light pull and the
scene formed; bright and Technicolor. He hissed into the
nearest ear. 'You, my dear are as straight as a telegraph
pole, I've never doubted it, and I have the strongest
possible objections to being used to help you establish
your own sexuality – one way or another. I engaged you
to crew this boat because of your sailing skills. Oh, for
your own satisfaction, I'll admit you are a decorative
child, easy on the eye, but I had and have no intention of
attempting a seduction. You are very much under
twenty-one and there is a law to protect even the dubi-
ously innocent – one has to be very careful. You could
well go home and cry rape to your outraged parent – no
doubt very prettily - perhaps you still will.'

Maddaver said, 'shut up, shut up, damn you! I really liked you, Simon, I thought you were different; I admired you, wanted to give you something of myself....' He ended in theatrical tones.

Bennetto was laughing outright now. 'Oh, bravo, my dear, bravo, you'll make a fine romantic novelist if you ever settle to anything. You are a very accomplished little liar. You were out for self-gratification – a notch of experience on the tree of life – a cheap and nasty thrill at my expense. But I'll give you your thrills, Davey!' The grip on the boy's left wrist was painful, unbreakable, and sent him sprawling on his face before his arm was twisted up behind him leaving him helpless whilst Bennetto's other hand briskly stripped away the last embrace of the satin sheet and cracked down across his buttocks, once, twice, maybe half a dozen times more and there was nothing Maddaver could do but submit to this humiliation like a rebellious nine year old. Bennetto returned his arm and gave him a long look which covered his length, satisfied with the blush of his handiwork, before pulling the sheet up again.

'You bastard! Oh, you bastard!' The boy had his head turned away, spitting fire. Bennetto said grimly. 'That, my dear is what your father should have given you years ago and repeated at quite frequent intervals! Now, I'll take a sleeping bag on deck where the air is a darned sight fresher!' He drew the curtain across the bunk, snatched what he wanted for the night and went on deck, slamming the hatch behind him.

David Maddaver woke to the smell and sounds of bacon sizzling in the galley and felt sick. Bennetto was whistling, clattering crockery, laying the table in the cabin. Eventually, he whisked aside the curtain covering the bunk.

'Good morning, David. Put something on and come and get your breakfast. How many eggs?'

'I don't want – '

'Just two for you then, back in a jiff.'

Maddaver was slumped at the table when he returned, zipped into jeans and enveloped in an outsize mohair sweater. He had his face sunk into a mug of tea and was further eclipsed by yesterday's copy of The Guardian. Simon slapped down a plate of bacon, eggs, kidneys, mushrooms and fried tomatoes; the aroma was out of this world. Maddaver picked at this feast for a while then his usual healthy appetite drove away enough of his chagrin for him to finish the plateful.

'Simon, I want to say something.'

'No, you don't.'

'Yes, I do.'

'Then put that paper down. I can't listen through newspapers, especially The Guardian.' He sat expectantly, arms folded.

Maddaver lowered his paper slowly but would not look at him.

'I suppose I want to say I'm sorry.'

'Are you saying it?'

'I didn't mean to insult you, I misjudged the situation. I thought it was what you wanted, what I wanted. I loathe myself this morning. Really.' He did indeed look chastened.

'Yes, well, I wasn't too fond of you myself last night, you young wretch. You look terrible. Did you howl all night, Davey? I suppose I behaved like a brute but you badly needed spanking – summary justice, a short, sharp, shock and all that.'

Maddaver looked up at him then. 'I'm seventeen. It was bloody embarrassing!'

'No need to have taken it quite so much to heart. I did mean to put you ashore but you'll only sell yourself to white slavers and end up in some eastern seraglio with various fixtures and fittings missing so you'd better stay.'

'Not if you're going to be like this the whole voyage!'

'No, I'm not. I shall work you damned hard. I'll make Captain Bligh look like Goldilocks. For starters you can do the washing up, and don't leave rings in the tea mugs like last time.'

'I haven't said I'd stay.'

'No, you'll play hard to get, which will make a pleasant change. Oh, cheer up, Davey, at least we both know where we stand and, admit it, if anything is bruised this morning it's your pride, not your arse! How do you feel about seconds?'

They came into Plymouth Sound under blazing blue skies, with white heat battering them from Picklecombe Point and every building upon the Hoe flashing a welcome from the aldis lamps of its windows.

'Where do we berth?' yelled Maddaver. Bennetto was engaged on his ship to shore link; feet on the cabin table, large cigar waving, like the Last Tycoon.

'Mayflower Steps,' he said airily.

'We can't,' said Maddaver 'without blocking half the Sound. All the pleasure boats disembark at the steps.'

'I'm not in my dotage yet, we're picking up a passenger. Then we'll take on enough fuel for Dartmouth. Plymouth on a hot Saturday is just too Piccadilly Circus!'

'You said nothing about a passenger.'

'Did I have to? Whose boat is this, pray? And who's piloting it now, God? Because God doesn't know we're too near Drake's Island!'

'We're on automatic.'

'Get up-along, you idiot and swing her hard over!'

Maddaver fled. Simon had been right.

Eventually, they glided into the Mayflower Steps, paintwork pristine. A row of faces pressed to multi-coloured ice cream cones looked down upon them. Maddaver tossed his painter to a likely looking old salt who ignored it and regarded him stonily. A blonde girl in gingham shorts and a pert pony tail grabbed for the retreating rope and put it round a metal stanchion with a perfect hitch.

'Thanks, love,' drawled David patronisingly 'the Navy couldn't have done better!'

'The Navy wouldn't have tossed it to a Trafalgar veteran in the first place,' said the blonde tartly and leapt lightly aboard. 'Is Simon at home, I expected him on the poop deck?'

'Well, yes,' said Maddaver, 'he's below. Who shall I say?'

'Why,' said Bennetto, emerging from the blissful shade of the cabin 'if it isn't the First Lady. David, let me introduce my sister.'

The girl said, 'Eve may have been first but I doubt if she was a lady. David and I have already met; we exchanged ropes, so to speak.' She did not offer him her hand. She was petite and very fair and golden with eyes the colour of wild violets. 'I must go and freshen up, the journey was ghastly,' she said. 'My bag is on the quay, would anyone mind?' Her eyes fastened upon David and appraised him from head to foot with a cool glance which gave nothing away of approval or dismissal. Then, confident that her wishes would be carried out, she ducked below.

'Eve,' said Bennetto 'will be on board until Dartmouth. She is convent educated, intelligent, nubile and, as you have no doubt noticed, has a figure most schoolgirls would die for. It would please me greatly if she could be returned to her mother more or less in the state in which she arrived – i.e. virgo intacta – with your recent predilection towards sexual experiment I rather fear she may be encouraged to speed up certain rites of passage – which I would find regrettable. I trust her implicitly of course, but you sadly, not a whit. Any hanky panky, Davey lad and it will be the bath brush this time – applied with vigour!'

'We don't have a bath brush,' Maddaver scowled, angry that he could feel the blush mounting to his cheeks again.

'You obviously haven't explored that battered suitcase in the forward cuddy – all manner of goodies in there – red satin basque, whips with chased silver handles, bondage chains, oh, and a pink feather duster!'

'Christ!' said Maddaver. 'Why am I still here, why don't I cut and run?'

'I don't know, old son, you'll have to examine your own heart about that, won't you!'

Salcombe was bursting at the seams. Simon sent David ashore for supplies and the wine order, watching him skull adroitly through a forest of masts.

Eve said, 'he is good looking. Isn't he rather young?'

Eve was only sixteen but unfortunately not too innocent to be aware of her brother's sexual proclivities.

He laughed. 'Have a heart, Evie. He's purely decorative and more than useful.'

'But I thought - the way he blushes when he speaks to you – the very breath of love.'

'I don't prey on schoolboys and he's little more. Oh, how can I put it, we have shared certain intimacies but never the ultimate. That glorious mantling of his cheeks merely denotes high embarrassment. I tease him unmercifully, which he deserves. One day he will 'put one on me' as they say in this nasty modern parlance. I rather hope he does. It will give him back his self-respect. So why the curiosity, little sister? Perhaps you are wishing to stake your own claim?'

'Simon, he's an arrogant brat! What on earth could I see in him?' But those clear, honest, violet eyes could not look at him. Simon only smiled to himself, a Machiavellian glint in his eyes.

'All is for the best,' he said 'in the best of all possible worlds. Salcombe is heaven. I've changed my mind, we'll go ashore.'

CHAPTER TWENTY

1966

One day, of course, he would have to take life seriously. There was a sad inevitability in the thought but just now it danced away upon the horizon, fickle and fugitive as the bright points of light coruscating on the fretted blue of the bay. Ambition, fortune, ominous words like 'settling down' rarely troubled Adam Colenso's existence. Even a wished-for fame would be a mere bagatelle.....

The old men leaning over the harbour wall were muttering darkly, heads together. He caught at a name – Davey Maddaver – but their talk was of no interest to him. Then the big man with the bobble hat said. 'There'll be no buyer, breaking her up they'll be, like as not. Poor old Waterwitch, one engine fair to being knackered and a hull like a sieve. Miss Deverel'd 'ave her preserved out of sentiment but she's got the sense to know that's all it would be; a leaky hull, moored somewhere out of sight and sinking lower at her moorings until the first high water spring, coming in on a brisk southerly, storm force, and she'd vanish for ever, give up the ghost and be grateful for it!'

Colenso followed that stabbing, accusing finger across the bay. It was the beginning of a perfect evening with wine-dark seas marked by tiny eddies and tired tides into shot taffeta. The blush of the sunset steeped the horizon, mounted to gold, to green and on into an indigo zenith. There were few sails to interrupt this scope of sea and sky. A cluster of toshers out of Mevagissey, riding to their nets with mizzens set and firefly lights winking at their mastheads, and the Waterwitch, swinging into the mouth of the bay, the ruby of her lamp, port side, flashing, the white of the bow wave, the whirr of wings at her stern as the last and most venturesome of gulls followed her home. The vestiges of the sunset warmed the rust of her sail.

'Vanish for ever' were the old man's words. Something stirred in Colenso's brash young heart that lay so lightly, so unburdened in his breast. Those vague thoughts which had accompanied him since he had left the heat of a London summer for the land this side of Lyonesse flashed through his mind again; the studio set high above the cliffs in a converted net loft; the cottage going cheaply because it wasn't on mains drains; the abandoned lighthouse; the ruins of the Palmerston Fort away towards Plymouth, obsolete before it was finished..... all vanished before the germination of a new idea. It budded as the Waterwitch straightened her course between the clashing rocks at the harbour mouth, until it flowered finally into the smile at the corners of the straight mouth.

As he watched from his cliff-top perch, the walkway above the crowding houses at the quayside, he saw the boat nose alongside the quay. There was a man on board, young by the lightness of his feet across the worn decking, Cornish dark. But out of the rose-glow and the shadows, swift on her feet, appeared another figure, a girl, small and slight and fair. Her plain white shift dress was expensive and understated, her long straight blonde hair, heavy and shining a la Jean Shrimpton. She caught the bow rope as she had been catching ropes for David Maddaver since the day she had met him beneath the Mayflower Stone. And when the boat was moored she scrambled lightly aboard and he caught her in his arms and kissed her.

'I must have her,' said Adam Colenso, out loud between his teeth, but whether he meant the girl or the boat was not really clear, even to himself!

Harry Colenso had left very little to Lillian's son. He had died on the verge of bankruptcy but his legacy of a stable, happy childhood and a life brimming with laughter and its full measure of serendipitous happenings was worth more than a bank account and Adam was wise enough to recognise it. Besides, he had the paintings; Harry's own and a small collection of Lillian's Cornish landscapes and her portraits: Harry in typical swaggering pose, a critical self-portrait which was too honest to deny her beauty and then there was the portrait which had taken pride of place in the London house, the man who had been their friend, Tristan Toller, who was spoken of with shared affection. Harry had said, 'Promise me, boy that you will hang onto that. Your mother set great store by it. I regard it as one of her finest.' And, of course, he had promised. Harry never did get to tell Lillian's son that he was not his father. He had meant to, of course, when the time was right, but perhaps he feared that he would lose him. He did tell him about Trevander and the cottage on the cliff top where Toller had been born, and it was curiosity about this young man, flotsam of a savage war, which had taken him, off track, to Trevander. He had often stood in front of the tall Edwardian mantle at home and gazed up at the enigmatic young face and been struck by a familiarity he could not fathom. He could not see that the face he probed with such intensity was his own and, even when the thought had crossed his mind in recent years, he shrugged it away, wondering if it was possible to absorb a man's features from too long an acquaintance with his face. The idea caught his fancy and he stood there often, vowing to make more of his own life than was given to this man to make of his. Further he did not question. But in his crowded little pad, sandwiched into the middle floor of a villa in Ealing, it was Lillian's last portrait of Harry which took pride of place.

So, he had found his way to Trevander and roamed its narrow streets and stood at the gates of Penolva and not known that Pog Toller, weeding the border, was his aunt. She smiled at him and he felt embarrassed by his own voyeurism and moved on. He had only meant to spend a night in Trevander, putting up at a B & B but they had stopped his moving on – the girl and the Waterwitch. He had nosed about the gallery in Fore Street where there were local views by local artists in every style you could wish for and he had chatted up the woman at the till. She was old enough and plain enough to value the attentions of this handsome, open-faced young man with his untidy mop of fair hair and guileless grey-green eyes.

Well, if he meant to stay for a while there wasn't much to offer by way of accommodation. Folks were realising that holiday lets were more lucrative these days but Miss Deverel, she who owned and ran the gallery, she let out a couple of rooms at the top of Fosfelle. Didn't he know Fosfelle? She would be pleased to meet him for his father's sake.

Adam had let fall his father's name in the natural way he always did. The kudos their relationship still brought him rarely came into it. Colenso was still so much a part of him that he could rarely keep him from popping up in conversation.

He crossed the bridge, making for The Strand. The tide was out but the morning sun found every water-filled hollow in the mud of the harbour floor and filled them with silver and glinted from the rain-washed coach roofs of the yachts, abandoned by the weekend sailors, and warmed the coloured hulls of the fishing fleet. The Waterwitch had her own place against the jetty, still wearing Annabel's green and gold livery; the colours she had chosen for Frank Toller's gift before this turbulent century began.

He strode along The Strand, hands in the pockets of faded jeans, sniffing at the salt air, happy with the unsavoury smells emanating from the harbour mud. He found the flight of stone steps described by the woman at the gallery; cut between two houses, dark and narrow and steep. At the top was an old wrought iron gate which swung at a crazy angle on creaking hinges as you opened it. From this point you could not see the house, only a tangle of garden, lovely in its neglect. Above him, lush semi-tropical greenery backed the cliff face. Below him were the higgledy-piggledy roofs of The Strand with their golden patches of lichen and the clumsy nests of importunate seagulls. He began to climb, following a path overgrown in places though here and there it was obvious that a flurry of gardening activity had taken place and there were neat rows of beans and onions. There were old apple trees with names like Sops in Wine, Sweet Larks and Cornish Gillyflowers. There was a small lily pool, green with weed, a clump of tamarisks, the stag's horns of a sumac tree, a soldierly row of delphiniums, heavenly blue, a little terrace with a rustic bench and a couple of canvas chairs. So, thought Adam, she does have visitors, the witch of the woods. He had feared she might be a recluse, shut away in her enchanted garden.

Another corner, another flight of crazy steps and there was Fosfelle, a grey blur behind its rioting roses; windows which struggled to peer across the harbour between pink Albertines and the large loose cups of Crimson Glories and the sulphur yellow heads of Mermaid, delicately fragrant. As Adam stood there hesitantly, delighted by it all, his artist's senses stirred; a Monet in the garden at Giverny, Van Gough amongst the sunflowers...... A woman came over to him from some dark recess of the house. He held out his hand. 'Miss Deverel?'

She took it and liked his confident grip: 'And you are Lillian Toft's son. I don't need to ask.'

'How?' he began.

'Oh, I met her once in London, during the War.'

'At Stuffs?'

'Yes, at Stuffs. I was curious, I suppose. Tristan Toller was one of our own; I grew up with him.'

'He was a friend of my father's.' Adam almost felt a need to defend his mother's honour. It had never occurred to him before that it would ever have been necessary. Gina did not say as they all said, 'he should have died here amongst his own. He should not have broken his mother's heart the way he did.' She had spoken briefly with Lillian but had found her remote, detached and could not fathom the fascination which had taken Tristan Toller away from them all. In this boy she could see an animation which Lillian had kept under lock and key. It had free rein in her son, in Harry Colenso's son but then, he wasn't Harry's son. Gina had grown up with the Tollers, she had known Tristan at this boy's age and she saw him again. She must be careful.

'You have come about the rooms? They're at the top of the house.'

He was looking her over; a woman in her forties, dressed in slacks and a faded shirt, red hair knotted on the nape of her neck, springing out on all sides as if it remembered the freedom of its youth. She might have been pretty once with it tumbling about her cheeks but now it was a plain country face. She wore no make-up and her limp was very pronounced.

'How much are you charging?'

'I hadn't thought. How much can you afford?'

He named a price but she shook her head. 'I don't think that is enough.'

'I paint. I paint well. If you can stand out of the extra for a while ...'

'How are you in the garden?'

'I'm sorry?'

'I need help in the garden. I have some young friends who come to my aid when they can but I am being overtaken. You can see.'

'Its glorious, I wouldn't pull up a weed if I were you,' he said 'but if that's what you want I shall prove all things to all men, Miss Deverel.'

'And women?' she thought idly to herself. 'You, my lamb are far too lethal a mix.' Instead, she said out loud, 'I'm Aunt George to everyone in the village. Miss

Deverel is far too formal. I did have my moments, many years ago; I would hate the label 'Miss' to preclude the possibility.'

He looked embarrassed as if he might bolt at any moment. Gina laughed, 'I'm sorry, I didn't mean to shock you. I just meant to convey that I'm rather a free spirit. There aren't any house rules. Would you like to look round?'

And he had loved it, up in the attics of Fosfelle. He did not know until much later that his room below the eaves had been Annabel Boase's nursery and Gina Deverel's sanctuary or that the narrow bed where he slept the easy sleep of youth had nursed her girlhood's passion for Lanty Maddaver and witnessed her coupling with Rob Ashley.

Gina said, 'I'm making tea; there are chairs on the terrace. I expect you could manage a cup.' And she went indoors leaving him standing under the sumacs, looking out across the bowl of the harbour. She appeared precariously carrying a large and loaded wooden tray. He hurried to take it from her. There were sandwiches and scones and real Cornish cream.

'Heaven!' he said.

'I'm afraid there's no Ginger Beer,' said Gina.

He gave her an odd glance.

'Sorry,' she said 'I though all your generation was reared on Enid Blyton. Now, tell me about your work. Is it good or are you a basker in reflected glory?' So he spent the next hour in animated discussion conveying an obvious belief in himself, and Gina smiled and nodded and watched him and enjoyed the rise and fall of the young, clear voice and the changing seasons of his face until he said. 'I must go and sign out and get my things. I shan't be long. Can I go down through the garden again?'

She watched him disappear through the tamarisks and beyond the spires of the delphiniums. Just above the lily pool he stopped, a splash of colour catching his eyes, a quick movement. He paused. It had not been there on his way up. It was the girl in the white dress; jeans clad now, a skinny sweater moulded to her perfect figure, the blonde hair about her like a golden cape. She was weeding the patch of blue-purple campanulas, the exact colour of her eyes, trowel flashing industriously. Her arms were lightly tanned and, where the long blonde strands of her hair had parted at the nape, her neck was smooth and golden.

'If you plan to stand there for any length of time you could empty the trug. The compost heap is a few steps further down.' She hadn't even paused to turn round to see who had come to spy upon her.

'I'm sorry; I was startled to find anyone here. She's got you at it too, has she? Gardening, I mean. I'm the new gardener designate. The Andre Le Notre of Ealing, that's me.'

'You don't sound very French.' She looked out from the curtain of her hair. You don't look very French. I suppose there could be a colony in Ealing. I suppose you could be of Huguenot descent.'

'I'm Cornish, both sides. Really!'

'I suppose that makes it all right then, stealing up on people.'

He ignored that and said. 'I'm Adam, Adam Colenso. I'm staying with Aunt George.'

'Oh, you must be one of her rent boys, so to speak.'

'What! No. That is, have there been many?'

'Only Geoffrey. He was a budding author. Then his Aunty Phoebe left him a legacy and he needed to bud no more so he went home to Bridgenorth.'

'I don't believe her name was Phoebe!'

'Probably you're right. I'm Eve, Eve Bennetto. I too have Cornish both sides. Isn't it a coincidence! Kissing Cousins probably.'

'Adam and Eve,' he said 'and a Garden of Eden all about us. How poetic can you get!

'*Eve with her basket was*
Deep in the bells and grass
Wading in bells and grass' he quoted.

'Ah, I suspected it all along,' she said, 'you're a dead ringer for the cobra.

Out of the boughs he came
Whispering still the same
Tumbling in twenty rings

I have only one as you can see and it's an engagement ring.'

'*Poor motherless Eve*,' he said with a sigh, still quoting.

'Oh mother's very well, thank you, and into the garden party season. That's why I have escaped up country to Trevander. Do you think you ought to go? If you're making your way through to the last verse it could well be dark before you get back.'

'I'll see you around then,' he said in what he hoped was a nonchalant voice.

'Oh, bound to.' She was back on her knees again, fully absorbed.

High on her terrace Gina watched them; Tristan Toller's son and Davey Maddaver's bright, brittle young fiancée. She watched them and she feared for them both.

But she was not Asmodeus; she did not know how to put the lid back on the box.

❧

The men of Trevander had started up a co-operative and there had been meetings with the White Fish Authority from Plymouth. They had a decent cold room now, a stout crane and a ramshackle van, bought for £50 to help transport the fish to market. They shipped out two loads a day, returning with ice for the next consignment.

David Maddaver, looking to the future, had plans to put the old Waterwitch out to pasture at the end of the summer season. The summer was lucrative with the red-lips pouring into the village, crowding down onto the quay, there to be seduced by boat rides and fishing trips. By the autumn and the start of the winter fishing, the Flower of the Winds would be seaworthy; a smart, fast little boat, fibre-glass hulled and economic on fuel. He couldn't expect much for the Waterwitch but with a good summer season and what he had prudently stashed away crewing for the racing yachts he would manage. After that there was the wedding to save for but Simon would take care of that. Simon took care of everything. Eve was still the cherished little sister. Her mother wanted the wedding at Mylor, in the old church where the Bennettos had worshipped for centuries, but Eve spent more time at Rosarrock with Simon and Trevander had become home so she would climb the hill to the little church where the Maddavers and Tollers lay beneath their grassy mounds. Mother would shrug her shoulders and fall in with Simon and all would be well.

David met up with Adam Colenso in the bar of the Moonraker one sultry July evening. Adam had sold a painting and was celebrating, spreading largesse and laughter in equal measure. He persuaded David to let him accompany him on a fishing trip out to the Eddystone. He would be taking his sketch book. The lighthouse itself was impressive, accompanied as it was by the stump of the older tower; monument to man's folly and the sea's overwhelming strength, but he also wanted to work on some action sketches. As it turned out, he was sea-sick most of the way there and all the way back. The lighthouse loomed above him from a wall of crashing waves and his pencils never came out of their box. Even David Maddaver felt sorry for him.

'I'll get over it. I'll be out again,' said Colenso.

'Some people never get used to the sea. Nelson never did.'

'I don't want to fight the bloody French!'

But he persevered and eventually some sketches did blossom from the experience. They looked good hanging up in Aunt George's gallery; the impassioned force of the waves tearing across his canvas; stark contrast to the neat water colours boasting colourful harbour-locked fishing boats and rose-spattered, white-washed cottages.

It was an enchanted summer. Looking back it would be remembered as the definitive bench-mark of summers. Gina and Pog would meet in The Strand and say ' Oh, it's not as good as 1966.' or 'I think its hotter than '66, don't you?' But through the days of superlative golden sunrises, tropic noons and sultry dusks ran an undercurrent of tension. Adam Colenso and David Maddaver had struck up a firm friendship and when David finished the season and the Flower of the Winds was launched from the stocks at Toms' Yard in Fowey, Adam would take over the Waterwitch and open a floating studio. They talked about it endlessly, David and Adam and Eve, lying out on the sands of a tiny beach in Lantic Bay, the Cornish cliffs above them, the gulls wheeling, the Waterwitch gently swaying at her moorings.

From the fringe of lashes too long and heavy for a young man, Adam watched Eve, tanned and golden in a brief bikini; pink gingham with a tiny bow between her swelling breasts.

'You should have had a summer wedding, Evie, summer suits you. September is a sad month.'

'A wedding,' said Eve 'tends to be based on the availability of churches, the whims of brides' mothers, aunts from the Outer Hebrides and the trauma of cake. There is very little romance to be extracted from it. David has the best policy; he keeps out of it entirely. He thought he might send a cardboard cut-out to the reception.'

'Why not live in sin instead?' said Adam. 'It's very fashionable.'

'Mother,' said Eve.

'Simon,' grimaced David.

'Oh yes, Simon. Simon doesn't like *me* at all,' said Adam.

'That could be a blessing,' said David and even Simon's sister had to laugh at that.

'I thought,' said Adam, testing the water rather 'that is, I want to give you a wedding present. Would you like me to paint Eve? If you don't care for it you can thank me nicely and use it to fill up a draughty corner somewhere.'

'Portrait of Eve,' said David. 'Yes, I like that. There's a certain cache about having an original portrait in the house. What about it, Eve?'

'I don't know. I'm not Dorian Grey; I might age quickly and have you keeping picking me up on it every time we have a row. I really don't think I want to. I don't think I have the time to keep still. You won't be terribly offended if I say 'no, thank you' very politely?'

Adam shrugged his shoulders, still watching her. This time he was on his stomach, peering out from the flop of his blond hair.

David said, 'Oh, go on, Eve, don't be a spoilsport. I'd like to have it even if it's awful. People would have to stop and say something clever and meaningful and be gushingly serious about it. It'll be fun!'

'Oh, it'll be fun,' echoed Eve. 'Dangerous fun,' said the violet eyes which met Adam's grey ones across the space of sand between them.

⌘

Gina privately thought Eve should get a job of some kind, a proper job. The Bennetto money did not require it. Mrs Bennetto, Romola Frayne that was, had raised her daughter for marriage and a position in society; the last of the debs perhaps. Simon over-indulged her. So she played at work, a dilettante princess nibbling at the edges of life, serving in boutiques and antique shops and knick-knack emporiums. Now she had joined the gallant little band of village elders who gave guided tours of Trevander to coach loads from the car park and Americans from the Guest Houses and children from the local schools; slick patter and jolly jokes interspersed with tales of haunted inns, smugglers caves and fishing lore. Eve was good for business. She was trailed along the quay by brash young Americans; band box fresh, paint box pretty, heels clicking, hips

swaying, blonde hair swinging, an English rose playing
Pied Piper.

❦

Gina was not one of nature's cooks but she could rustle
up a mean casserole when the occasion required and,
because she was aware that food rarely features top of an
artist's agenda, she prepared supper for Adam every
Tuesday. It was so hot that day that she had laid the table
on the shady terrace, covered it with a white linen cloth,
lace bordered, and served the meal on the remains of Mrs
Boase's dinner service, passed through the family from
Annabel.

The whole village seemed to be sleeping in the heat,
enervated and listless. The only sound came from the
restless owls in the tall trees above the cliff. Gina ladled
out the casserole. Colenso wondered if it were chicken or
pork. Gina's casseroles all tasted the same but they were
filling and he knew she needed someone to mother.

'And how is the portrait?' she asked, as he had known
she would.

'Oh, progressing, you know.'

'And you and Eve? Progressing too, I suppose?'

'I'm sorry; I'm not quite with you.'

Gina smiled. 'No, I imagine you're well ahead.'

'You're going to say I'm playing a dangerous game.
Please say it, they always do in fiction.'

'If,' said Gina with a dangerous glint in her green eyes
'you were half the age you are, you'd be over my knee
and you wouldn't sit down for a very long time. Didn't
Harry ever tan you?'

'No, never. Sorry to disappoint you. I had a well-
meaning aunt though. She threatened me constantly

with a clothes brush. I hid it in the garden shed once after I'd been particularly obnoxious. She got the Kleeneze Man to trawl the country for another one. He was completely in thrall to her, managed to get one from the north of Scotland.'

'Don't,' said Gina 'do this to me. Stop playing with Eve.'

'Oh, I'm not playing,' said Adam 'we're made for each other. Were you waiting for me to say that?'

'Yes. No! I wish you hadn't.'

'You're very fond of David, aren't you?'

'Yes, very.'

'Are you going to order me to leave your house, never again to darken your door?'

'No, I'll be around to pick up the pieces, I suppose.'

Adam shrugged. 'He'll get over it. People always do.'

'You're an arrogant little toad, Adam!'

'Do I get seconds? You know, I sometimes feel that if *you* were half the age you are now we might have made out well together.'

And because Gina had been thinking the same thing precisely she caught him across the ear with a rolled up copy of the Cornish Times and had to rush to make coffee before her laughter got the better of her. The casserole had gone by the time she got back.

'That was chicken, wasn't it?'

'You know very well it wasn't! You sold that rather green canvas of the Wolf Rock; I need something to fill the gap.'

He grinned. 'You mean that the more time I have to spend on bread and butter art the less time I shall have to ogle Eve.'

'Precisely! Now go before I get really angry. And yes, I know, I'm beautiful when I'm angry but just scram!'

※

Adam was minding the stall for the Tregenza woman. The mournful face with hair like a yard of pump water had taken itself off to a local funeral and he had agreed to sit in at the gallery for a morning. It was ferociously hot outside and all anyone wanted to do was to grab a crab sandwich and a coke and take it into the nearest patch of shade. No one was in a mood for art. Adam was sketching idly when the doorbell rang, followed by a succession of wind chimes.

Simon Bennetto ducked under the lintel and entered alone. Usually he was accompanied by members of his entourage; his aloneness boded ill. He prowled, panther like, about the racks of smaller prints, the sort you took for Auntie Maggie because it packed flat for the train. He stopped finally before a sunset, a blood red sky behind the angry teeth of rocks at the mouth of the harbour.

'It's good. I hate to say it, but it's good.' He addressed the air rather than the youthful artist.

'Why don't you,' said Adam 'come out with what you really came to say?'

Simon spun on his heels. The panther had stopped prowling and turned to stalk toward the counter which separated him from his prey.

Colenso thought: 'He really has a wonderful face. I should like to paint him but it would do nothing for my reputation with the girls of Trevander.'

Simon lunged forward then and grabbed both of his wrists, shaking his hands. 'Keep away from my sister if you value these!'

Adam sighed, 'How tiresomely theatrical. You could just push me off a cliff and no one would know. Verdict - accidental death.'

'Too good for you, my dear. What, come up behind you one dark night and toss you from some Tarpeian Cornish rock? You might never know what had hit you!'

Adam could not stop himself from saying very coarsely. 'But coming up from behind is surely your forte, dear Simon?' He expected the man to hit him then but instead Bennetto tossed back his head and roared with laughter, turned on his heels and left the shop.

'One down to me, I think,' said Adam with a smile.

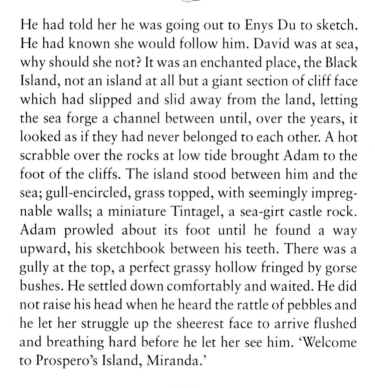

He had told her he was going out to Enys Du to sketch. He had known she would follow him. David was at sea, why should she not? It was an enchanted place, the Black Island, not an island at all but a giant section of cliff face which had slipped and slid away from the land, letting the sea forge a channel between until, over the years, it looked as if they had never belonged to each other. A hot scrabble over the rocks at low tide brought Adam to the foot of the cliffs. The island stood between him and the sea; gull-encircled, grass topped, with seemingly impregnable walls; a miniature Tintagel, a sea-girt castle rock. Adam prowled about its foot until he found a way upward, his sketchbook between his teeth. There was a gully at the top, a perfect grassy hollow fringed by gorse bushes. He settled down comfortably and waited. He did not raise his head when he heard the rattle of pebbles and he let her struggle up the sheerest face to arrive flushed and breathing hard before he let her see him. 'Welcome to Prospero's Island, Miranda.'

'Beast!' she said. 'You could have given me a hand. I don't know why I came.'

'Don't you?' He watched her sink down upon the soft, springy turf, dotted here and there with sea pinks.

'It's a beautiful day. I was at a loose end,' she said dismissively. She wore pristine white shorts and a striped matelot sweater. The blonde hair swung about her in a shining silk curtain, her legs were smooth and brown. She shook off her golden sandals and wiggled her toes.

'Very stylish, very nautical,' he said 'like the Greek princess who put to sea in a pirate sloop - *and all the jolly mariners were gallant little girls.*'

She knew the line, of course. She knew all his poetical allusions:

'*And would you like the yellow boat or would you like the red*

Or would you take myself and mine, the gold and green instead?' The Waterwitch was gold and green, she always thought of the Waterwitch when she read Flecker.

'You can't marry David,' said Adam. He had not moved any closer. He lay on his back, arms linked beneath his fair head, skin as golden brown as her own.

'Can't?' said Eve. 'I suppose it is my destiny. It's in our stars, has been for years, if not from the moment of conception at least from that of our first mediocre, inauspicious meeting. Simon willed it so the hour he and David met and I grew up believing that Simon would always know what was best for me and, in all honesty, he usually did – nothing to kick against there. Perhaps it was a little incestuous, like the old Egyptian dynasties. Simon couldn't have him; he knew that, so he did the next best thing to keep him in the family, he groomed him for his sister. I expect he'll dance at our wedding.'

Adam grinned. 'The spurned lover lusting after the groom instead of the bride? You can't seriously go through with this!' He rolled over onto his stomach, put out a hand and took hers.

'Kiss me, Eve and prove you don't love me.'

She laughed, quoting again: '*Sir, handsome fellow as you are, it's curious you know,*
To ask a maid for kisses in mid archipelago.'

'Here on this fledgling island,' he said 'I can hold onto thistledown dreams.' He drew her to him then and kissed her gently, so gently that she could have easily pushed him away but she did not have the will or the courage. 'I think I have proved my point, princess,' he said after a long time lying silently beside her.

'You did not need to prove it to me,' said Eve quietly. 'I love you, Adam but I intend to marry David.'

'That's madness! So you came here only to taunt me!'

'I came here to explain. No, that is a lie. I came here because I could not keep away. The bright eyes of danger beckoning, I suppose. I want to love you Adam and I want to remember it for ever!'

'No, you want to defeat Simon and his wizardry. What a triumph, the virgin bride deflowered before being offered as a sacrifice upon her brother's altar. Find someone else for your games, pretty lady.' He turned away from her, gazing out to sea. A lone gull swooped down, crying plaintively, its wandering witch-notes fading into the distance.

'Adam, I never meant to love you. My life was planned out and I was content with it. You will find a better woman than I will ever be who will share your vagrant, gypsy days and fill your nights with love and laughter.'

He shook his head. 'There is no room for another, not now, not ever. You would always come between us.'

'Then make love to me Adam, for the first time and the last time. It's what I came for. It's what I want, here with the wind in my hair and the salt upon my lips and the sorcery of summer all about us!'

'I can't lose you, Eve.'

'You will never leave me after today, I promise.' She wound her fingers into his hair and pulled him down beside her so that the mermaid weeds of her own mingled with his. Finally, they lay naked together, cleansed by the wind off the sea, golden limbs entwined, breast to breast, heart to heart. And, long afterwards, they walked back across the rocks, hand in hand. Alone, he climbed the path to Fosfelle. Aunt George met him at the Vantage and he could not face her out, guilt started from every pore. He tried to dodge around her, to flee on and upwards, to seek solitude in the room under the eaves.

She only said, 'For Heaven's sake, boy, you're as awkward as a cow with a musket!'

'I'm sorry, perhaps I've laid too long i' the sun.'

She grabbed one brown wrist and turned it over. 'Is that all it was? I thought perhaps you'd been caught with your fingers in the jam pot.'

But he only raised his eyebrows and smiled that louche heart-stopping smile of his that angered her so much because she was well over forty and not impervious to it. And so she let him go and watched him shin up the last of the steps to the door behind the roses. Suddenly she wanted to keep them all safe, Adam and David and Eve Bennetto but she could only wait helplessly until they needed her. After all, picking up the pieces was what she was so good at! Everyone said so.

Chapter Twenty One

The Flower of the Winds would be launched the next week, bedecked with Chinese lanterns. There was to be a party over to Polruan, champagne as she slipped into the harbour, no expense spared; Simon's treat. David and Adam had spent the night talking enthusiastically about the celebration and whether there was to be bunting and who would smash the bottle.

'Eve, of course,' said Adam as they lounged about on the Waterwitch's deck, nets payed out and their work done for the night. It was a beautiful night. Above them every star in the northern hemisphere burnt silver and blue and all about them the sea was brimming. It would be a good catch, a fitting catch for her last. Later, their backs would be breaking as they hauled in but now was a time for relaxation, for jokes and stories and confidences.

'Eve,' said David 'will do very well. She'll put on her princess airs and wear a hat. Poor old Waterwitch, nose out of joint.'

Adam patted the bulwarks. 'We've had a talk, Waterwitch and I. No more storms for her, a safe haven and happy landings. I'll have my office down below; somewhere ship-shape for the signing of cheques and all my exhibits will fit neatly into the fish holds. In the summer I shall sail into the smart harbours and sell my wares. In

the winter maybe we'll hole up in some hidden creek off
the Fowey River and I'll divide my time between stormy
landscapes and portraits of bored society beauties
wintering in Cornish resorts. Paradise!'

'We shan't know you any more, Eve and I,' laughed
David.

'No, you'll be working far too hard to know anyone.
Eve wasn't made for a fish widow. If she were mine I
would take her with me.'

'But she isn't, is she?' said Maddaver suddenly. 'And
I'm going below for some shut-eye. Can you keep the
watch for an hour or two without drifting off into some
Impressionist dream?'

'I might be able to but I need to say something important.'

'Really? That sounds ominous. We'll be hauling, it'll
have to wait.'

Adam shrugged and watched him go below. 'I have
tried,' he said to the stars. 'He doesn't want to hear.'

David was right, it was a magnificent catch. They
hauled and cleared, filling the fish hold with living silver.
It was all going so well until the last of the nets came
aboard and fouled up as it came in contact with the
rollers.

'We've got problems!' sang out Adam. 'Hold hard for
a moment!'

David came round to have a look. 'That'll be a dirty
great hole to repair tomorrow.'

'Scrap iron, Dave, from a wreck d'you think?' He
helped Maddaver to jerk it inboard, rusty and heavy and
sinister.

'Christ!' said David, 'it's some kind of explosive.
The Lady Lucy brought one in like this last winter. The

Ministry took it very seriously, grim faces all round, bomb disposal people muttering incantations, the lot. Eventually they dismantled it. Alan Cluett's mother has it on her sideboard.'

'Which war?'

'Oh, the last. Our air crews jettisoned a lot of iron-mongery out there before they made landfall. You don't want a bomb in the bomb bay before you make a hasty let down!'

'I suppose not. It's a very small bomb.'

'They come in all sizes. Believe me, its big enough to be lethal!'

'It's not ticking. Do they tick or is that fiction? Let's chuck it back.'

'We can't. Someone else might dredge it up, someone less fortunate. We'll head for home. We've done here anyway. I'll ring in as soon as we get back, have it checked out.'

Adam shrugged. 'If you say so, it looks innocuous enough.'

'Just let it be and give me a hand. We might get a round of drinks out of the story.'

And so they sailed through a dazzling morning, the gulls about them, the sky a cloudless paint box blue.

'What did you want to discuss?' asked David, tanned and dark and happy.

'Oh, it'll keep,' said Adam faintly, cowardice gripping him by the throat.

The quay was deserted; the bomb lay dark and silent in its corner of the deck, cradled in the mesh of their last net. Maddaver leapt ashore, flinging the bow rope about a stanchion.

'I'll make that call before we unload.'

Waterwitch rocked her stern moving gently out from the wall. Adam lay down on the warm deck, hands beneath his head. He closed his eyes. Minutes later, the chatter of voices round him, children's voices, caused him to open one eye. Eve was touring Junior Three, trailing them through their village, pointing out the local landmarks, filling them with effortless history. They clustered around her excitedly; glad to be out of the classroom. Eve raised a hand and waved. He felt guilty, he had not spoken to David as he had meant. He was pathetic. He did not deserve her; she was right to insist that she marry David. And perhaps he was too warm and full of sleep to care. How quiet it was, just the murmur of Eve's voice, spellbinding, the lap of the water about the keel, the buzz of a fly around the fish hold, the tick of his watch. Funny, he had not noticed that before. He shook it and put it to his ear. It wasn't his watch; it was that dark, evil piece of jetsam, inches from his head. Was it true? Did bombs really tick? Surely they would have to use a stethoscope to detect activity beneath that solid, impenetrable core? He listened again. Nothing. He had an overactive imagination that was all. But, in spite of the heat of the sun on the nape of his neck, he found he was shivering.

The thing lay there, silent, menacing, and suddenly he knew there was danger; some primeval instinct was urging him to cut and run. He sprang up then. The children were running up and down the quay. In a second he knew what he had to do. Hauling the Waterwitch in by the bow rope he scrambled to unhitch it, ran to put the engine in reverse, turned her and made for the harbour entrance.

'Adam,' Eve was shouting 'where's David?'

'Gone ashore. Tell him I couldn't wait and get them out of here!' He gestured to the children from the deck house. For a moment she saw the panic in his eyes but he relaxed for a minute. Waterwitch glided through the harbour entrance. 'I love you, Evie.' He blew her a kiss. Surprised, she watched him move toward the sea.

Eve Bennetto and David Maddaver married in September. Trevander was in the midst of an Indian Summer, clinging on to its clear blue skies and leaf gilding sunlight for all as if spring would never come round again and bring another golden summer in its train.

Between them, Simon and Mrs Bennetto had seen to it that Eve lacked for nothing befitting a princess bride, the daughter of their house. Her dress was expensively simple, the high bodice of its Empire Line embroidered with seed pearls.

'Pearls for tears,' sniffed Cynthia Toller, to be immediately shushed by a happy, tearful Aunt Pog.

David was nervous but not as nervous as Gina and Simon who had wondered if the bride would ever reach the church or if she would flee at the last minute like so many brides of legend. Bright and obedient she had appeared on Simon's arm and paced the aisle surrounded by the men and women who had grown up with David Maddaver and who wished them both well. Perhaps it was significant that when the Reverend Vellacott, in rather sonorous tones, had said:

'You may now kiss the bride,' and David had gently lifted her veil, her eyes were closed as his mouth found hers. And then they were out in the sunshine at the top of the hill. The bay was all about them, a blue fret untroubled by white crests. The cliff top was golden with the late flowering of gorse and the distant mournful cries of the gulls were drowned by a robin's pure song from the heart of a scarlet fuchsia, just below the church tower.

The photographs were over. They were showering confetti now, laughing, waiting for Eve to take David's arm and lead the way down the winding path toward the road. Only Gina knew that the blue-purple bells in her bridal bouquet, gleaned from the gardens of Fosfelle, signified more than a bride's fancy for something a little different. As Eve moved forward between the soft green mounds of Trevander's sleeping dead, she was aware of the ghost brides who had taken this path before her, of the presence of Annabel Boase and Tabby Cluett, of Emelynne Deverel and Lowena Maddaver. But beyond the haunted path and the mossed graves, below a newly planted pear tree which would weep snowy petals in the spring, the clean face of a new monument, faced with Delabole slate, stood out from the short daisy sprinkled turf about it. Eve hesitated and the bridal procession came to a sudden halt behind her. She looked at David with eyes that were blank of appeal but he knew what she wanted, as he would always know, and he nodded. She lifted her skirts, her veil rippling behind her in the light breeze from the sea, her white satin shoes printing the morning dew, and she laid her bouquet, bright with its bells before the stone cairn which the people of Trevander had erected to the memory of the man who had saved their children. It was simply, inevitably inscribed:

'Adam Colenso
Greater love hath no man'

Down with the bells and grass she murmured, 'Sleep easy, Adam, easier than I ever will.' Then she rose gracefully to her feet. 'Farewell Eve Bennetto, now turn Eve Maddaver and look them all in the eye and smile and smile.....' And she held out her hand to David and stepped lightly down.

Envoi

1967

Like most of the Cornish, heirs to the Wreckers and the smuggling trade, David Maddaver had spent his life retrieving from the sea the flotsam and jetsam of retreating tides. It was hardly surprising to Eve when, in the second year of their marriage, he had brought home his latest find.

Chy an Lor, whitewashed and sturdy and cheerful with bright hanging baskets, had been their home since they returned from their honeymoon. It had seen the births and deaths of Tollers and Maddavers since Frank Toller and Annabel had taken up residence after their own marriage. Mathey Toller had been borne there. Johnny Fortnight had wooed and won his recalcitrant bride and both Drew and Lowena Maddaver had first seen the light of day in the best bedroom overlooking the harbour. Drew and Emlynne's boys, Lanty and Tim, had woken to the cacophonous sound of gulls crying from every chimney round and had dragged themselves from bed to toil up the hill to the village school on many a wet and windy morning. Only Pamela Denbow had elected to have David in hospital thus breaking with tradition. Now Eve too was pregnant, awaiting the birth of the child she knew would be a daughter. She had got slowly to her feet, languid on the sofa by the fire, at David's impatient knocking at the door. She turned off the gramophone. Why didn't he use his key? She went into the hall and prepared to let in the gusting gale. It had been a wild October. All the leaves were gone from the trees in the gardens on the hillside, the streams were running rivers and there hadn't been enough blue in the sky to make a sailor a pair of trousers in over a week; the fleet was harbour-locked. David had gone out for a breath of air but Eve, dreamy and warm, had decided to stay behind.

David stood dripping on the doorstep. He had been unable to reach for his key because he was supporting a young girl, as drenched as he was. Her short brown hair was plastered to a little heart-shaped face, her eyes were enormous and dark shadowed. The simple dress she wore, far too thin for the October weather, was plastered to her swollen body for she was as far advanced in pregnancy as Eve herself.

'I'm sorry,' yelled David above the storm. 'I had nowhere else to take her.'

Eve stood back then. 'Come in, oh, do come in. Come by the fire. Let me get you some towels. You'll have to take that dress off. I'll find a dressing gown or something.' She moved swiftly then, fussing around the girl.

'Who is she? Where did you find her?' They talked over this child of the storm as if she was a dumb animal, unable to speak for herself.

'I went up along The Burrows. She was over at the Devil's Leap, she was....' He paused.

The girl said in a clear American drawl. 'Don't be afraid to say it. I was going to jump. I was going to kill myself. It would have been better if he had not stopped me!' She glared momentarily at David then she burst into tears.

Much later, cocooned in a dressing gown of David's and tucked up on the sofa with a mug of hot cocoa, she told them her story. It was an old one and a familiar one. She came from Baltimore, had been studying at Exeter University. She had met a young man. She had married him and they had lived idyllically in a bed-sit in Bristol. He had walked out on her. He had abandoned her for a Swedish blonde. He was thought to be in Australia. She had found that she was pregnant. She had no money left. She could not go home to Baltimore and let them all see what a mess she had made of her life. She did not want the child, it was his child.

Eve, who very much wanted David's baby said. 'It's your child. You're his mother. He'll be half American. That's enough of a good half to see him through life.'

'How do you know it will be a boy?'

Eve smiled, 'Well, maybe I'm wrong. Let's take a bet on it. Do we get to know your name in exchange for another mug of cocoa?'

'Its Revel,' said the girl 'Revel Caine. I guess I'm having a bad day. I guess I'll sleep on it and things will look better in the morning.'

'I think they just might,' said Eve. 'We do have a spare bed. You can't go out again in this. You're very welcome to stay, isn't she, David?'

And so, Revel Caine stayed the night and the next and telephoned the folks in Baltimore and had money sent out. But still she lodged at the house on The Strand, company for Eve whilst David faced the winter weather. She was a delightful girl, artless and honest and, some-how, the rhythms of their lives marched together and when David drove Eve over to the cottage hospital in his battered Mini Cooper, Revel sat beside her, holding her hand. By the time Eve reached the labour ward Revel's pains too were beginning. Her son was born two hours after Eve gave birth to a daughter.

'Mothers and babies are both doing well!' shouted David down the crackling line from the hospital to Aunt George at the other end. She too had to shout over a southerly gale. 'For God's sake, David! She didn't have twins!'

'No, I'm talking about both of the girls.'

'Not twins? You mean you have two wives!'

'She's got hair.'

'Who has dear, Matron?'

'Annabel.'

'Annabel who?'

'We're going to call her Annabel. She's perfect.'

'When can I come over? I think I ought to come over, don't you?'

'Oh, tomorrow. No, it's tomorrow already. You can come today. Will you bring flowers?'

'Well, I might.'

'Will you bring a bunch for Revel, she won't have any visitors. They're together you see, side by side in a little ward of their own.'

'What's she had?'

'Who?'

'Revel, you idiot!'

'Oh, I see. It seems to be a boy. I must go now. Tell everyone!'

So Gina Deverel appeared laden with flowers. Eve was propped up against her pillows wearing a pink negligee and a serene smile. Gina kissed her.

'So you were right. And she has the carrot-red hair too. That's a real throw-back to grandmother.'

'Yes, I know. I thought you'd be pleased.' They were almost whispering as Revel was sleeping, her child silent in the cot beside her. David had been sent out for a walk.

'He's so happy about it all,' said Eve 'I never thought he'd take to the idea of fatherhood.'

'Too selfish?' laughed Gina. 'But you, are you happy, Eve?'

'Yes, this makes us a real family, brings a sense of completeness. It lays the demons to rest.'

Gina knew that she was thinking of Adam Colenso; that she would always think of him but they would be all right now, David and Eve. She leant over the baby. They say that the eyes don't focus for a while but something stirred in the little body and the tiny fists waved up at her.

Gina laughed, 'It's my necklace!' She didn't wear much jewellery but when Lowena died she had had Consuela's earring threaded onto a fine silver chain and, sometimes, she wore it, whether in memory of her dead mother or the worthless father who had wrecked so many lives she did not really know. Or perhaps she wore it for her own brother-lover who had kept its fellow close to his heart all those years ago.

'So Revel had a boy,' she said suddenly.

'Oh yes, he's to be Ashley. That's quite a nice name, isn't it?'

And when Gina looked startled she said. 'You know, 'Gone with the Wind', that awful boring man Scarlet O'Hara was besotted with. It is one of their greatest novels, you know.'

Revel stirred and without opening her eyes said with a smile. 'Not 'Gone with the Wind'. I never could stand all the frilly frocks. Come and look at him, Aunt George. Oh, your necklace, it reminds me.... Oh, more than that, it is the same!' Gina was stooping over the sleeping child. 'Pass me my purse, please.' Revel waved toward the window sill.

Eve said, 'That's handbag in English.'

Gina fetched it. For a girl who hated frills it was surprisingly ornate; a mesh of yellow wooden beads, bulging with every conceivable make-up aid. Revel fumbled about in it for some time and triumphantly pulled out a screw of tissue paper. 'Here, take a look at that. I'm sure they're the same.'

Gina parted the folds and took out the fellow to her own bauble, still as shiny as the day Jack Toller had taken them from the dead girl's body on the night the Mohegan went down. She sank onto the bed.

'Where did you get this?'

'Oh, Mark gave it to me. It was a family heirloom. I don't know why I kept it after he went.'

'It belonged to his mother?'

'To Susan? No. Well, I suppose she passed it on to him. What use is one earring? Anyway, she wasn't that sort of a woman. I mean, wasn't one for things that dangle. I liked her, she was sensible, practical. It came from his father so I think that's why I kept it. Robert Ashley was a war hero and I like that. It was amongst his belongings in his locker after he was shot down over Germany. He had a load of adventures, dived into the sea once, got rescued and they brought him ashore here. That's why I came that day. I couldn't fathom why Mark should be such a heel with a father like that. But now, well whoever he was he has a grandson. I don't want any part of Mark so he'll be brought up a Caine but I'll let him keep his grandfather. When he grows up he'll probably marry Annabel.

What fun that would be. Aunt George, are you sure you're all right?'

Gina thought to herself: 'Its all happening again, as it will go on happening down the centuries; Maddavers and Tollers, for Rob Ashley had been a Toller after all. But she smiled and touched the baby's forehead and he opened his eyes and made a slight sound. A tiny life built upon the legacy of so many ghosts; red-headed Annabel Boase moving through the gardens of Fosfelle, bad Jack Toller and the libidinous Alfie O'Brien, Lanty Maddaver and the Sea-Beggars and the old Waterwitch taking Adam Colenso to an unmarked grave.

'Ashley Caine,' she said 'meet Annabel Maddaver.' And if Consuela's shade hovered for a moment about their happiness, they did not heed it.

Printed in the United Kingdom by
Lightning Source UK Ltd., Milton Keynes
136640UK00001B/13-42/P